BROTHER

JOHN LODWICK was born at Chelter
father died at sea before his birth, an
and grandfather. After spending most ot his ......,
was sent at age 8 to Cheltenham College preparatory school, where ne
acquired a penchant for British naval history, a hobby that led his guard-
ians to dispatch him into the Royal Navy. He attended the Royal Naval
College of Dartmouth, and after spending some time at sea Lodwick left
the Navy at age 18 to become a writer. His literary agent, Curtis Brown,
encouraged him to experience more of life before attempting to write
novels, and he accordingly relocated to Dublin for three years, where he
was an advertising agent, journalist, and playwright.

When the Second World War broke out, Lodwick was living in
France, and he immediately volunteered for the French army, serving in
the Foreign Legion. His first novel, *Running to Paradise* (1943), drew on his
wartime experiences and won the $1,000 War Novel Prize.

Between 1943 and 1960, sixteen more novels followed, as well as works
of nonfiction and autobiography. Lodwick's prolific output included war
novels, thrillers, adventure novels, and comic fiction; most of his works
were published both in both England and America, and many of them
were translated into foreign languages. During the 1940s and '50s, Lodwick was one of the top sellers for publisher William Heinemann on a list
that also included Somerset Maugham, J. B. Priestley, and Graham Greene.
Critical reactions to Lodwick's books were mixed. Though reviewers were
unanimous in praising his fine style, wit, and sardonic humour, he was
sometimes rebuked for the cynical tone of his books and the unpleasantness of his characters. Nonetheless, his many admirers included Maugham,
John Betjeman, and Anthony Burgess.

John Lodwick died at age 43 in 1959 in a car crash in Spain. At the
time of his death, he had been working on a volume of autobiography, a
fragment of which was published posthumously in 1960 as *The Asparagus
Trench* to rave reviews, with critics agreeing that, had it been completed,
it would have ranked as one of the great autobiographies of its time.

BROTHER DEATH

A Novel

BY

JOHN LODWICK

With a new introduction by
CHRIS PETIT

VALANCOURT BOOKS

Brother Death by John Lodwick
First published London: Heinemann, 1948
First Valancourt Books edition, January 2014

Published by Valancourt Books, Richmond, Virginia
Publisher & Editor: JAMES D. JENKINS
20th Century Series Editor: SIMON STERN, University of Toronto
http://www.valancourtbooks.com

ISBN 978-1-939140-85-2 *(trade paperback)*
Also available as an electronic book.

All Valancourt Books publications are printed on acid free paper
that meets all ANSI standards for archival quality paper.

Cover by M. S. Corley
Set in Dante MT 11/13.5

INTRODUCTION

JOHN LODWICK was one of those English adventurers, along with Geoffrey Household and Simon Raven, who could write because they'd had a life before; experience, in a word. Lodwick belonged to a generation both made and ruined by the Second World War, unable to settle after; an ex-public schoolboy (Cheltenham) who had found himself in France where he joined the Foreign Legion, was interned after the German invasion of 1940 but escaped to return after training in England to act as a saboteur behind enemy lines. In his autobiography, *Bid the Soldiers Shoot*, he introduces himself in typically insouciant terms: "When war broke out, I was living in St. Rémy-de-Provence and, because my money was very low, sleeping in the back of a car belonging to a man called Tintin Blanchin. I was twenty-three years old, and in many ways retarded."

He went on to become a best-selling author for Heinemann, producing seventeen novels, drawing from his war experience (including *Peal of Ordnance*) before embarking on books with mainly foreign and often Iberian settings. Somewhere along the way he became friends with the ostracised Irish writer Francis Stuart, one of the great intransigent authors of the twentieth century. Stuart was in disgrace after abandoning a wife in narrow-minded Ireland and taking up teaching in Nazi Berlin for the dura-tion of the war where he compromised himself broadcasting pro-German propaganda, an act of collaboration that had ended in execution for others. Stuart dedicated his autobiographical masterpiece *Black List, Section H* to the memory of Lodwick after Lodwick, in a broadminded gesture, had dedicated *Somewhere a Voice Is Calling* to Stuart.

The relationship with Stuart suggests a man uncaring of conven-tion and operating outside the usual canons. In fact, Lodwick's literary efforts were well recognised. John Betjeman praised his richness of invention, debunking wit and a command of words equal to Evelyn Waugh. Anthony Burgess in *The Novel Now* (1967) put Lodwick in danger of being forgotten following his death in 1959, after a car crash in Spain. Lodwick had positioned himself as a writer deeply embedded in French and Spanish culture, which resulted in a special kind of fiction, "giving a violent English hero—one who could hardly survive a day in suburban Britain— the only kind of background for the release of his passionate talents". Burgess notes the European quality of Lodwick's rhetoric, grandiloquence, knowledge of foreign literature and subtle irony, which repelled readers more used to anodyne English fare. The negative review of *Brother Death* in the *Times Literary Supplement* in 1948 found parallels to Graham Greene, Conrad and Simenon, only because they operated in what the disdainful critic consid- ered the same dreary territory, where in fact Lodwick was richer in texture than Greene, wilder and more loquacious than Simenon, had something of the cosmopolitanism of Conrad but probably owed more to the restless adventure of Céline, not mentioned by the reviewer but whom Lodwick, given his Francophile persua- sion, would almost certainly have read.

Today Lodwick's work seems just as informed by the doomed romanticism and dysfunctional anti-heroes of film noir, with its cinematic treatment of landscape and psychological terrain of emotional autism caused when the sanctioned violence of war ceases and becomes institutionalised or domestic. One is reminded of the post-traumatic stress, fugue states and violent eruption of the returning war veteran played by William Bendix in the film of *The Blue Dahlia*, as well as the compromises of exile and collabora- tion in *Casablanca*.

Lodwick remained his own man, but the writer who cast the longest shadow was Ian Fleming, whose books can be read as exercises in the acclimatisation of violence that left Lodwick's characters in a more doomed space, *Brother Death* especially. Flem- ing's first Bond novel, *Casino Royale*, written five years later, laid down the next commercial template, a flattened combination of travel journalism, snobbery and sadism. How damned and stuck (and authentic) Lodwick's world seems in its grubby dustiness, selling nothing, compared to Fleming's consummate exercises in branding, anticipating the consumerism of 1960s, where personal choice was not moral decision but an exercise in style, leaving Lodwick's troubled men looking lost in time. No one asks Bond to murder a child, as they do Lodwick's anti-hero, Rumbold (such a hobbled, askance name compared to Bond), punished in the end less for his crimes than not knowing his place.

The story is pretty much a jazz riff—a mercenary adventurer adrift in the back streets of Marseilles, night-life in Madrid, a fatal encounter (a woman, of course), what the Panther paperback calls "a terror-haunted cliff top in the West of England", pursuit and escape, the enemy within, sickly loathing, drink taken, a hypochondriac lover ("Kill me then. Oh, I don't care"), the grisliest ménage-à-trois, a sense of inescapable doom and the trap of life snapping shut on a desolate Scottish moor.

There is a legitimate desire to shock, not just with erudition against provincial Britain (philosophy, art, literature), but in the relentless exposure of hypocrisy and failure of rehabilitation. The plain misanthropy and forensic nastiness seem to come naturally; utterly gripping is Lodwick's casualness in negotiating the reader into untenable areas. His set pieces are terrific, especially the pivotal one in the Madrid night club. The way he covers his ground is impressive: afternoon brothels, schoolgirls smelling of urine, nuns in railway carriages, and all within a few lines. There are asides on lesbians, art, paintings and even an unexpected reference to Mrs. Gaskell. What Lodwick nails is that bled-dry feeling of post-war exhaustion, its psychosis, misogyny and austerity of emotional impoverishment, without in any way being nostalgic or decadent. He is exactly the kind of writer of whom the late Roberto Bolaño would have approved, as one of the clumsy, poetic questers. His obscurity is a great indicator of the unfairness of what doesn't get remembered, but if one rightly carries on reading Muriel Spark and Daphne du Maurier then why not John Lodwick, who for all his troubled machismo was also curiously feminine in sensibility.

Chris Petit
London

November 12, 2013

BROTHER DEATH

To
DIANA AND ALEX BELL

"Let us have a quiet hour,
Hob-and-Nob with brother Death."

TENNYSON

"I describe, not men, but manners; not
an individual, but a species."

HENRY FIELDING

One

LONG, long . . . long ago, when he had been aged about ten years, his mother had said to him: "Your father is a brave man although his life has not been happy. There are some things to which honourable men do not stoop, but you, in your time, will stoop to all of them."

These words had been spoken in anger, the fruit of some forgotten and childish misdemeanour. Yet in every gust of anger there lies the germ of prophecy. His mother had been right. He had stooped low, indeed.

Marseilles, the British Consulate in the Rue d'Arcole, the 20th day of December, in the year 1946. Rumbold had come straight to this waiting-room from the Pelican bar.

Grey the walls of the ante-chamber, and dusty the bookcases with their cargo of geographical magazines, marine text-books, company law. Apart from Rumbold, four persons were present. These were: a Maltese seaman who had lost his ship, and who stood, therefore, in need of cash, two ladies of the governess class, and a time-bedraggled old gentleman—almost certainly a retired major—who perhaps owned a bridge club along the coast.

These persons did not address each other in any way, nor did they address Rumbold, who, after staring for some moments at a photograph of the late King George V which hung above the mantelpiece, stared at his suède shoes. Meanwhile the old ladies stared at the major, in the belief that they had once seen him emerging drunk from Charley's Bar in Nice, and the major, who had not seen a real coffee-coloured dago for many years, stared contemptuously at the Maltese seaman, his fingers fumbling as if for some absent horse-whip. The Maltese seaman, conscious of his lowly station, did not stare at all, but instead played with some poker dice which he held in his right hand.

The door opened: "Mr. Rumbold."

Rumbold, who had known that he would be called first, rose casually to his feet. He confronted the furious glances of his fellow-citizens. He followed the clerk.

"Mr. Pearce will see you now."

"Yes, I thought he might," said Rumbold. He was shown into a large and well furnished office. The Vice-Consul, a tall man still red from his lunch, waved him to a chair.

"Good afternoon," said Rumbold affably.

"Good afternoon. I have now received authority to issue you with a passport."

"Yes, I thought you might," said Rumbold.

"Here it is," said the Vice-Consul. He pushed the document across the desk. "You will find it in order," he said. "The photograph has been inserted and stamped. The visas you must get for yourself . . . that is, if you still intend to travel through Spain."

"It is a route to which I am accustomed," said Rumbold.

The Vice-Consul played with a paper-knife. "In the passport," he continued, "there is a slip of paper with an address. I am instructed to tell you that you must report to that address upon arrival in England."

"Ah, the pound of flesh," said Rumbold.

The Vice-Consul shrugged. "You know best," he said.

Rumbold looked at the slip of paper. "You were in the Internment Camp at St. Denis, weren't you?" he said, suddenly.

"Yes," said the Vice-Consul, "I was."

"You don't remember me, do you?"

"No," said the Vice-Consul. "I know your face, but the name conveys nothing to me."

"It wouldn't," said Rumbold. "But you lent me 200 francs in 1940. Here they are." He tossed the notes across the desk.

"Well, I'll take your word for it. Much obliged."

"What did they say about me in the cable?" asked Rumbold.

"They didn't say anything. They merely instructed me to issue you with a passport."

"Very kind of them," said Rumbold.

"I should look out if I were you," said the Vice-Consul. "You're sailing into tricky waters. Somebody doesn't care for you. I can tell you that much."

"I take great care of myself," said Rumbold. "That's why I'm alive to-day."

"And prosperous, too, I believe," said the Vice-Consul.

"And prosperous, too," confirmed Rumbold. "You know a lot, don't you . . . Pearce?"

"Well, it would be odd if I didn't," said the Vice-Consul. "I have lived in this town for twenty-six years, and I have a French wife who is . . . how shall I put it? . . . a good listener in a butcher's queue."

There was a short silence. Both men regarded one another carefully. Then: "I'd better go now," said Rumbold. "You'll be wanting to see the major."

"Not the major . . . the Maltese," said the Vice-Consul. "All are equal in the sight of this God."

Rumbold rose. "Well, goodbye, Pearce," he said. "I know you, though you don't know me. You were the man who stayed here six years ago."

"I think you're wise to get out," said the Vice-Consul. "Over-confidence is fatal. One can print just one meat ticket too many."

"How right you are!" said Rumbold. He extended his hand. "Well, goodbye again. I should imagine this is our last meeting."

"Yes," said the Vice-Consul. "I should imagine it is."

Rumbold left the office and entered the annexe. With a swivel-movement of his thumb he indicated the invitation of the open door to the dice-juggling Maltese. The major glared. The two ladies cast down their eyes, as they had been taught to do in the days of their lissom youth; in Edwardian times.

Rumbold was amused to note that a coal-black West African had taken his place beside the major.

He descended the stairs. In the street, in the Rue d'Arcole, he turned left. He walked with even strides towards the Spanish Consulate.

"*Arriba,*" he said, as he stood before the grille.

"Do not be funny," said the man behind it. "Your transit visa is here. Where is your passport?" Rumbold handed it over, saw it

stamped, and paid. Emerging, he turned right, towards the Portuguese Consulate.

And now that we have him in the street once again we may as
well take a first and last comprehensive glance at him: Rumbold,
Christian names Eric Waterman, almost six feet tall, twenty-nine
years old, educated at Guildford Grammar School. His hair is
golden, fine in texture, unthinned by time, by nature wavy. His
eyes are the slate-grey of the English Channel: small grey eyes,
hard and piercing, which, by their very lack of size, lend a quality
mesmeric to his always well-calculated stare. The hands, well
cared for, are wide of palm, with tufted digits. The legs are long,
the biceps have done press-ups . . . the whole body is, indeed,
athletic. This is a man, perhaps not devoid of natural kindness, but
with whom it would be far from safe to trifle. The instinct of self-
preservation is too evident.

The Portuguese Consulate, another fusty little office with its
flagpole for fête-days, its tarnished coat-of-arms.

The clerk knew Rumbold. They had done business together:
"Your visa is ready for you," he said. "How long do you intend to
stay in Lisbon?"

"I don't know; a week, two weeks perhaps. Do I have to tell
you?"

"Don't forget to visit the medical authorities," said the clerk.

"What do you think I am . . . a typhus carrier?" said Rumbold.

The clerk waved his hand in deprecation. "You will like my
country," he said.

"I already know your smelly little country," said Rumbold.

He paid the sum required of him, pocketed his now well illustrated passport, and turned down the street towards the *Cours
Pierre Puget*. The day was leaden-faced and Arctic. From the direction of L'Estaque the mistral blew with savage vigour, whipping up
the dead leaves beneath the naked plane trees, buffeting the shop
fronts, matching its din with the din of the tram cars. Rumbold
turned up the collar of his overcoat. He thrust his hands deep into
the pockets. He walked with his head down, avoiding other pedestrians by sound.

In the Rue Grignan, a sordid little street of gown and scent and pet shops, Rumbold entered a side passage. He ascended two flights of uncarpeted stairs and opened a door labelled *MAX . . . Couturier.* Inside the room, at a long table covered with some white material, seven girls were working. Some of the girls were sewing; others were measuring finished dresses against brown paper silhouettes. Rumbold paid no attention to the girls, but instead walked straight through the long room and into a smaller one behind it. In this room a bald Jew with a black moustache was ironing a pair of riding breeches. On a sofa a fat woman, with dark and luminous eyes, blew over a cup of tea, causing a slice of lemon to circle languidly.

"Hullo Max," said Rumbold. "Hullo Yvonne."

"Got your passport?" said the Jew. There was a note of grievance in his voice. He continued to iron the riding breeches.

"Yes," said Rumbold. "Is there any more of that tea?"

The woman pointed to a pot and a glass which stood in the fireplace.

"Nippy outside it, isn't it?" said the Jew. He licked his finger, rubbed it against a small crease in the riding breeches, then ironed gently where the wet mark showed against the cloth.

Rumbold filled himself a glass of tea, then sat down on the sofa beside the woman. He removed the slice of lemon from her cup with his fingers and placed it in his own glass. Then he pinched the woman's buttocks.

"Well . . . and how are we to-day?" he said.

"Don't do that unless you want this tea in your face," she said. She stared at the Jew, who was her husband, as if suddenly exasperated by him. "What do you want to stand there ironing like that for?" she said. "Haven't you got any pride? Why don't you get somebody else to do it?"

"I like to keep my hand in," said the Jew amiably. "This is how I started. Maybe this is how I'll finish." He turned to Rumbold:

"You going to-day?" he asked.

"Yes."

"What train are you catching?" Again the note of grievance in his voice.

Rumbold smiled. "Does it interest you?" he said.

"Certainly it does. Dédé will be here soon. Don't you want to see him?"

"No," said Rumbold.

"Well, we shall miss you," said the Jew. He laid aside his iron, folded the riding breeches and gazed at Rumbold quizzically. Rumbold sipped his tea.

"Have you got what I want?" he said.

The Jew opened a cupboard. He produced a pair of heavy brown golfing shoes. He laid these on the sofa.

"How do they work?" said Rumbold.

"You press," said the Jew. "See . . . here, on the instep," and, indeed, as he pressed, a semi-circular portion of each heel swung free.

"Very clever," said Rumbold.

"It's done by a spring," said the Jew. "Amazing what the human mind can devise, isn't it?"

"Amazing," agreed Rumbold. "But the cavity seems a bit small to me."

"Don't you believe it," said the Jew: "You could fit the English Crown jewels in there if you had them."

"I'm interested in dollars, not jewels," said Rumbold.

"Well, here they are," said the Jew. He produced and laid two stacks of notes upon the sofa.

"Those are the *escudos*," he said, indicating the smaller pile.

"So I see," said Rumbold. He began to pleat the notes into batches of five, stuffing them into the cavities.

"Aren't you going to count?" said the Jew.

"I never count," said Rumbold. "If there's anything wrong, I'll come back and have a chat with you." He took off his own shoes and threw them across the floor into the fireplace.

"How do I close these?" he asked, indicating the semi-circular hinges of leather in the new pair.

"Just press again," said the Jew. "It's quite simple."

Rumbold pressed. He satisfied himself that the device, when closed, was unobtrusive. Then he put on the new shoes, and stood up.

"You're not going already?" said the Jew, alarmed.

"Certainly, I'm going."

"But you can't clear out like that . . . without a word. We must have a talk. Surely you see that?"

"Let him go," said the woman Yvonne. She had finished her tea, and now lay back on the sofa smoking a cigarette.

Rumbold gazed at her appreciatively. "She understands," he said pointing to her.

"Listen," said the Jew. "You're clearing out . . . all right. You feel the call of your dear fatherland . . . all right again. *I'm* not stopping you. *I'm* not putting any obstacle in your way. On the contrary, I'm splitting even with you. But don't go without giving me some advice. Tell me at least what you think I ought to do."

"The best advice I can give you, Max," said Rumbold, "is to clear out yourself."

"And the printing-press?" said the Jew.

"Sell it."

"And Dédé, and the workmen, and the distributors?"

"Pay them off. Take a holiday at Cannes. In this game you've got to know when to stop. Bread's finished. Meat's finished. The penalties are getting too severe and the market's flooded. That leaves you tobacco cards and clothing coupons. Small stuff: I wouldn't waste my time on it."

"I can't sit around here and do nothing," said the Jew pathetically.

"No," said Rumbold. "I don't suppose you can. That's the trouble with you Yids. You don't do it to make money. You do it to show how clever you are. But you're not clever at all . . . not really. Even when you've got it you can think of nothing better to do with it than to cover young fingers and your wife's tits with the wrong kind of diamonds. Take my advice, Max . . . retire. Make some dirndls for a change, instead of as a cover story."

"You can sneer at us if you like," said the Jew, "but it takes a Goy to walk out on a pal without a word of regret or even thanks."

"I don't go much for sentiment," said Rumbold. "I don't care for it. We've been useful to each other. We've had some good times. Right . . . it's over now and we cut the painter."

"Cut the painter," said the Jew. "That's all it means to you . . .

cut the painter." He gazed at Rumbold. There were tears in his eyes.

"Don't snivel, for Christ's sake," said Rumbold. "Look at her," he said, pointing to the woman. "She doesn't give a damn."

"Goodbye, you bastard," said the woman calmly.

Rumbold laughed gently. "That's the spirit," he said. "Well, goodbye, Max." He held out his hand. "Try wine," he said. "Get some Algerian into Monaco and sell it as Nuits St. Georges."

The Jew turned aside and looked down at the floor. Rumbold shrugged. "Have it your own way," he said. "I'll leave you my shoes. You can cry over them in secret whenever you feel lonely."

Rumbold left the office. He closed the door behind him. "Goodbye, girls," he called to the women in the workshop.

"Goodbye, Eric."

In the street, Rumbold tested his new shoes. The leather, he found, did not yield easily to the flex of his instep. The shoes were heavy. Also they made an undue noise. He wished that he had caused them to be soled with rubber. He did not wish to remain continuously aware of them.

In the Rue Paradis, Rumbold picked his way through the crowds of afternoon shoppers. He sidestepped, then forged ahead, side-stepped, swerved, then forged ahead again. He was in no hurry, yet he could not bear to have his pace dictated by the slow surge of these idlers, could not *bear* it. He clenched his fists in exasperation as a couple of women paused before him to argue. He yearned to kick their drooping buttocks. He yearned to send their shopping baskets flying. Stepping off the gutter into the street, he walked on swiftly, oblivious of the traffic.

Paradis . . . St. Ferréol . . . the Rue de Rome . . . these are the arteries of that squalid city, here the disease which infects it pulses strong on its way to the outer network. The mistral, seasoned by the bite of the distant alps, punched the last roses of summer in the hats of fashionable women, made bold inside carelessly buttoned blouses and drew a chilly hand across thighs crisped in gooseflesh. The mistral would blow for two more days. Then rain would come from Corsica, then ice. Little boys from the Lycées would slide down the curving hill by the hospital. The stall-holders in the side-streets would put away their snails and sell, instead, roast chestnuts.

Rumbold walked on, each step a long farewell. Marseilles before the German war, with *pastis* at four francs a glass, the Anglo-Indians en route for Blighty ashore for one day of vicious dissipation, the flowered dresses of young women making, of a Sunday, for a *Cabanon* in the hills; the interminable jokes about Marius . . . Marseilles on the morrow of the sudden armistice, the clusters of rich but frightened Jews in the lounges of the Noailles and the Louvre; the denunciations, the rumours, the first tentative transactions in illicit olive oil . . . Marseilles when the enemy came at last, his Spandaus pointing towards the Cannebière from the station; the perquisitions, the round-ups, the awe of the Italianate inhabitants at the discovery of a race more corrupt than themselves . . . Marseilles liberated (had it ever been enslaved?); the Yanks, bored, impatient, waiting with brandy in their pockets for a ship to take them home . . . Marseilles, the fundament of Europe, the last port of the emigrant, the whore-house of the sailor, the haven of the card-sharper, the clearing-house of every venal and some mortal sins.

Rumbold walked on. He would not pass this way again. There was no love in his heart, and no regret. He knew this town in all of its material, and some even of its spiritual, aspects. He knew and shared the delight of its population in the surrounding countryside, the sea. He knew where to eat the best *bouillabaisse* and where to experiment with hashish. He knew everything about Marseilles and, knowing all, knew that the town was but what the come and flow of foreigners had made it.

Belsance . . . Dominicaines . . . Cours Lieutaud . . . for others these streets represented but the path towards the railway station, but for Rumbold they were the stations of the Cross. For others they contained shops, and flower stalls and fashionable flats, but to Rumbold they were the bland façade behind which the tortuosities of his business had been conducted . . . here a second floor back bedroom where it was always safe to leave a letter; here another, with brass bedstead and cracked *bidet*, a room eminently suitable for the consummation or the rupture of a secondary love affair (he would leave now without paying this month's rent). And beneath these rooms, in cellars, in garnished out-houses, the nightclubs; some legal, some illegal, but all prepared to substitute Mousseux for Champagne at the first sign of inebriety in a client.

Rumbold turned into *Dan's* now: he had left his valise in the cloakroom. He parted the blue curtains and confronted the commissionaire, who, divested of his uniform, and in shirt-sleeves, was polishing the brasswork of his dais. *Dan's* did not open until six, but from beyond further blue curtains came the sound of music. An audition was in progress.

"Hullo! Eric," said the commissionaire. He spat copiously upon his cleaning rag, using his own saliva in preference to the tin of metal polish beside him.

"Hullo! what's up?"

"Just a crowd of amateur Carusos with laryngitis," said the commissionaire. He thought poorly of all singers, being obliged to listen to them, without a drink in front of him, for four hours every evening. "You want your bag?"

"Not yet," said Rumbold. "Where's Dan?"

"Baptising the brandy," said the commissionaire; "we don't want folks to get too drunk over Christmas. It don't seem right somehow."

"Ah, yes, Christmas," said Rumbold. From his wallet he took two thousand-franc notes and laid them on the dais. "Buy yourself some lottery tickets," he said.

"You become a Christian or something?" said the commissionaire. "I never seen you do that before."

"You'll never see me do it again," said Rumbold. He parted the inner curtains and entered the cabaret. Only at the far end of the long room did signs of life exist. Here, upon the stage, beneath a single amber spotlight, a number of young men were standing. One of them was singing, watched with mingled boredom and malevolence by the others. To the right of the stage, in almost total obscurity, a three-piece band accompanied the singer. A yard or two away from the footlights, a small group of theatrical producers, commission agents, and lyric writers were arguing loudly about some musical score. None of them were paying any attention to the singer:

"Serre ma poitrine contre toi, ma brune,
Ferme tes jolis yeux, car les heures sont brèves,
A l'autre côté de la lune
Au doux pays des rêves."

The young man sang well, but perhaps conscious of the inattention of the audience, overpitched his vibrato.

"Next please," came a voice from the circle of producers.

"But that's only the first verse," protested the young man.

"It's one too many," said the producer. "Next."

Another young man, in no way dissimilar to the first, stepped forward and began to give an imitation of Charles Trénet. Rumbold, who had been watching the scene with amusement, now turned away, and leaning over the deserted bar, looked down through the trap door behind the beer taps. Beneath him, in the cellar, he could see Dan at work. He selected a peanut from a tray and dropped it neatly upon Dan's bald head.

"Don't muck about, man," said Dan; "come down if you don't want to speak to me."

Rumbold obeyed. Dan was recorking and sealing brandy bottles, for a part of the original contents of which he had substituted water.

"Oh, it's you, is it?" he said. "Well, I wish you wouldn't leave your bag here. The police have been in twice this morning, to go through it."

"I hope they didn't steal anything," said Rumbold.

"No. They just admired your pyjamas. There's one of them waiting up there now for you. He's drinking coffee . . . *coffee.*" Dan's face revealed his disgust. "I had to send out for it," he added.

Dan was a dapper little man, and like many another dapper little man he wore a bow-tie. His social position was equi-distant between the Arts and Grand Larceny. The dominating feature of Dan's face was the mouth; no doubt a sensitive organ originally (traces of the original Cupid's bow remained) but one which time had crabbed with the taste of insults swallowed unavenged. But why describe the face . . . was there ever convention more empty? The centre of Dan's life lay in his diaphragm, swollen by constipation and easy living, its swelling controlled to some extent by abdominal exercises.

"Have some brandy," he said.

"I'll take the champagne," said Rumbold, observing that the crates due for consumption that evening had not yet been tampered with by the addition of lemonade.

"Just as you wish," said Dan (his real name was Mariano, and he came from Murcia, in Spain). He opened a bottle, watching the cork curve as it sped towards regions where spiders reigned supreme.

A young woman, who, unseen by Rumbold, had been sitting on an empty beer barrel in the obscurity, now stepped forward.

"I'll have some of that, Dan," she said, indicating the bottle of champagne.

"Why, hullo, Odette," said Rumbold amiably. "Fancy meeting you here."

"Shall I leave you two lovebirds alone?" said Dan.

"Not if you value your cellar," said Rumbold. He stared at Odette, watching her hands for the first sign of trouble.

Dan poured out three glasses of Piper-Heidsieck.

"Well, Eric, here's luck," said the girl. "I hear that you're leaving us."

"You heard quite correctly," said Rumbold. He sipped his champagne, remembering that he had eaten no lunch.

"I think I have some business upstairs," said Dan. He ascended the ladder which led to the bar. They watched the oscillations of his buttocks.

"What a bastard you are, aren't you?" said the girl.

"The question is debatable," said Rumbold. He gazed at the girl's nose, which he himself had broken. The nose now lay supine, its bulb casting a shadow across the freckled upper lip. She was a big girl, a Brynhilda, not really very young but with a profusion of flesh upon chest and hip which, cushion-like, would always lure the jaded head.

"What a bastard you are," she repeated.

"Here," said Rumbold, and from his wallet he removed thousand-franc notes to the number of ten. He laid them fanwise on the ruptured champagne case.

The girl watched him for a moment, then seized the first two notes. She began to tear them.

"Not like that," said Rumbold. "Tear straight across. You'll find them easier to repair."

He walked up the stairs. "Where's the copper?" he said to Dan.

Dan nodded towards the corner of the bar, beside the band. Rumbold advanced. A face clutching a pipe between false teeth sprang out at him.

"Hullo! Archambaud," he said. "Your coffee looks cold."

"I get no expenses on this job," said the detective. "You may order me a *Fine à l'eau.*"

Rumbold sat down.

"Been waiting long?" he enquired politely.

"Two hours," said the detective.

"You must be very ill-informed," said Rumbold. "I have been at my consulate half the morning." He shouted to Dan, who came over from the bar bearing a tray and two drinks. "Thank you, Dan," said Rumbold. Behind him the orchestra were packing their instruments. The musical part of the audition was over, and the stage was now occupied by a young man telling dirty stories in rhyme.

"So you are leaving us at last," said the detective Archambaud. "We shall miss you."

"It's funny you should say that," said Rumbold. "Quite a number of people have said it and—do you know—I think that some of them actually mean it."

"It is but good manners to express regret at your departure," said Archambaud.

Rumbold grinned. "Yet for you it's something more than good manners, is it not?" he said. "For you, it is a matter for *relief.*"

Archambaud said nothing. Rumbold considered the man with amusement. It always amused him to consider Archambaud for he knew so much about him. In appearance, the detective was squat, broad-shouldered, bow-legged, with dark hair, a low forehead and heavy eyebrows. He resembled a caricature of Daladier in the role of Bonaparte, and, like the politician, he had been born in the Vaucluse. Archambaud had not always been attached to the squad dealing with Black Market activities. Before the war he had been in the drug squad, specialising in the arrest and interrogation of Chinese seamen. Archambaud had been very good at interrogations. After the armistice, his zeal and efficiency had been brought to the attention of the Vichy authorities with the result that Archambaud had been transferred to duties connected with the suppression of patriotic and anti-German activity. As a politically enlightened citizen, with an eye for the main chance, Archambaud had of course realised that the precarious political equilibrium of Pétain's last years was unlikely to endure. He had taken his precautions, and in Resistance circles the thought had been pretty general (encouraged by a couple of spectacular escapes) that Archambaud was a good fellow, who merely pretended to do his duty, and who, in secret, was a friend of the free.

At the liberation, Archambaud had been awarded the rosette of the *Légion d'honneur*. Life had appeared to smile upon him, and life, indeed, might have continued to smile upon him, because dead men tell no tales. Unfortunately, two of the men whom Archambaud had reason to believe buried beneath six inches of lime were alive, and in singularly robust health.

These men had been friends—colleagues even—of Rumbold's. We cannot, at this early stage in a long book, go into the details of their relationship here, but take my word for it that it existed, that it was close, binding, and that in consequence of it Rumbold knew a great deal more about Archambaud than Archambaud would have preferred.

For Archambaud had no desire . . . no desire whatever to be arrested, to be tried upon a charge of collaboration, to spend twenty years at Clairvaux, or . . . more dreadful alternative . . . to take hesitant steps in the dawn between a cell and the guillotine.

Rumbold, the knowledge in his possession, had been quick to point out the situation to Archambaud; and Archambaud, who was, after all, no fool, had acquiesced. And this is why it always amused Rumbold so intensely merely to look at Archambaud, for he considered it ineffably funny that the detective, who should have arrested him months before for the distribution of forged food tickets, was unable to do so through fear of the counter-accusations which Rumbold might make.

Rumbold thought all this very droll indeed. He considered it even more droll that he was now about to extract—under a vow of eternal silence, and conditional upon his departure—the sum of 90,000 francs from Archambaud, who, having no private income of his own, had almost certainly stolen the money from the Police Pension fund.

He liked to think (for few men had a more acute sense of justice than Rumbold) of the day, eighteen months, perhaps two years hence, when Archambaud would be arrested and suspended from his duties for the defalcation of public funds.

"Have you brought the money?" he said now pleasantly.

"I have brought it," said Archambaud.

"Converted into *pesetas*, I hope," said Rumbold.

"Converted into *pesetas*," said Archambaud.

"I have been thinking," said Rumbold. "The journey to the Spanish frontier is a long one. I would not like anything untoward . . . my arrest, for example . . . to take place upon that journey!"

"Nothing untoward will occur," said Archambaud.

"I am grateful for that assurance," said Rumbold.

Archambaud leant forward. He knocked over his *Fine à l'eau*. "Nothing will happen, Rumbold," he said. "But I, too, need an assurance. You have persecuted me long enough. I must be certain that I shall never set eyes upon you again."

"Pass over the cash, will you?" said Rumbold. Archambaud did so. Rumbold pocketed the envelope. "But, my dear fellow," he said, "with the best will in the world, how can I give you such a guarantee? Circumstances may throw us together again. Marseilles is a big city. It is always possible that I shall revisit it."

And he gazed at the detective mockingly. Archambaud decided to essay another argument.

"The Gentlemen in London will be glad to see you, I expect," he said.

"I wouldn't count on that if I were you, Archambaud," said Rumbold. "Long-distance treachery very seldom succeeds. The affair is, I can assure you, purely domestic. It is between me and them. I am not, as I have several times warned you, an ordinary deserter. If you attempt to harm me when I am gone it is yourself who will be destroyed, and that very speedily."

"You are a cunning devil, aren't you?" said the detective.

"A compliment such as that, from you," said Rumbold, "deserves a drink. Shall we have one?"

He waved to Dan. "The Inspector looks tired, Dan," he said. "I think you should mix him one of your specials."

"I am always glad to do anything for the Inspector," said Dan. "The Inspector and I are good friends . . . aren't we good friends, Inspector?"

"Oh, by the way, Dan," said Rumbold, "I shall be leaving a sealed envelope with you. Here it is. It concerns the Inspector. Break the seal sometime and show him the contents, I'm sure he will find them most interesting."

"Anything you say, Eric," said Dan. He took the envelope, winking.

"Yes," said Rumbold, when Dan had withdrawn. "Yes, I hate to leave with a guilty conscience, Inspector. The thought, in fact, is most distasteful to me."

"Is that so?" said Archambaud.

"It is very much so," said Rumbold. "For example, I would not like to think that, when I am gone, you might proceed to the arrest of certain of my late and now defenceless confederates."

"And what makes you think that?" said Archambaud.

Rumbold grinned. "Because you earn quite a large salary, my friend, and are obliged to justify it by results . . . even at some small risk to yourself."

"What is in that letter?" said Archambaud.

"Oh, never fear: Dan is most discreet. He would never stoop to blackmail, which is why I have chosen him in preference to our mutual friend, Max. No . . . Dan will be a kind of trustee for me, Inspector. That's all."

"Rumbold," said Archambaud heavily. "There is no man in Marseilles whom I would better like to kill than you."

"Interrogate, Inspector . . . you mean 'interrogate', surely? Ah, here are the drinks. You'd better have mine as well as yours. I'm in a hurry. No . . . don't get up. Let our farewell be as informal as our long association. Goodbye, Dan; look me up in London sometime . . . and Inspector, *not* too many plain clothes men on the station, please. You know I prefer to travel incognito."

He rose. He shook hands with Dan, and smiled at the Inspector, who scowled in return. He left the room. On the stage the young *raconteur* paused in the middle of an obscene poem to watch him leave.

"*Flack.*" As he parted the curtains which led to the vestibule, the girl, Odette, stepped forward. The blow was neatly delivered. An embossed ring on her finger grazed his nose. He stepped back, surveying her.

"A Spitfire to the last, I see," he said. With his handkerchief he dabbed at the trickle of blood upon his nostrils. He moved over to the counter, handed across his check, received in return his valise from the commissionaire.

The girl stood watching him. Her fists were clenched.

"Have you succeeded in piecing the torn notes together yet?" he said. "I can recommend stamp paper. It's admirably adhesive . . . like yourself, dear."

"You're very pleased with yourself now," she said. "But you'll come to a bad end one day."

"You think so, dear? I disagree. I fear that I have flourished too long to be easily uprooted."

He stepped out upon the pavement. Behind him the swing doors of the club circulated lazily. A passing taxi slowed down, its driver touting for custom. Rumbold waved the man away. The station lay near-by and his valise was not heavy.

At the corner of the *Cours Devilliers* he stood looking for a moment at the church of St. Vincent de Paul. On the steps of the church a great fir-tree had been set up in preparation for Christmas, and even now, in the last light of the murky afternoon, children were decorating the tree with silver streamers, with Chinese lanterns and with globes of many colours.

Rumbold watched the children for a while; then he ascended

the steps and entered the porch of the church. A priest was standing in the porch, making pencil corrections to a notice. Rumbold nudged him.

"Is there anywhere I can leave my bag for a moment?" he said.

"You may leave it here, my son," said the priest. "No one will steal it."

"Well, I'll take a chance," said Rumbold. "I'm sure you believe what you're saying."

He set down his bag and entered the church. The hour for Benediction was drawing near, and over the altar, far away, two vergers fussed about a pile of sacred accoutrements. On the right of the church, in the Lady Chapel, the Crèche had been set up, and a workman under the supervision of two ladies was unloading a sack of straw and spreading it artistically about the Manger. Rumbold moved slowly down the aisle, stepping carefully to avoid two women kneeling before the seventh Station of the Cross. A cluster of seated penitents, who were awaiting confession, eyed him furtively, fearful lest he might forestall them with their chosen confessors.

Rumbold installed himself two or three pews behind these people. He sat quietly, not kneeling, listening to the murmur of voices from the confessionals. Several priests were evidently in session. From the nearest box, only a few yards away, the conversation was quite audible:

"Bless me, Father, for I have sinned. . . ."

"In what did your sin consist, my son?"

Resolutely, determined not to hear, Rumbold turned away his head. His eyes met those of St. Joseph, who, bearded, soberly clad, and holding the Child in his arms, looked down at Rumbold from a niche.

"Courage," said Rumbold, "Courage." He returned the stare of St. Joseph with distaste.

Two

At the beginning of the Second World War there lived in the little town of Hasselt, in Belgium, a furniture maker named Sluys, his English wife and their eighteen-year-old son.

Denis Sluys, the father, a man of Flemish stock, who spoke French only with difficulty and always unwillingly, had served with some distinction in the Belgian Army during the First Great War. Wounded, he had been evacuated to England, where, passing from one convalescent camp to another, he had stayed long enough at last in Yorkshire to enable him to court and to marry a Miss Colclough, the not unattractive daughter of a Bradford baker.

The war at an end, the couple had returned to Hasselt, where, assisted by some slight transfer of capital from Yorkshire, the husband had set himself up firmly, and to his growing advantage, in the furniture trade.

He was never to become a rich man, but he did achieve that small degree of affluence and that position of respectability to which his talents entitled him and his circumstances demanded of him.

In 1932 the old man, the Yorkshire baker, died from a cancer of the throat after a lingering illness, to be followed to the crematorium by his wife, not six months later. Up to this time, the visits of the Belgian family to England had been fulfilled as an annual duty. Now, however, though they did not cease altogether, they became more infrequent, for the baker having spawned no other child save this one who had married the foreigner, surviving relatives of the English line were scarce: consisting, indeed, only of some second cousins and an aunt.

So far, so good. These are facts, easily verified, and verified, indeed, some years later when a Court of Inquiry was established . . . by which time both Sluys and his wife were dead in their turn, and their son Pieter was also about to die: though this not of his own free will.

The rest, particularly in regard to the character of the son, and of the motives which inspired him, must remain a matter of speculation. It is easy to believe that he was shocked by the threat to his mother, for example, but this in no way explains his subsequent actions nor the zeal with which he performed them.

In 1940, at the time of the German occupation of the Netherlands and Belgium, Pieter Sluys was reaching manhood. Sexually he had reached what he believed to be manhood very much earlier . . . at the achievement of puberty, perhaps. A fumbler beneath servant girls' skirts, a ripper of waitresses' bodices, he revealed himself in these, as in other, pursuits a savage. With that extreme blondness, almost whiteness, of hair which the Germans admire, but which the Flemings distrust; with his squat but sturdy and far from ungainly body, his blue eyes, Pieter even then had admirers who believed that butter could not melt in his mouth.

One day, not very long after the German invasion, and following a check through the registers of the Town Hall—a check which had resulted in the discovery of his mother's English birth—young Pieter Sluys was summoned to the *Kommandantur*. Here he met a certain Colonel von Krebs, a man, it would seem, of many parts and much initiative. What passed between the pair is not known, but a few days later Pieter, who had in the meantime been spending money freely, approached his father with the information that, Belgium proving unbearable under the German occupation, he intended to make his way immediately to England.

The father, who was certainly no Germanophile, approved of this intention, overcame the natural scruples of his wife, and provided the boy with a considerable sum in ready money. Poor man, he did not know, and thanks to his early death he never did know, of the true facts behind his son's decision.

In August of 1940 young Pieter left Hasselt on foot for the French frontier. Beyond the confines of the town, however, a car drew up beside him, and he stepped into it. This car took young Pieter to Givet, on the French frontier of the Ardennes. At Givet, Pieter transferred to a second car, which took him to Paris, and in Paris, after a night of exuberance in the Rue Mouffetard, Pieter joined a third car which took him by easy stages as far as St. Jean-

Pied-de-Port, on the Spanish frontier, where, after receiving, reading and returning the contents of an envelope, he was left to his own devices. All the cars in which he had taken passage had been German.

The intelligence, the cunning and the wiliness of the Germans in this matter of Pieter Sluys deserve great praise. Yet this praise will not easily be accorded by the reader unless he is first made aware of certain facts.

In the first years of that war the German organisation in England was competent and widespread; yet, at the same time, timid, unadventurous and easily "blown". The reasons for this were twofold. First, agents had been established in their territory too long in advance of the outbreak of war, with the result that the opposition had got to know of the presence of some, who, shadowed, had revealed the presence of others. Secondly, all the men employed (with three exceptions of very inferior capabilities) were German by birth, having in consequence to add the pretence of being English to the pretence of being book-keepers, newsagents or whatever role had been allotted to them.

Experiments with false refugees, with enthusiastic Swedes, Afrikaners and Chinese, conducted upon a cash down and bonus-for-action basis had always proved unsuccessful: the devotion of the agent to his cause being in the last resort unequal to the strain of life in enemy territory.

A textbook could be written about German attempts to infiltrate British subversive organisations. A second textbook could be written about the training to which agents were subjected in either country. King's Regulations being, however, likely to intervene, the place of neither textbook can be here. Suffice it to say, by way of contrasting the two methods, that if an Englishman designed for despatch to France were described upon his false identity card as a waiter, he would wear, when he set off upon his mission, clothes in keeping with his supposed income level, would have endured, had he been previously ignorant of the profession, a course in waiting, and would have been fully conversant with the peculiar *argot* of that trade.

The Germans, despite their supposed reputation for thoroughness, knew nothing of such subtleties. One has only to recall the case of the gentleman, arrested at Bristol upon some trivial charge, who claimed to be a salesman for a Tyneside fish-canning firm. Upon examination it was found that he knew the name of no fish to be found in the Tyne estuary, nor indeed in the entire North Sea.

This is why the case of Pieter Sluys stands—and, as far as that war is concerned, will always stand—alone. No great credit can be allowed to the Germans for discovering Pieter. He discovered himself, and his advantages were only too obvious: he was young, impressionable, superficially innocent, and, by birth at least, half an Englishman. No! the credit must go to the Germans, not upon these counts, but because of the superb way in which, within the course of a few days, they first awakened, then directed down well prepared channels, the latent cupidity, the brutality, and the yearning of the boy for adventure.

Forty-nine persons were later executed as the result of direct betrayal or of information laid by Pieter Sluys. Many more were tortured, transported or killed, as the result of the torture of these forty-nine. An organisation previously regarded, in the country of its origin at least, as impregnable was all but shattered. So that now . . . since it concerns the main stream of this story very intimately we might as well see how it was done.

Sluys entered Spain through the Urepel gap. He took no trouble to conceal himself, and was immediately arrested and interned, together with some thousands of fellow-refugees from Fascism, in the concentration camp of Miranda-del-Ebro. The arrangements between the British and Spanish Governments were at that time of a vague, yet, in the last resort, of a gentlemanly nature. In return for a monthly quota of petrol, the Madrid authorities were prepared to release from their camps a monthly quota of human beings. This quota was never very large, and was also subject to sudden reductions when the Spaniards, under pressure from Berlin, became intransigent. British Embassy officials visited the camps and established lists of priority. Sluys' priority was not very high.

Thus, he did not leave Miranda for seven months, and then it was to travel to England the dangerous way, as supernumerary passenger in a tanker from Gibraltar. On reaching England he was examined by immigration and other authorities. His story concerning relatives in Yorkshire was checked and found to be true. Asked what he now wished to do, Sluys, after some hesitation, required to be allowed to enlist in a North Country regiment. This request was granted, and Sluys was drafted to a training depot. He spent the greater part of the next year in Yorkshire, in Lancashire, and finally near Carlisle. In accent, in appearance and in behaviour he was quite indistinguishable from his fellow soldiers.

Sluys' state of mind during this period must have been curious. It seems likely that, although he had not forgotten his interviews at Hasselt with von Krebs, he was quite content with things as they were: to be an Englishman now among Englishmen; a German, at some future date, among Germans. On arrival he had no doubt been led to expect an approach from one or other of the mysterious organisations, the activities of which had been outlined to him. When no such approach was made, he adapted himself without difficulty to his new circumstances, for though a brutal he was far from being either an intelligent or an introspective young man. Certainly, during that year, he possessed no contacts with other agents, and it is unlikely that he had ever been entrusted with any. Popular with his comrades, a favourite with his officers, he passed twelve months in obscurity. He did, it is true, have an affair with a girl, employed in an Army cipher office, but this appears to have been irrelevant to his subsequent activities.

Von Krebs, having decided that the English had ignored the bait, had probably written off Sluys as a loss. If this is so, he was too impatient. The talent spotters, whose task was to choose the few from among the many, took a long time to find Sluys, but they found him in the end. They examined his credentials, which were good. They reviewed his brief army career, and were satisfied by it. They investigated the aunt and the three second cousins who were all that remained of his English relatives. Finally, they called him to London, where, having put certain propositions to him, they obtained his immediate agreement.

They could not know that this was what the Germans hoped

they would do. They could not know because Sluys was fool-and-
security proof. His youth, his English birth, his apparent innocence:
all these were in his favour; but overshadowing them, lulling any
suspicions which might have been entertained, was the fact that he
had already spent over a year in the country, during all of which
time his behaviour had been irreproachable.

And this is where Rumbold comes in ... Lance-Corporal
Rumbold, recruited from his tank depot at Catterick, marked
down by the scouts by reason of his evident intrepidity and long
service in a Paris bank.

The pair, together with about fifteen others (Armenians, Mediterranean Jews, French-speakers from Mauritius: surprisingly few
Englishmen), were given their first month of sabotage-training at a
country house in Surrey. Then they went North, beyond the Cale-
donian Canal, then came South again to parachute at Ringway,
then dispersed to attend the lectures of the theorists.

At this stage, before the pupils took the field in earnest, it was
customary to classify them; to adapt the pegs, few of which were
entirely round, to the shape of hole which would suit each best.
Thus men of the greatest strength of character and initiative
were chosen to be organisers, to take over existing movements, to
direct and attune the efforts of these movements to the common
aim. Others, no less talented, but of a more mechanical turn of
mind, became radio operators and endured further training to
this end. Still others ... we are in the middle ranks of talent now
... worked in a more restricted sphere: they were couriers: they
were selectors of landing strips for parachute supplies: they were
pay-masters (travelling with fabulous sums with which to sweeten
the faithful): they were pamphleteers, scribbling for some ancient
printing press concealed in a hayloft or a lady's bedchamber.

But when all these had been disposed of, there still remained
the hard, the irreducible core of near-unemployables; the timid,
the temperamentally unsuitable, the fractious and the slow of
thought. The timid and the temperamental did not long enjoy
their pay in ease and comfort. They left—sometimes willingly,
sometimes helped upon their way by polite threats of sanctions—
and afterwards were to be encountered, shorn of their glory, in the

most surprising places: an Army bakery, for example, the workshop of a jobbing tailor, the cloakroom of a night club. But for the fractious and the slow of thought a hope would still remain . . . a lowly hope, it is true, but still a hope, a future, and in its humble way, a calling.

They were the hit-and-run men, the in-and-out boys. Not for them the heavy pay-packets, the swift rise in rank, the Military Cross. They were the simple Myrmidons, the *condottieri*, the licensed brigands of their age: five days in France (or Belgium, or Holland . . . name the country that you please), a simple objective and a swift run across the border, where, if you were lucky, you reached your Consulate; if unlucky, suffered your head to be shaved and ate bean soup in a Spanish prison for a month.

Such a one, an aristocrat of his profession, was Rumbold. People liked Rumbold, and they liked him the better because he was successful and preferred to work alone. Three times in ten months Rumbold went to France, and not once was he caught in Spain on his way out: Rumbold always made Bilbao even if, as on the first occasion, he had to push two policemen aside as he ran in through the doors of the Consulate. And after Bilbao . . . Lisbon. Rumbold used to spend rather a lot of money in Lisbon, but in the opinion of the firm, his achievements justified it.

Rumbold was generators . . . dynamos and generators, electrical equipment always easy to replace on the Clyde or in Pittsburgh, but not so easy to replace in the occupied Europe of that time. Not *any* generator, of course, not any dynamo, but, for preference, a dozen of each in a locomotive factory, which meant that no locomotive would leave the factory until the wrecked equipment had been replaced . . . four months later. Which saved the lives of a number of airmen, who would otherwise have had to dive daily, with uncertain rocket aim, above the *flak* guns of armoured trains.

A sideline of Rumbold's which, circumstances permitting, he might have carried further had been E-boats. On his first job, dropping near Meulan, a small town upon the River Seine, he had there destroyed, with thermite charges, ten out of thirteen hulls ready to be floated down to the sea.

This had meant a certain decrease in German shipping protection in the English Channel.

But, while Rumbold had been thus employed, Pieter Sluys, and several others with him, had done nothing ... not, to be sure, from any lack of enthusiasm upon their part, but rather because the authorities did not care to entrust them with independent endeavour. The authorities were retaining them for the Invasion, that period in which the foot-soldier would realise that the war had begun and in the anarchy of which their lack of talent and perspicacity might well pass unnoticed.

Rumbold met Sluys several times during his short rests in England. He met him at that gloomy Elizabethan mansion near Oxford, upon the banks of the sluggish Cherwell, where prospective "in-and-out" men were detained. The pair were not fond of one another. Sluys envied Rumbold his success, his assurance. Rumbold, though divining nothing of the truth, disliked Sluys for the freedom of his behaviour before women, his general coarseness, his entire lack of the quality which the gentry call breeding. Rumbold, it must be remembered, was seven years older than Sluys.

Ah! those damp November days of mid-war in the Thames Valley, when the mist would not rise from the ground until the sun was at its zenith. At nine in the morning, before the explosives class, the Instructor Fernandez, a Spaniard with admixture of Devonian blood, would call the reluctant residents from breakfast, to box: "Hit me! Hit me with your right, man." The pupil, a young Jew, would strike out, indenting the Spaniard's thorax with feeble force, to be immediately felled by an uppercut. "What are you? Corner-house Commandos or cry-babies? Is there nobody here who has guts?"

Rumbold, watching Pieter Sluys step forward to be battered in his turn, decided that the child possessed courage. He decided that he might take him upon his next job, if official opinion would permit it.

Official opinion not only permitted but even encouraged the idea, for, as it so happened, Rumbold's next job was not one which could conveniently be performed alone. A system of canal locks near Valenciennes, affecting two main waterways from Belgium into France, had been marked down for early destruction. A very considerable weight of explosive would be necessary together with its transport from the dropping ground to the target area, seven kilometres distant. Four others, besides Sluys, were designated to accompany Rumbold.

At first, all went according to plan. The party dropped, towards the end of a moon period, from two Halifax bombers. The drop was without incident. The containers were salvaged, buried, the explosive transferred to individual valises. Before dawn on the same day, all six men were lying up within sight of the objective. They lay up separately, as a precaution, several hundred yards apart, with a rendezvous fixed for their meeting at dark. The attack was to be made that same night.

Throughout the early part of the day there was no special activity in the neighbourhood of the locks, but in the late afternoon, Rumbold, inspecting the scene through binoculars, was amazed to see a full company of German infantry moving along the canal banks, halting, dragging up field-kitchens and settling down as if to bivouac.

At the evening conference, fully persuaded that the arrival of the Germans was an unlucky mischance and that they would move off in the morning, Rumbold postponed the attack for twenty-four hours. He was quite comfortable in his wood, and he was prepared to wait.

But the Germans did not move on the following morning, nor upon the morning after that. If anything, their numbers were reinforced, and it became clear that intelligence of the proposed attack must have reached them. Such, in any case, was Rumbold's conclusion, although he found it hard to reconcile it with the absolute inactivity of the enemy and their failure to search the surrounding countryside.

He was not to know that the capture of six men crouching in brambly thickets was of small importance to the Germans when set beside that of the organisation to which the men might lead them when they set off upon their journey to the South.

On the fourth day Rumbold cancelled the attack. He buried

the explosive and instructed the party to disperse. His own escape route, and that of one other man, lay through Soissons and Auxerre. This saved their lives. Sluys, with three companions, was to travel to Paris. They travelled separately, to be sure, but in the capital they were to meet, and to be lodged in the same "safehouse", before attempting the long journey to Spain.

None of those four, apart from Sluys, ever reached Spain. The "safe-house", it was learnt later, had been blown; Sluys' story being that, returning to it one evening, he had found the place in the hands of the Gestapo, his companions arrested, and himself with just sufficient time to scuttle round a street corner in order to avoid a similar fate.

Oh, it was very artistically done, very thoroughly. Sluys had even gone to the trouble to have himself arrested in Spain, so that he arrived in London with a shaven head and a month's delay. Everybody believed him. Everybody was rather sympathetic, in fact. *Poor* little Pieter Sluys, they said, for the arrests had gone just far enough: they were not so widespread and so crippling as to cause doubts to arise.

In Paris Sluys was interviewed by Germans very much more important than his original acquaintance, von Krebs. These gentlemen were well satisfied with his performance, his loyalty, but somewhat less satisfied with the information which he was able to give them . . . nearly all of which they knew already. To be brief, they were not prepared to rest content with the capture of a few unimportant "in-and-out" men, with the liquidation of a safehouse, with the trimming of small corners from the vast pattern of the Underground. They wanted the big men. They wanted the couriers, and the false names employed by them; the date of departure from London of radio operators, their description, the area to which they had been directed.

And this, of course, was precisely the kind of information with which Sluys was unable to provide them. A humble and hitherto unemployed operative, his opportunities for research work were far from brilliant. True, upon his occasional visits to London, his long waits in a flat close to Selfridge's, he had seen men whose faces he had attempted to memorise, but the rules governing security in that overcrowded and unfurnished flat were such that he could never hope, without dangerous indiscretion, to learn more.

But the Germans were no longer interested in descriptions of life in British sabotage schools, any more than the British were interested in the parallel establishments at Potsdam. Each was well aware of the methods of the other, each well aware, too, of the numbers, the facial peculiarities of the pupils introduced into both each month. The Germans wished to know where the trained agent was going. His face they knew, his antecedents they knew. But the one thing they did not know, was . . . where he was going, what he would have to do, and under what name he would pass.

They relied upon Pieter Sluys for that information. His explanations, his excuses, they brushed aside. For now they had him, and that firmly, in their grip, for even a brief note, allowed casually to fall into the hands of Resistance circles, would have meant his doom. Of this they were well aware. They returned him to England. "Come back with something better," were their last words to him.

If Sluys had been unaware previously of the magnitude of his undertaking, he became aware of it now. He was trapped. Just one word too many, just one impulse towards virtue, and his German employers would have had no further qualms about betraying him. He was trapped, indeed, but this is not to say that Sluys felt greater remorse than that of any wrongdoer threatened from two sides.

He was a most practical young man, with his baby blue eyes and his crinkled hair and his nails bitten down to the quick. He was most practical . . . and also most unsentimental.

When he arrived in London Sluys was granted leave. His leave expired, he should by rights have returned to the Holding School, near Oxford, there to await his next briefing. He contrived, however—upon some such pretext as the requirement of dental treatment—to remain in London, and not only to remain there, but also to pay frequent visits to the flat which was used as the Organisational briefing rooms.

His presence there excited no suspicion: on one day he would call to arrange some difficulty concerning his army allowances, on the second to complain that the shoulder-padding of a French suit issued to him was excessive, on the third to present a supplement to the report of his escape.

Unnoticed, he prowled the long uncarpeted passages, sat in the waiting rooms and there, shyly admiring, engaged in coy conversation men who, with folders outspread upon their knees, would yet spare time to listen.

In this work—which was certainly most dangerous—Sluys was served at once by luck and by his own natural audacity. The trained agent, uncommunicative at normal times, is most liable to indiscretion upon the eve of his operational departure. Even then, of course, he will reveal nothing of the first importance, but emotional disturbance, the too long suppressed desire to boast and the craving for friendship may draw from him in those last hours, through tactful enquiry, his field name, for example, and a general indication of the area to which he is going.

Sluys, well placed to enquire, and even better placed to win confidence, was able to secure seven such names; including three of quite exceptional importance. His memory for faces being excellent, he now needed only an operation which would take him back to France.

Nor was this slow in forthcoming: upon several occasions, notably at the time of the North African landings, it had been thought in London that the Germans might attempt their long-prepared invasion of Spain. Plans had been laid . . . plans involving the despatch of a single sabotage group to wreck railway lines leading south from Bordeaux, Agen and Toulouse. The job was the sweeter, the more worth while of performance, because the railway lines in question were electrified.

The derailment of a train, and the destruction of even a dozen electrical pylons on either side of it, might well hold up traffic for a week.

At the time of which we are writing, however, the totality of France lay under enemy occupation, an offensive was in progress against Rome, while, in the West, the invasion seemed imminent. The question of a breach of Spanish neutrality by the Germans no longer arose.

Nevertheless, the authorities, having had their plan in the pending file for so long, decided, at this late juncture, to bring it out . . . perhaps because they desired to see how it would work, perhaps because it represented an excellent training exercise for inexperienced men, of whom greater things would soon be required.

The operation involved less than normal risks to the personnel involved, for all three objectives chosen lay close to the Spanish front, while the surrounding countryside of Landes and Basses-Pyrénées was thickly wooded, confused of contour, and most difficult to search. Also, French resistance in that area was weak, and in need of encouragement.

Rumbold, with seven companions, dropped near Morcenx, between Labouheyre and Dax on the Bordeaux-Bayonne line. Of the seven men who went with him only one—Sluys—possessed previous experience, and he was obliged to leave the party immediately, having been chosen to execute a subsidiary operation between Mont-de-Marsan and Orthez. This selection, very fortunate for Sluys, since it enabled him to proceed without hindrance to the nearest German Headquarters, resulted in the surprise and near extermination of the main party before their attack had been made.

Lying up in pine woods not far from the railway line, they were surrounded by a company of Field Gendarmerie, with armoured cars and dogs. Five men were killed outright. Rumbold, wounded in the hip by a grenade burst, survived to be taken by his captors to Dax.

Here he was confronted with Sluys: a dramatic scene, in its way, but of the circumstances of which neither, perhaps, made full advantage.

"So your career with us is over, I take it?" said Rumbold, after formal evidence of identification had been taken.

"It is," replied Sluys. "And I am sorry it had to involve you, Rumbold. I'm genuinely sorry about that."

"Well, I must say I admire your nerve," said Rumbold. "How much do you get paid, if the question is not indelicate?"

"I have not yet been paid at all," said Sluys. "But I shall look into the question when I get back to Paris."

"And also denounce a number of people, I take it," said Rumbold. "*How* many, if you will pardon my curiosity?"

"Oh, not many," said Sluys. "But one thing leads to another, you know. The labourer is worthy of his hire. As for you, Rumbold, I could make things quite easy for you, if you cared."

Rumbold replied that he was too old to change his allegiance at that stage of the game.

Sluys said that there was no question of Rumbold being offered alternative employment, but rather . . . thanks to his past kindness to Sluys . . . of his having an easier time in prison, and of escaping the death sentence.

Rumbold remarked that he was glad to hear this, as he was accustomed to a life of comfort, and had no desire to die. This concluded the conversation, which was held in the presence of several German officers. The pair never met again.

Rumbold was taken, under escort, from Dax to Toulouse. On the way, somewhere near Auch, he jumped the train while it was travelling at reduced speed, by the ancient but simple expedient of asking permission to relieve nature, and then flinging open a door and himself out of it, while his escort stood undecided.

Escaping further capture, he made his way slowly up-country towards the mountainous and inaccessible department of the Ardèche. He was without contacts, without money, without food tickets and without identity cards, and for the first few days—until a patriotic doctor gave him lodging—suffered acute pain from the wound in his hip.

Arrived in the Ardèche, Rumbold took refuge in the small town of Lamastre, where he was known, having spent fishing holidays there before the war when an employee of the bank in Paris. Lamastre was unoccupied, and but rarely visited by the enemy. The townspeople were safe, and those of them who might have been inclined to talk intimidated by the presence of a large and successful *maquis* in the near-by hills.

Rumbold did not join this *maquis*. He had no further interest in the war, and no desire whatever to reach Spain for the fourth time and certainly none to return to his own country. His wound healed slowly. To the curious he explained that he was a bomber pilot who had been shot down, adding, with rather more truth, that he now considered his nerves unequal to further strain. He gained a living, at first, by serving as a kitchen hand in a hotel. When he had sufficient money put by, he bought forged papers and, moving to Marseilles, embarked upon the career of which some hint has already been given. His fate remained unknown in London, and until he came forward to demand passport facilities it was thought that he had perished with the rest.

For many . . . very many had perished in that last summer before the Liberation. Sluys did his work conscientiously and well. Of the seven men whom he had been able to identify, six were located and captured, their capture leading through the breaking down of cells, the interception of couriers and the neutralisation of radio operators to a degree of a disorganisation of which the Germans had good cause to pride themselves.

Strangely . . . yet not so strangely when one comes to consider his twofold position . . . Sluys remained for a long time unidenti-fied as the root of these disasters. Enlightenment came much later, and, as might be expected, accidentally.

One day, in the early spring of 1944, a young woman who had had the misfortune to be arrested in Paris during an incident outside the Metro Station, Porte-Maillot, while carrying certain documents, was brought into the presence of a very senior German official. The interview was of an exploratory nature, for the documents carried by the young lady, while of a curious and equivocal complexion, were not in themselves absolutely compromising.

Towards the end of the interview, the German official turned suddenly towards a young man in S.S. uniform who had been seated upon the window-sill throughout it, and who, so far, had said not one word.

"Do you know this lady?" asked the German official.

"No," replied the young man briefly and—as it was later to turn out—most inadvisedly.

For if the young man did not know the young woman, *she* at least knew him, having seen him several times in the flat behind Selfridge's. The young man was Sluys and the young woman,

released upon the recommendation of his single negative, was
later to return to London: there to expose him.

Sluys, of whose subsequent movements a constant tally was
kept, was arrested in Hamburg in the last days of the European
war. He was tried by summary court-martial and shot. He died
bravely, and to this day his relatives are unaware that he lived other
than as a Belgian patriot.

For to Sluys' credit let it be said that, his choice once made, he
never again attempted to get in touch with his English mother.

In this story, confined to bare facts, the motives which inspire
men have been most deliberately relegated to a secondary plane.
Sluys produced Rumbold as he was later to become . . . and of that
dark career we must now again speak.

Three

THE train, although theoretically a *rapide*, made slow time. At
Tarascon half an hour was wasted, at Sète another half hour.
Rumbold, who had no intention of enduring the tiresome rigma-
role of customs examination by night, abandoned his corner seat
at Narbonne and booked accommodation in a local hotel. He ate
his dinner, drank two glasses of Armagnac, and wandered down
by the canal. The evening was very clear. He could discern the
Pyrenees and the bald peak of the Prats de Mollo, fifty miles away.

He had stood in this same spot, by the drifting weeds of this
canal, nearly four years earlier, upon the occasion of his second
clandestine visit to France. Diverted from his normal escape route,
he had been sent here to attempt the rescue of a colleague held
in Perpignan prison. This colleague, an amateur photographer,
demanded that crystals of sulphate of chrome be sent to him concealed in a package of tobacco. With the aid of a pin he would
then prick raw a portion of his leg muscle equal in area to the size
of a postage stamp, and rub in the chemical. The leg would swell
and a sore would develop, indistinguishable in nature from a syphi-
litic outbreak of the tertiary period. The imprisoned man was the

more certain of these facts because he had already escaped once while under remand before the war in Mexico City by the employment of this same subterfuge. On that occasion he had been transferred to the prison hospital, where supervision had been slack, and departure easy. He hoped to be transferred to the prison hospital again now. The hospital was near Narbonne.

Unfortunately, Rumbold had been unable to procure any sulphate of chrome. He had sent copper sulphate instead. The prisoner, dosing himself with this, had observed that his symptoms were less those of counterfeit syphilis than those of genuine leg gangrene. He had died in considerable agony after the emergency amputation of the affected limb.

Rumbold, who had not learnt the reason for the miscarriage of his plan until his return to London, some weeks later, had been shocked.

He gazed at the Pyrenees now, and gazed at them with a certain irony. To-morrow he would pass through Perpignan. From the train he would even see the prison . . . the last prison in France, and the last link with a period of his life which it was Rumbold's earnest desire to forget.

Yet he knew very well, even in the secret formulation of the wish, that it was impossible of realisation; that he was chained and tied to views and opinions concerning existence which he had not willingly made his own, which had been thrust upon him by circumstance, never to be withdrawn.

His health was good. His liver, his bile ducts, his bowels functioned better than those of most town dwellers. There was no history of hypochondria in his family—what better proof of this than his endurance, when very young, of three years of life as a bank clerk?—nor was he emotionally exercised by religious questions or the fear of hell fire. Tall, well built, even handsome in an austere manner, he had never lacked women, never been obliged to return, by way of compensation, to the habits of his boyhood. Of moral scruples he had few, and of principles no more than those which exercise at Christmas time the minds of men who pass from the nappy to the coffin in the belief that the acquisition of wealth is the sole justification of life.

Yet for some time, for some months now, he had been considering the question of killing himself, restrained from this act, in the last resort, only by a certain latent curiosity, an unwillingness to leave the world without observing the fate which he believed to be imminent for it.

For this reason he was now travelling to Madrid, where memories would sap, to Lisbon, where they would carry by assault the last faculties which he retained for normal human intercourse. The grey horrors of London would achieve his ruin, and step by step he would descend, with aimlessness, lack of purpose and self-loathing his companions, to the level of gibbering imbecility.

"You have no luggage other than this one valise?"

"Nothing."

"You are carrying neither oils nor spirits, gunpowder, cartridges, percussion caps nor other material of a dangerous nature?"

"Nothing."

"Then be so good as to go into that room which you see on the right of the corridor."

Six paces. A knock, a turn of the door handle.

"You have been in Spain before?"

"Yes."

"Then why is the fact not marked upon your passport?"

"Because it is a new passport."

"When were you in Spain?"

"During the war."

"To which war are you referring? There are many wars. There was one here, if you remember."

"I am referring to the more recent, and more general holocaust."

The official wetted his finger. He opened the good book and turned the closely printed pages until he came to the letter R.

"What a lot of Rubinsteins you have," said Rumbold. It was true: a whole column and a half lay devoted to bearers of this inoffensive name.

"You should see the Cohens," said the official. He wetted his finger, flicked paper, peered.

"Ah, here we are . . . Rumgold. You are a trade unionist, a Marxist."

"Excuse me, but the name is Rumbold."

"To be sure, to be sure . . . I apologise. You have not been in the hands of the police but you have passed twice through Spain as an escaped prisoner of war."

"Three times, to be precise. On the last occasion I changed my name."

"You should have changed it the second time. Look at the trouble you put us to: there are no less than four lines about you."

"It was not for me to draw attention to the situation."

"Well, this time be more circumspect. In Madrid you must report to the Police Prefecture. You will not be permitted to leave Spain until you have done so. You understand?"

"I understand perfectly."

Rumbold hired a porter and walked down the platform. There were not many travellers, and very few indeed who had booked first-class seats. Apart from two Civil Guards, who were whispering in a corner, Rumbold had an entire pullman coach to himself. He threw his valise on the rack and went towards the open platform at the end of the coach. He stood looking at the bomb-scarred villas on the hill. Beyond the hill lay Cerbère and France. With a shudder, a jolt, the train started. The hill became smaller, blending into perspective with the hills beside it. Rumbold returned to his seat, and ignoring the frowns of the Civil Guards, stretched out upon it. He slept.

At Gerona he awoke, cold and hungry, and went out to purchase rolls and coffee. A small boy pestered him to buy peanuts. He bought some and sat munching as the train rolled on again. He now regretted that he had seen nothing of Northern Catalonia, and blamed himself for having slept. He had always considered it the height of bad manners and boorishness in a traveller that he should ignore or remain indifferent to the country through which he passed. Not every field could be interesting, of course, but everywhere men lived and each hedge, each brook was the backcloth to a life.

Rumbold produced his map and examined the route ahead, noting the bridges, the level crossings, and checking them with satisfaction when reached. The wildness, the peculiar lush grandeur of Catalonia excited him. He did not like it quite as much as Navarre, but it was new, and his heart constricted happily at the thought of the long journey before him. In no circumstances would he have agreed to travel by air: rather, he determined, even at the cost of inconvenience, to enter Portugal by a longer route. Narvao might do: he would look up the time-tables.

Arrived at Barcelona, he ignored the appeals of taxi-drivers, hiring instead an open cab, and causing himself to be driven across the town towards the port. He was charmed and impressed . . . as all must be who enter it from Marseilles . . . by the spaciousness, the industry, the quiet of this first of Mediterranean cities. Consulting his guide, he discovered that he need not leave for Madrid until the evening. He ate his lunch on the balcony of a restaurant overlooking the harbour. His coffee finished, he made enquiries of the waiter concerning a suitable brothel. The waiter obliged.

There was a certain effervescence that evening, upon the platform, as the train for Madrid shunted backside-in from the siding. A party of Catalonian girl guides, smelling vilely of urine, were the cause. These girl guides were travelling to the capital, there to attend a conference. No compartmental reservations had been made for them, and in consequence they invaded the train at its entrance with all the agility of youth, dragging nuns, rosaries, valises, tennis racquets behind them, staking claims supported by schoolgirlish scowls to corner seats. Rumbold, pummeled between plump buttocks and vestal breasts, lunged forward through sweaty serge to secure a corner for himself. He had failed to secure a sleeper, failed to secure a first-class seat. He would spend the night and a portion of the forenoon studying three female Carmelites, and two adolescents, one of whom was a sufferer from acne in its encrusted form.

The train drew out, puffing slowly to achieve its full momentum of forty miles an hour. The vinous coastal plains traversed, the train turned, at Tarragona, towards sacred Saragossa and the mountains. Here, in these dunes smoothed daily by the wind, the forces of General Franco had reached the sea in their offensive of 1938. But who now cared, who remembered even, the blood sucked in beneath the sleepers of the track? The heads of the nuns were nodding: their chins kissed the sober habit, beneath layers of which, beneath flannel, their useless tits were shrivelling. The two schoolgirls, having exchanged photographs and discussed the holiday in hand, sucked acid drops with expressions ruminant.

At Fuentes del Ebro, a country station not far from Saragossa, a girl entered the carriage and, diving beneath the obligingly raised feet of the nuns, secreted herself behind their calves and the plush.

Presently, the ticket collector appeared. The nuns, fussing deep in their purses, said nothing. The schoolgirls said nothing, either. Rumbold, who could hear the breathing of the fugitive, passed across his ticket with a trembling hand.

He could see very well the dilated eyes, the dusty cheeks, the cramped arms of the girl. "If you will only come out of there," he said, when the official had gone, "I will willingly pay your ticket to Madrid."

"I am not going to Madrid," said the girl, "I am going to Alcolea."

"It is best to leave her alone," said one of the nuns. "She will come to no harm. Here," she said, and she passed a flask of coffee down to the girl, who drank eagerly.

"But the train does not stop at Alcolea," persisted Rumbold. "There is no stop between Saragossa and Guadalajara."

"Then she must jump off," said the nun. "In the early morning, when we pass Alcolea, the train will be going slowly, for it is there that the mechanics eat their breakfast."

Rumbold was defeated. He stared at the girl and the girl stared at him. Her eyes were very dark and seemed, in the obscurity of the carriage, to be immobile. Presently she turned on her side, so that he could see no more than a portion of her dress, and one hand, outstretched and grimy.

The train rolled on. The nuns slept. They slept sedately, with hands folded upon their laps, fingers in contact with the beads. The schoolgirls also slept, their mouths open and twitching from time to time in uneasy dream. Only Rumbold remained awake.

He studied his map, but beyond Saragossa, where a further mob of passengers invaded the train, staring resentfully into the full carriage from the corridor . . . beyond Saragossa the light was dimmed. At four o'clock in the morning the ticket-inspector made his second round.

"Where are we?" said Rumbold.

"Vargas." The man seized the shoulder of the nearest nun and shook her. "Wake up, Sister. Whatever will you do when the last Trump sounds?"

The nuns wrestled with their many garments, blinding each other with a swing of a crucifix, with the folds of their sleeves, as they attempted to find their tickets. Neither schoolgirl could find her ticket at all, and ten minutes passed before Rumbold, with sudden intuition, pointed to the abandoned bag of acid drops.

"That was Vargas," he said, when peace had been restored. "If the girl wishes to leave at Alcolea it is time for her to be woken."

A nun bent down and tapped the girl's knee. There was no response, and presently it was discovered that she was unconscious, having been overcome by the fumes of the radiator system.

"Well that settles it," said Rumbold. "She must lie on the seat. If the man comes round again I will pay her fare."

"What is she to you?" said one of the nuns.

"Sister, she is nothing to me," and to prove it, he stood up and averted his head as they fumbled with her clothing. A crowd of excited soldiers peered in at the scene from the corridor. One of the schoolgirls began to snivel.

"She shouldn't have come in here . . . she shouldn't have come in here. Why can't she pay her fare?"

"Here, give her some of this," said Rumbold. He unlocked his valise and passed across a brandy bottle. "The first thing to do, of course, is to open the window." He strode across the carriage and lowered the sash a foot. The nuns raised their hands in horror as the night breeze dispersed the fug.

"You will kill her. She will catch her death of cold."

"Nonsense, if you take the trouble to look, you will see that she has opened her eyes."

"Don't hurt me . . . don't hurt me," the girl was saying. "I have done no wrong."

"Oh, give her the brandy for God's sake," said Rumbold. He looked at the girl for the first time, and was disconcerted to receive a wink in reply. She was about sixteen years of age, very poorly dressed, very dirty; with an accent which, to him at least, was almost incomprehensible. She was not beautiful, being cursed with a thickness of leg and ankle which matched ill with the lines of her waist and neck.

"What is your name?" he said.

"My name is Mañuela."

"Señor," said one of the nuns. "You must leave the carriage. This is an affair which concerns women alone. We shall look after your luggage. Pull down the blinds as you leave."

"As you wish," said Rumbold. He looked at the girl, and again received in reply something tantamount to a wink. He stepped into the corridor. The soldiers were excited.

"What's up, man? What's going on in there?"

"A woman has fainted. It is nothing."

"Then why have you left? Is there a seat vacant?" They jostled him, attempting to seize the handle of the door. Rumbold planted his feet apart, occupying the maximum amount of floor space. "Stand back," he said. "There is no seat. You can see for yourselves that she is lying down in my place."

"Cursed foreigner," they grumbled. "Why can he not book a sleeper like the rest of his kind?" Rumbold paid no attention to them. He looked out of the window. The darkness was fading. Already it was possible to distinguish the outlines of culverts and bushes. In the interval between the lighting of a cigarette and the last puff drawn from it, the whole plateau of Guadalajara became visible, with the peaks of the Guadarrama in the distance. A cold prospect, a cheerless prospect: the sun not yet being risen, scrag, scrub fields and streams alike remained a lifeless grey.

It was very cold in the corridor. On the outer glass the soldiers had drawn pictures and inscriptions with their fingers. But that had been done during the night, and at a lower altitude. Now the frost of the morning seized the trickling moisture, congealing it into ice so that the pictures and rude words were formed anew, and in intaglio.

Wine flasks were produced, and mouths grimaced to swallow, for the wine, too, was now icy and had lost the power to warm. And some there were ate bread and cheese, masticating slowly, without enjoyment, but from habit, because the day must begin with a meal.

The ticket inspector reappeared. Rumbold, glancing into the carriage met the stare of the girl. She was awake, lying outstretched, her head pillowed upon what appeared to be his hat.

"I shouldn't go in there if I were you," he said to the official.

"Eh . . . how's that . . . what do you mean?"

"You see that girl? She's a typhoid case. Those nuns are taking her to Madrid. I came out here rather than run the risk of infection."

"My God, and I've been in there twice already," said the inspector. He hurried on.

The train was travelling very slowly now. After consulting his map, Rumbold opened the inner door. The nuns were asleep.

"You must be close to Alcolea now," he said to the girl.

"I don't wish to go to Alcolea any more. I shall go on to Madrid."

"Very well. Do as you wish, but allow me to point out that you are ruining my hat."

She grinned. "What are you?" she said, "French? Why did you pay my fare?"

"I didn't pay it. I merely bluffed the inspector. Are you really ill, or were you shamming?"

"I was shamming. It was uncomfortable beneath those nuns. Their feet tickled me."

He considered her attentively. "Do you mind if I sit down?" he said. She said no, she did not mind. He could not make her out at all. There were elements which clashed: the extreme poverty of her clothes with the assurance of her manner; certain indications of good breeding which did not harmonise with her smelliness, her evident aversion to the use of soap and water.

"I have been sleeping in the fields for three nights," she said.

"Ah?"

"It is because I have run away from school."

"Indeed?"

"Don't say 'indeed' like that," she said. "If you think I am lying, you should speak up. It is more manly."

"I have no opinion. Perhaps you have never been at school at all? What is the past participle of the French verb 'surseoir,' to suspend. . . . ?"

"Sursis," she said.

"And the capital of Peru?"

"Oh, for a Spaniard, that is easy: it is Lima."

"Well, well," he said admiringly. "Now tell me more about this school. Why have you run away, for example?"

"Because I hated the place. It is an establishment to train orphans for the teaching profession. I am an orphan myself. My father was killed in the Civil War . . . with the Republicans. He was a notary."

"Just a minute," said Rumbold. "Before you tell me the complete story of your life, and so lose the advantage of surprise, let us get one important point clear. What do you want . . . why were you winking at me?"

"Well, I had read that this was the way in which to attract a man's attention."

"But for what purpose?"

"Well, I thought, since you had already offered, that you might as well pay my fare to Madrid. So I winked to encourage you . . . to be kind, as you might say."

"Wait . . . excuse me for mentioning the matter . . . but I thought your original intention was to drop off at Alcolea."

"Certainly . . . but, as I told you, I have changed my mind. I have an aunt at Alcolea, but I see, upon reflection, that she is not a suitable person to have charge of me."

"And you think that I am more suitable?"

"Oh, I don't say that. You will pay my fare in the first place. After that, we shall see."

"What shall we see?" said Rumbold.

"Well . . . you are a foreigner. Therefore you have no opportunity of placing me in a brothel, for example, or of using me in any other way of which I do not approve, for, if you misbehave, I can denounce you."

"You seem," said Rumbold, "extraordinarily sure of your personal charms."

"Oh," she said, "I look better when I am clean. It is this cursed carriage floor. When I am clean I am even elegant."

"Now listen to me," said Rumbold. "Here are two hundred pesetas. Return to your school. Inflict your presence upon your aunt. Do what you please, but abandon any designs which you may have upon me. I am travelling through Spain. I am only staying for a few days. I have no time in which to complete the education of young ladies."

"But," she said, pocketing the money, "don't you *want* to see more of me? Perhaps you are shy, perhaps I have not given you sufficient encouragement. At my school there was a book of deportment: 'Young ladies,' it said, 'whose interest has been aroused, may indicate the nature of their feelings by any means consistent with propriety.'"

"It is not," said Rumbold, "a book of deportment you require, but one containing a few straightforward moral precepts. Please allow me to take my bag and my hat . . . no, don't detain me or I will drop both on the floor and wake these admirable nuns. At present, it is true, I can go no further than the corridor, but if you molest me out there I shall shout for help."

He rose and, grasping his baggage, stared at her with deep mistrust. Up to this point both had been speaking in low tones, in whispers almost, but now Rumbold raised his voice, causing the nuns to stir and the schoolgirls to stretch their legs as consciousness returned.

"You see," he said. "Ten seconds more and they will be fully awake. You had better lie down again, hadn't you? You certainly won't retain your seat unless you keep up the pretence of being ill."

The girl stuck out her tongue at him . . . but, all the same, she lay down. Rumbold went out into the corridor with his baggage. He burst out laughing.

Four

IN Madrid, he had booked a room in advance at the Mora: this not because of some special preference . . . rather the reverse indeed . . . but because here it was that he had stayed in the old days, here that the corridors contained memories.

He was given room number twenty-four, with French windows and a balcony, and a view overlooking the outer shrubberies of the Retiro. Number twenty-eight, on the same floor, had once lodged his friend, Jacques de Menthon, who had died in a scuffle for a fallen Sten gun in the backyard of a *Kommandantur*. In number thirty-seven, down the corridor, by the bathroom, Marcelle, luckiest and most long-lived of women couriers, had received her lovers with impartiality and ardour. In those days the Mora—surely the most uncomfortable and pretentious of all Madrilene hotels—had been a recognised staging post on the road to London. Ancient governesses evacuated from the Riviera by the inexorable pressure of German circumstance, could be heard calling for tea as they returned from ceremonial visits to the Cathedral, the Prado. Whole bomber crews, dressed in non-Iberian reach-me-downs, the lusts of their flesh unsatisfied by the niggardly Embassy allowance, had played poker all day beneath the dropping palms of the lounge, for stakes measured in fractions of a peseta. At the more exclusive tables in the restaurant, old gentlemen of military . . . and sometimes of diplomatic . . . appearance crumbled their bread, asked in low voices for *Anis* or *Pastis* or *Slivovitz*, depending upon the country of their origin, and sketched in pencil upon the table cloth the main features of the various theatres of hostilities (the management was eventually obliged to hang a notice in the restaurant, asking clients not to use indelible pencils for this purpose). These old gentlemen—Liberal members of the Belgian Senate, French generals on the retired list who had decided that patriotism might be more remunerative in Great Britain, the occasional

Italian Communist moving from one set of hard times to another, the dispossessed but still vocal Jewish business men, the fashionable violinists whose long and expensively prepared conversion to democratic principles was now expected to yield dividends in would-be clever propaganda—these gentlemen, supported by the British taxpayer, were on their way to the current Land of Promise. The main question in their minds was whether they would travel by Gibraltar, which was dull, or by Lisbon, which was lively.

Their destinies, together with those of returning agents, of escaped airmen and soldiers, of the governesses, and of the thousand odds and coloured sods (the Parsee stranded for some inexplicable reason in Milan, the West African in Liechtenstein) . . . these destinies had been in the hands of certain young gentlemen at the Embassy, more remarkable for their good breeding than for either tact or perspicacity. A sliding scale of beneficence existed: the French general, the successful agent received one sum for living expenses each day; the Parsee, and the Yid without security, quite another.

In so much, that that portion of the British treasury reserve, those few thousands of Victorian and Edwardian gold sovereigns which were not being scattered in the Balkans to corrupt the already corrupt and to provide mules and Turkish delight for use of liaison officers . . . that remnant was being scattered here.

Madrid in 1942, in 1943 . . . oh, of course, to claim the real putty medal of democracy one must have seen it in 1936—but at that time Rumbold had already acquired the conviction that all men are bastards ("there are bastards in all nations", the German officer had told him shortly after a sentry had struck him when manacled). He had acquired that conviction and was uninterested and unable to associate himself with a struggle between certain reactionary elements and other elements who, without travelling to the front, succeeded in decimating themselves in Barcelona. Franco, in Rumbold's opinion, had been the best solution. Presently he would go, having spent much blood but having spent it in an unpharisaic manner. And this was important, very important to persons like Rumbold who had observed that, with the gentle evolution of the world, it was now impossible to declare one's dislike of certain races, certain creeds, without being called, in turn, a Fascist.

Madrid in '42 and '43 . . . a wide, a so very airy city, a kind of Perpignan transported without rhyme or reason to the level of mid-Sierra, and then chopped by ten leafy variants of the Boulevard Haussmann. The suburbs drop off into dung heaps and piles of rusting petrol cans. Within a mile of all three railway stations, carts, manned by peasants, wend their way towards the outer wilderness. The occupants bear flowers to be laid upon graves, and carbines with which to shoot rabbits.

And Madrid in 1946 was not so very different. Such, at least, was Rumbold's discovery. The season, to be sure, was now winter: chestnuts had replaced figs upon the carts of street vendors, but the contrast between splendour and squalor remained: a contrast without its parallel in any other city except Cairo.

At the hotel, although the administrative staff was unchanged, the manager did not recognise Rumbold, and paid no particular attention to him, apart from enquiries concerning the cost of living in France. Rumbold took a bath, ate a lunch enlivened by the excellent red wine of Navarre, and went out with the intention of passing the afternoon in pedestrian re-exploration of the city. Fifty yards down the street, he turned into a wine-shop, drank several glasses of *Manzanilla*, threw dice for half an hour with the proprietor, and losing, decided to go to the bank to change his French money in order to save himself the trouble of broaching the secret hoard in his shoes. Somewhat heavy on his feet from much wine, he travelled to the bank by taxi.

Stone steps flaring outwards flanked by urn-bearing balustrades . . . a portico of the mid-Baring period . . . swing doors that were genuine modern Rothschild. Some people suffer a depression of the spirit in railway-stations, in barber shops, in the cascade and antiseptic drip of lavatories. The nose is the Judas of the sensory organs. Immune elsewhere, Rumbold had, from his earliest days as a junior clerk, been susceptible to this *malaise* in banks. Therefore, he paused before the swing doors, hesitating until driven forward by the arrival of two messengers, whose path he blocked.

He walked straight to the Chief Cashier's grille.

"Hullo, Barnard," he said, without surprise.

The man peered at him from behind thick lenses. "Why, Rumbold," he said. "It is Rumbold, isn't it? We thought you were dead."

"No," said Rumbold. "Not dead."

"Well, what brings you here?" said Barnard. He had heard something about Rumbold, but couldn't remember quite what. He was certain that the man was supposed to be dead, though. "What brings you here?" he repeated. In his trouser pocket his fingers closed defensively upon coins. He feared a touch.

"Just a little question of currency exchange," said Rumbold. He indicated the wad of notes which he had flung on the counter. There was a great deal of money in the wad.

"Ah," said the cashier. His expression of caution did not relax, but underwent a mutation from private to official suspicion. Where had this man, once a clerk, obtained this considerable sum? "You want pesetas?" he said.

"Naturally."

"Just a moment then." The chief clerk handed the notes to an assistant behind him. The assistant disappeared from view. "Shan't keep you a second," said the chief cashier.

Rumbold watched with amusement the mummery taking place behind the bars. He was perfectly well aware that Barnard suspected that the notes were either forgeries, or hot.

"Well, Barnard," he said. "You've come up in the world, I see."

"You, too, perhaps," said Barnard.

"Yes and no, old man . . . yes and no. But chief cashier! Well, that *is* something to be proud of. How do you like it in Madrid? Better than Paris, eh? I suppose you were here throughout the war?"

"I was," said Barnard. "The military wouldn't take me. My chest, you know."

"I remember your chest," said Rumbold. "Ah, how I wish that I, too, had had a chest."

The assistant returned and whispered something to Barnard. "Oh," said Barnard, "all right. How will you take it?" he said to Rumbold. "In tens, or fifties?"

"Any way you like, old man," said Rumbold. "You see, you shouldn't be so suspicious of an old colleague. But I forgive you, Barnard. I have a generous nature. Here's a little something to prove it."

From the new notes handed to him he extracted one, of fifty pesetas value, and laid it on the counter. He began to walk away.

"Take your money back at once," shouted the chief cashier. He positively pranced with rage, clawing the woodwork, and thrusting a thin wrist through the grille in an attempt to strike the note to the floor.

"Now, now," said Rumbold. "Remember where you are, and that you're behind the bars. You'll never get out from behind those bars, Barnard. A pity, because you look to me as if you had cirrhosis."

"You watch your step," hissed the chief cashier. "I know you, Rumbold. There was always something fishy about you. Take my advice and check with the Spanish police. We can make things pretty hot for you here."

"Funny you should say that," replied Rumbold. "You've reminded me of something I have to do."

He raised his hat solemnly, and bowed, watched with amusement by fellow clients, with apprehension by the chief cashier.

"Goodbye, Barnard," he said. "I'll be in again tomorrow to change some more of the loot."

Outside the bank, he hailed another taxi. He instructed the driver to take him to the Police Prefecture.

"Yes?" said the duty clerk in the Aliens' room.

Rumbold extended his passport. "Transit visa," he said. "Any pretty stamp you care to put upon it will be welcome."

The duty clerk reached for the thick black book of names.

"You can save yourself the trouble," said Rumbold. "Somebody has already taken a look at it at Portbou. As a consequence, I was asked to call here most particularly . . . most particularly."

"Ah," said the clerk. "In that case you had better follow me." He lifted a detachable section of the counter, and beckoned Rumbold to pass. Rumbold followed the man through the office, through an inner office in which two women typists wearing eye-shades were sipping coffee and gossiping, and into a long and cold white corridor.

"Please wait here a moment," said the clerk. He knocked upon a door, entered, and closed it behind him. Left alone, Rumbold inspected the pictures in the passage. These were reproductions of Goya's "Horrors of the War". Abstractedly, Rumbold noticed that one of the men in the firing squad was not holding his musket correctly.

The clerk came out of the office: "The Director will see you now," he said.

"The Director?" said Rumbold. "This is choice . . . very choice. Am I to take it that I enjoy priority?"

The clerk did not answer. He scowled. Rumbold entered the office, which was small, but comfortably furnished . . . electric fire with imitation coals, massive paperweights, less than usually distasteful photograph of General Franco, curtains of heavy green material, spittoon, and easy-chair for visitors.

Behind a roll-top desk in need of dusting sat a man with a non-secular face.

"Mr. Rumbold, good morning," he said in English. "You are a very interesting man and I am glad to make your acquaintance. Please sit down."

Rumbold sat down. "From your manner," he said, "I infer that you have some proposition to make to me. I have no idea what this can be, but trust that it will be in keeping with those principles to which I subscribe."

"'Subscribe,' is, of course, the *mot juste*," said the man behind the roll-top desk. "I shall come to my proposition presently. Meanwhile let us re-examine the history of certain incidents familiar to both of us."

From a drawer the man produced a pink folder. He consulted this folder: "On the 16th July, 1942," he said, "at the entrance to the British Consulate, Bilbao, you assaulted the uniformed Civil Guards, Zuloaga and Arrese. The Guard Zuloaga suffered a fractured jaw, the Guard Arrese multiple contusions. By reason of the diplomatic immunity which you then enjoyed, you were never called upon to answer for this crime. Correct?"

"Correct," said Rumbold.

The man turned a page of the folder. "On the 16th November, 1942," he continued, "upon the occasion of your third visit within eight months to our country, you deflated the tyres of a German military staff car which was parked in the Calle Major. Asked what you were doing by a police agent who had observed you at work, you struck this man, and made off at full speed on foot. Chased, you took refuge in the British Embassy, where you remained . . . once again enjoying extra-territorial protection . . . until your departure from Spain in an Embassy car. Correct?"

"Perfectly correct," said Rumbold. "Tell me, have you many such delightful case histories, and are they all housed in pink folders?"

"We have a great many such histories," said the man behind the roll-top desk, "but the colour of the folders varies considerably. Yours, as you have observed, is pink: this pleasant pastel shade indicating that the crimes of which you are accused are not taken very seriously."

"I am glad to hear that," said Rumbold. "Your intention in recalling them was, I take it, to impress me with your efficiency."

"Yes," said the man behind the desk, "I confess that such was my aim. You see, Mr. Rumbold, despite the fact that the New Spain has been in existence for some years, there are many abroad who believe that the slothfulness, the . . . how shall I put it . . . the spirit of *mañana* still rules supreme. I would not like you to think this, Mr. Rumbold. I would not like you to think this at all."

"Oh, believe me," said Rumbold politely, "I have the greatest respect for your police."

At this point in the conversation a short silence ensued. Rumbold stared out of the window at an asphalt courtyard flanked by plane trees. A workman was sweeping leaves into heaps with a broom, and loading these heaps upon a wheelbarrow.

"You are a Catholic, I believe, Mr. Rumbold," said the man behind the desk.

"I was born a Catholic," admitted Rumbold.

"Then you will also die a Catholic. In the meantime, however, you are going home to England . . . is that not so?"

"Yes," said Rumbold.

"Where you will be arrested and tried as a deserter, I believe? Is this not also correct?"

"Oh, I very much doubt that, you know," said Rumbold pleasantly. "English methods are considerably more lax than your own. However, don't let me interrupt you. Please continue. I see perfectly what you are driving at and am watching your approach with interest and even . . . if you will permit me to say so . . . with amusement."

The man behind the roll-top desk smiled. He wore square, rimless glasses of American manufacture, and when he smiled his face underwent an owlish metamorphosis which was far from unpleasing.

"You speak Spanish so well," he said. "In an Englishman that is unusual. Yet you were not here during the Civil War, I understand?"

"No," said Rumbold. "I learnt it for commercial purposes . . . to obtain an increase in pay, as a matter of fact. In the banking business linguists are valuable."

The man behind the roll-top desk removed his glasses. He began to polish them. His eyes, which Rumbold now saw clearly, were dark and lustrous, illuminating the steep brow, the thin and questing nose with a suggestion of magnanimity. In the cornea of every short-sighted man there lies the stuff of dreams.

"With your knowledge of the language," he said gently, "you could do well in Spain."

"You are suggesting that I stay here?"

"I am suggesting that you might do very much worse."

Rumbold selected a cigarette from his case, and lit it. He offered the case to the man behind the desk, who refused. "You forget that I am a poor man," he said. "The current exchange rate is not favourable to prolonged residence here."

"The exchange rate," said the man, "does not affect people who reside permanently in this country, and who earn their living here."

Rumbold was astonished: "Surely you don't propose that I should accept Spanish nationality?" he said.

"Why not? Of course, there would be a period of probation . . .

on both sides . . . but in the end I am sure that it would suggest itself to you as the most logical and sensible of steps."

"Well, well," said Rumbold. "This is most intriguing. Please be more explicit."

"Certainly." The man crossed his legs. He pushed his swivel chair several inches away from the desk. "By the way, my name is Aranjuez," he said.

"I was afraid it might be Torquemada," said Rumbold.

Both laughed. "No," said Aranjuez, "I am not the Grand Inquisitor, but still less am I Don Quixote. My proposition is a sensible one because I am a practical man with a position to consider." He paused. "Are you aware, Mr. Rumbold," he said, "that there is a certain measure of dissidence in this country, that there exist persons who are dissatisfied with the Government, and who would be glad to change it?"

"How can one fail to be aware of it?" said Rumbold.

"Precisely. Your answer pleases me. How, as you say, can one fail? Now you, Mr. Rumbold, are a man whose courage is not in doubt and who, in addition, have received training of a particular nature."

"You mean, I suppose, in sabotage, and underground work in general?"

"That is what I mean, Mr. Rumbold. Oh, I realise that we poor neutrals are not supposed to be aware of these things, but, during the war, our very position as neutrals, with a foot in both camps, enabled us to learn much that was going on. I have here, for example, a report of the activities of your organisation. It does them, if I may say so, great credit."

"Wait a minute," said Rumbold. "If I interpret you correctly, you are offering me employment on the principle that reformed burglars make the best policemen. Is that so?"

"Yes, Mr. Rumbold, it is so. Instead of working underground you would work for us in the *counter*-underground. Your knowledge of explosives alone would make you invaluable to me, while the fact that you are a foreigner . . . far from being a handicap . . . might prove a positive advantage. I have been waiting to engage somebody like you for a long time, Mr. Rumbold."

"Yes, I daresay you have," said Rumbold. "What's more, you think I'm the more likely to accept because of certain difficulties which may await me in England."

"Well, Mr. Rumbold, you put it rather bluntly, but I confess that you interpret my thought. Besides, even if you have no trouble, what future is there for you in England? You are a man of action. You surely do not wish to return to your bank?"

"No," conceded Rumbold. "I do not, nor do I intend to do so. But that is no reason why you should assume that I should jump at the employment you mention in Spain. I find your optimism rather ... rather *insulting*, Señor Aranjuez. You have evidently made up your mind that I am a man devoid of scruples."

"You have no political scruples, surely, Mr. Rumbold?

"None whatever, but I nevertheless object to hounding down my fellow men, while disguised, no doubt, as an innocent tourist. I have been hounded down too often myself, Señor, to find your proposition alluring."

The man, Aranjuez, was silent for a moment. He appeared to be considering some question irrelevant to the subject under discussion. A small and fleeting smile caused his lips to droop.

"Good pay," he said at length. "Good prospects. A position of honour and confidence, the reasonable certainty of a long and happy life and the bourgeois fear of destitution removed by the promise of a pension in old age ... these arguments, Mr. Rumbold, are, I know, unlikely to influence you, but before you commit yourself let me remind you that the profession of mercenary is as ancient as it is dignified. The words in which I make this offer are mine but the spirit is that of a Lorenzo de Medici, of a Bourbon monarch in parley with Dupleix. I have need of you, Mr. Rumbold. I need your independence of mind for myself, and your technical knowledge for the training of my men."

"In that case," said Rumbold, "you should choose your historic parallels with more care. Dupleix died in squalor. The hired men of Lorenzo were almost always assassinated."

"*Tiens*," said Aranjuez. "So you are also a historian? I did not know that you added intellectual pretensions to your other accomplishments."

"I have small intellect," said Rumbold, "and my pretensions are all uniquely sensual. But I have observed in the course of the last few months . . . and particularly in the last few days . . . that people are continually trying to *engage* me, to oblige me to associate myself with their desires, their plans, their way of Life."

"You imagine that you can remain aloof from Life, then?" said Aranjuez, ironically. He glanced at his watch, but seeing that Rumbold had observed him and made as if to rise, waved him back to his seat. "No, no," he said. "Please forgive me. It was a reflex action. I do not want to get rid of you. On the contrary, I am interested, and am learning much. Please continue. . . ."

"Very well," said Rumbold, recrossing his legs. "Yes, I do confess that it is my hope to remain aloof. That is the lesson which my formative years, all spent in war, have taught me. I despise the world. I cannot accept its conventions. I do not wish to be driven, *cornered*, the victim of chance and circumstance and the whims of others financially more powerful than myself."

"That," said Aranjuez, "is exactly why you are the man for me."

"Even though I be sick of heart, and mind?" replied Rumbold, in his turn ironical.

"Doubly so for that reason."

"But wait," said Rumbold. "You have not heard all, though you appear to have some general knowledge of it. Tired of grand larceny I determine to return to England. *Immediately*, I am caught up in the toils of a previous existence. My Consul warns me. My original employers in London make it plain that, upon landing, I must see them. Meanwhile, my business associates attempt to retain me, and I have the greatest difficulty in leaving at all. On the train I consider myself safe, but no . . . within an hour or two I very nearly become involved with a young woman in search of a Protector. . . ."

"Who is this young woman?" interposed Aranjuez. "She is Spanish?"

"It's of no importance. She won't find me again. If I mention her at all it is merely to illustrate the pressure of circumstance upon me."

"Ah, forgive me, but now you are being silly," said Aranjuez, repolishing his spectacles. "You are ill: this I grant, but you are ill of your own volition . . . because you wish to be ill. I can cure you, for your illness is the result of unemployment."

"Is it?" said Rumbold. "You thinking men have a definition for everything of course, but I am not so fortunate."

He uncrossed his legs, extinguished his cigarette, and this time, rose frankly to his feet.

"You are not going?" said Aranjuez.

"I'm afraid that I must."

"Well," said Aranjuez. He displayed a fine white palm, the fingers outspread in evidence of civilised resignation. "Well, I shall not attempt to detain you, nor, though it is within my power, shall I prevent you leaving Spain. I appreciate that you must ascertain how you stand with the British authorities. When you have done so, make a call at the Spanish Embassy in London and mention my name. I think we shall have many more instructive conversations, Mr. Rumbold."

"You are so sure of that?"

"I have never been so sure of anything in my life."

"You think you know the kind of man I am, then?" Rumbold felt depressed: he had no reason to suppose that the estimate of Aranjuez was other than correct.

"I have been dealing all my working life with the kind of man you are, Mr. Rumbold," said Aranjuez. "You are a man of violence."

Five

RAIN was falling. The wind blew in gusts from the north. Beneath the wand-like shape of the great telephone building the cafés gleamed cosy; for electricity is cheap in the Peninsula. Passing with mackintosh flung loose about his shoulders, Rumbold peeped at the chess players whose haunches indented the plush.

At the Puerta he turned left. He knew his way . . . "Escapada" . . . the ribbon lighting of the sign shone blue, reflected impartially upon the streaming pavements and upon the faces of urchins still attempting to sell waterlogged copies of the evening press.

A queer bloody name for a *boîte*. . . .

Rumbold turned into the café next door. He ordered a *fine*. Members of the night-club's feminine orchestra, who were enjoying a last coffee here before attuning their instruments, ignored him. They were an unattractive bunch. Piano, drums, accordion and effects, the soft flesh just above and just beneath their eyes was baggy; their complexions, though smooth with fard, chlorotic from the prolonged inhalation of an atmosphere alien to health.

His misery coagulating, Rumbold tapped his glass upon the zinc and received a second *fine*. He drank it and his thoughts soared away into realms of profundity and recollection, untapped except by this means. The world was once again explainable.

He watched the coffee-drinkers depart, allowing them ten minutes advance. The intervening wall was thin, the repertoire of the band not new. Throughout *Sweet Sue* he waited patiently. At the second chorus of *Some of These Days*, he made his entrance.

Swing doors. Beyond them a long room, as bare of surplus fittings as a garage, and as cold. A bar flanked by quasi-inaccessible stools, from which, once seated, it would be a case of mountaineering to descend. Tables with dirty covers, with for all furniture a pepper-pot, an ash-tray and an unpolished champagne bucket. Some of these tables were favourably placed, being near the rostrum of the band and by the touch-line of the dance floor, upon which, in due course certain artistes would perform. Other tables ranged away into a smoky gloom which, by reason of the early hour, it had not yet been thought necessary to illuminate. In the farthest reaches of this hinterland neon lights bespoke the offices . . . "Telephone" and "Gents" and "Ladies Cloakroom". The mural decorations, parodies of classics (the Miaya Vêtue, the Miaya Nue, Los Borrachos, the View of Zaragoza) were witty in intention, in execution lamentable.

Between the bar (at which some half dozen deadheads were knocking back Amontillado on the house) and the tables, ladies of the Sapphic persuasion circulated; their impregnability to mankind *affiché* by the tie, the stiff collar, the cropped nape and the ill-fitting tailor-made.

For the lusts of the flesh are not sinful when sterile, and the

"Escapada" enjoyed the patronage of Ministers—no less—as well as that of the entire foreign colony.

Choosing a table equidistant between the din of the band and the lounging wine waiter, Rumbold sat down. The latter sprang forward. The eyes of the two men met, in mutual respect of a right of choice that was in fact no right at all, but simply a convention.

"Champagne," said Rumbold.

When the bottle came the cork flew seven metres. It was Navarrese white wine, heavily aerated, and the Mumm label had been clumsily affixed.

Sipping the gaseous mixture (eighty-five pesetas for one bottle, the contents of which had been squeezed from the grapes by the black toes of peasants, working at fifty centimos to the hour), sipping, Rumbold surveyed the dancing scene.

Jig-a-jig-a-jig. Low heels, high heels. The whirling swish of dirndls, the dull sound of trouser turn-ups as they encountered the hiatus between male shoe and sock. The proprietress, a woman who would have made no mean figure in a catch-as-catch-can ring, picked her way from table to table, attempting to sell roses to clients not yet sufficiently sentimental to buy.

At Rumbold's entrance there had not been many genuine clients, but by the time he had emptied his first bottle and been once to the toilet the local colour in the house had become swamped by those who were prepared to pay for these sad pleasures. South American diplomats, newly dined, cigars between their canines, their wives imperious but a little flustered by the attentions of the intermediate sex to which they were immediately subjected . . . the odd American from the airport ground staff, a few British of apparently Consular status, even some Spaniards, though these latter exclusively of the theatrical profession.

The drums rolled. The spotlight, inexpertly handled, settled upon the bosom of the proprietress, who made an announcement inaudible beneath the clinking of glasses and the chatter of the men at the bar. A dancer appeared, a thin and earnest woman wearing a mantilla, a brassière, and a full skirt of floral design. She was not a very good performer but such talent as she possessed was not aided by the refusal of various guests to vacate the dance floor. Confined within an area of some twenty square feet, greeted with indifference, the poor woman pranced, pirouetted, sank beneath the weight of an insufficiently suggested misfortune, and crouched at last at ground level to the reward of ironic hand-claps.

Something in the hostility of this reception seemed to find a response in the dancer, whom Rumbold now perceived to be drunk. Brushing aside the hand of the proprietress who had come to lead her away, she rose to her feet. Gone now was the languor, gone the resignation. The confusion of styles was absolute, but the effect not without a certain comic value. The navel oscillated in homage to the Can-Can. The fingers flexed and rippled some-where in the Indian ocean between the Dravidians and Bali. The buttocks, unassisted by a bustle, yet contrived to play their part, while the feet, twirling ever faster, caused even the drinkers to turn in delicious anticipation of an accident.

Allez-oop . . . the high heel rose four feet three inches. *Allez* . . . *oop*; this time it was four foot nine. Fed by rage, the woman's employment of the small area at her disposal was masterly, but this same rage was to be her undoing. Turning to reply to the indeli-cate aside of some man immediately behind her she lost balance, fell, and falling, carried Rumbold's champagne bucket and his table cloth in a fine cascade of froth and linen to the floor.

A roar of applause arose. The dancer did not appear to hear it. She sat, crying, in the mess. Blood dropped from her chin and from a finger. Rising, Rumbold offered her his handkerchief amid sniggers. The woman looked at him with hate, seized the handker-chief, and fled.

Peace returned. The band struck up. The dancers circulated, grinning. The wine waiter approached, replaced the dripping cloth, replaced the broken bottle. Several people peered curiously at Rumbold, among them a woman who was sitting at a table on the other side of the dance floor with two men, both obviously Span-ish, and a girl. The woman, however, seemed to be either English or American. Looking up, Rumbold found that she was inspect-ing him with an intensity unwarranted by the circumstances. He shifted position slightly, ducked his head behind the screen of dancers, and lit a cigarette. As he did so, the wine waiter reappeared, holding a pleated theatre programme.

"For me?" said Rumbold.

"For you, Señor."

Rumbold smoothed down the crinkled art-paper. "Would you," the note ran, "care to join us at our table?"

The writing was rhomboid, schoolgirlish and in English.

"Keep this," said Rumbold, indicating his bottle, "for me."

"I cannot retain the table for you if you leave it, Señor," said the wine waiter.

"No?" said Rumbold. He held out a bank-note.

"I will reserve both bottle and table, Señor," said the wine waiter.

Rumbold crossed the floor. "How did you know that I was English?" he said, still standing.

"By your tie," she said. "My cousin was at Harrow."

"Then I must disappoint you. I wear the tie for business purposes, and from snobbishness."

"Well, at least you are frank," she said. "Won't you sit down? Don't let my companions alarm you. I only met them an hour ago. This," she continued, indicating the man upon her right, "is Mariano, and this . . . ." She pointed to the young man on her left:

"Juan," said this one, bowing slightly.

"He took a Berlitz course in languages two years ago," explained the Englishwoman. "The girl is named Inez. The three of them work the clubs together. Something for every taste, you know, with just the hint of blackmail thrown in. They are really most disconcerted at your arrival, I can tell you."

"Not at all," said the young man called Juan, his enunciation of each syllable both luscious and correct. "If you wish to talk with this gentleman, Inez and I will dance."

"It is a pity that Mariano cannot dance too," said the Englishwoman.

Juan said something to Mariano in Catalan.

"I will drink at the bar," said Mariano, rising with tragic dignity.

"Well now," she said, when all three had gone, and Rumbold had sat down. "Don't you think that was rather neatly done? They would be off for good, of course, if they knew that I had only three hundred pesetas in my purse."

Rumbold surveyed the two empty bottles of champagne upon the table, the third in its bucket, already more than half-way gone. "So that's how it is, is it?" he said.

"That's how it is," she confirmed.

Rumbold took the champagne bottle, and poured himself a glass. "I am not in the habit of assisting my compatriots," he said.

"Don't worry," she said. "I have much more in my hotel."

"That fairy tale, too, I have heard before."

"You don't like me, then," she said. She lit a cigarette and blew a smoke ring, which burst.

"You have two legs and certain attributes," he said, "but I've seen hundreds."

He gazed at her. She was a well-built woman, big of bone, wide-hipped, long-legged. Her height, in her nylons, might have been a full five feet seven, her weight ten stone, of which the last fourteen pounds was an interim dividend of advancing years and inattention to simple exercise. This surplus weight was distributed between hip and thigh and ankle. Her hair was a rich mouse colour, neither russet, nor, except in certain areas bleached by the sun, true blonde. Some grey hairs were present and no attempt had been made either to remove or to disguise them. The eyes were green, not the colour of grapes, but that of goose droppings. The nose was blunt and formless, the lips generous; but of a generosity inherited rather than acquired. Seen from a distance of five yards, with her white complexion touched by freckles, her great eyes tragic, and as tragically blank, she reminded Rumbold of the moon on the second day of its declension from the full. Her age he estimated at twenty-nine: he was to learn that she was thirty-two.

"Fiona Lampeter," she said, acknowledging his inspection with an ironical bow.

"Rumbold," said Rumbold.

There was a short silence. Among the dancers Rumbold observed Inez and Juan. The girl, Inez, was watching him.

"I cannot lend you any money," he said.

"No? And yet you gave your handkerchief to that poor woman when she fell. . . ."

"That was different. No commitment was involved."

"Look," said the Englishwoman suddenly. She opened her bag and displayed it. Amid the confusion of compact and lipstick, of papers and photographs and pieces of string lay a bundle of one hundred peseta notes. She began to laugh.

"I am glad you find the joke amusing," he said.

"Amusing? No . . . deadly serious, I promise you. I like to find out about people from the first."

"It is time that I returned to my table," said Rumbold.

He made as if to rise. She laid a hand upon his forearm. Her nails were very long, the colour of betel nut juice, the shape of almonds.

"Don't go," she said. "I apologise."

"You are surely not going to pretend that you are incapable of dealing with a couple of ponces?"

"Yes, I am," she said humbly.

"In that case you have no business to pick up such people."

"No."

"Where are you going?" he said. "What are you doing here?"

"You want the story of my life?"

"I feel sure that it is coming."

And come it did, to the accompaniment of a further bottle of champagne, for which Rumbold paid. She had been born in the year of the First Great War, in Peterhead:

"I know. There is a convict prison there."

"There are also some resident gentry and an east wind from Norway which blows for half the year."

Good family. Sound Scottish Presbyterian stock with a claim to have fought for Charlie at Culloden, and an engraving of John Knox among the bric-a-brac of the best bedroom. Her father had been a Macleod: a *fils unique*, much pampered, much be-whiskered; a poor fellow, it would seem, but a man of good will and some latent courage, who, enlisting at the outbreak, had died, a subaltern, in the carnage of First Arras.

"Mother said she often dreamed of him hanging on the barbed wire. I don't remember him, and so can tell you nothing."

"Mother," while not possessing the social connections of her husband (she was a Curtis and the daughter of a draper), had family in Australia, and, in consequence, some stock and expectations in sheep farms, and four per cent Commonwealth Government bonds. This was just as well, for the Macleods, despite their large and hideous house, were in reality as poor as church mice—a metaphor which is by no means inapposite, for the grandmother was a most regular attendant at matins.

"Thank you, God, for my good dinner."

When the dinner was poor, as it often was (the barbarous *cuisine* North of the Border must be tasted to be believed), the two little girls, of whom, Peggy, the junior, had been born three months after her father's death, would abbreviate the text to:

"Thank you, God, for my dinner."

The First Great War, the Zeppelins, the sugar ration. "Mother," a hot-blooded and intrepid woman, sought refuge from the sexual chagrin of her husband's death upon the front of Salonika. Here she contracted congenital malaria, and stank of quinine ever after. The war over, she appeared at Peterhead only at long intervals, touring the world meanwhile upon funds inherited from a brother, by then fortunately defunct. The two small children, now six and seven years of age, remained with their paternal grandmother, subject to all the whims of that rigid Scottish conscience.

Books, apart from the Waverley novels, Robbie Burns, some (but not all) of Compton Mackenzie, and the massive family bible, were forbidden. The butcher's boy must touch his cap before laying meat upon the kitchen table. Life was conducted upon the North-British principle that if a man is left alone with a girl, he will immediately whip up her skirts.

There was an aunt, sister to the grandmother, in the background, and also an Irish nurse, picturesque and voluble in the role of family retainer. But neither of these personalities impinge. The most that one can say in their favour is that it was in their rooms that the children cried.

The mother, who though destined to pay the fees, had expressed her entire lack of interest (she had just married an Australian book-maker, and was much preoccupied by the payment of his debts), the girls, at an age somewhat below that of puberty, were des-patched to a public school which shall be nameless, but of which it must be said that the worst faults of the male system were there multiplied.

"By which you mean?" said Rumbold.

"If I didn't sew well, if my French dictée was bad, I would be sent, in summer, to the nets. Horrid girls, members of the first eleven, would bowl at me. It didn't matter how often my stumps were broken. The point was to find the bump in the pitch and bruise me. My mother was paying one hundred and fifty pounds a year for this. In winter, when they played hockey, I was always goalkeeper. That's the place to get hurt, I can tell you. And all that goes on . . . still . . . still."

"I'd no idea women could be so sadistic," he said.

"Then you've a remarkably poor knowledge of the human mind, my friend."

Expelled for indolence (she had never been able to learn to crochet, and could, in fact, do nothing with her hands) she had fallen readily into the role of idle, as opposed to her younger sis-ter's industrious, apprentice. Months of semi-imprisonment fol-lowed, in which the discovery of Shelley was made:

> "Human pride
> Is skilful to invent most serious names
> To hide its ignorance."

"But was she so very terrible, your grandmother?" he enquired.

"Not fundamentally, I believe, but born into that narrow world, she had made no effort to break her bonds and saw to it as a point of honour that others should be similarly bound. Her own husband had died young. There was some mystery about that which I have never clarified: they say that he committed suicide. Be that as it may, she lived on for fifty-seven years without a man. You can see what that meant: it meant the Bible and . . . oh! . . . her sago puddings, you should have seen them. The funny thing is that when we went abroad, as we sometimes did—on my mother's money, of course—granny showed quite excellent taste. She had a passion for opera, which meant Milan and Salzburg. In those places she positively glowed. She had admirers, but at home she was mean: the kind who think that all servants steal and write the word *slut* in the dust of the drawing-room mantelpiece."

"I suppose your mother took you away from all that eventually?"

"Yes, she did. For some reason she always liked me best, but of course another motive was to spite my grandmother, who detested her. My sister was always worthy and girl-guidy: you know: knots, lanyards, little whistles and black stockings. At bottom, I don't think my mother could have cared less, but I suppose she thought she might as well save one of us for hell-fire. She chose me, and took me with her to Australia. I was then sixteen."

"And Australia?"

"Hip-flasks and high tea, and meat . . . meat . . . *meat*. Mother sent me to a finishing school near Melbourne. The educational standard was about the level of a British elementary school. The one idea of every girl was to go as far as she could with a boy in the back seat of a car without actually allowing him to give her the works. The worst aspects of America, with a touch of Leeds thrown in."

"Yet Australians fight well," he demurred.

"That doesn't surprise me: they have no other cultural resources."

"And your mother's second husband?"

"A cipher, with occasional appearances in the bankruptcy court. In the end, she pensioned him off. Later, he died of cancer."

"You have a charming family."

"*N'est-ce pas?* But look carefully into anyone else's, and you'll see the maggots wriggling."

"And your mother? She must have had a lot of money?"

"Oh, it grew and grew as sheep were sheared. Mind you, she'd never done a hand's turn herself; a blackhearted brother had made the pile. Mother's part was to supervise his home life, to prevent him marrying. She succeeded, all right."

That year (it must have been about '31, though concerning dates she was vague) the mother, an inveterate globe-trotter (what can have spurred her on from palm to palm, and one Hotel Bristol to another?) had made a trip through Tahiti to Hawaii and Los Angeles. Returning, with baggage multi-coloured, she had issued her edict to the girl:

"You are wasting your time here. You shall go to Lausanne and be finished properly. I shall join you in six months."

Oh, the arrogance, the bestiality of the very rich: the imperious telephone calls to Cook's, the ten-franc, the ten-peseta, the twenty-zloty notes flung unheeding to doormen with dirty collars and seven children. Yet it needs a Calvinistic mind, indeed, to disapprove the pleasure which was hers upon arrival in Switzerland.

"On the voyage I had my first affair. He was an engineer cadet. No stripes . . . just a patch upon his collar. He took me to the sick bay . . . what a climb! I couldn't do it now. It wasn't very successful, really. The ship was rolling."

At Lausanne she discovered Life. Until that moment, as she now perceived, she had not truly breathed. She took philosophy, her natural bent: first Kant and Hegel, venerables perhaps too quickly discarded, then Heidegger and the elusive Kierkegaard. In her hours of ease she met a pianist in the street. One wink was sufficient. He took her to an *hôtel meublé*, and completed the work begun by the engineer cadet.

But mother was once again upon the way:

"You are dissipating your youth here. Go back to Scotland and get married. You shall have five pounds a week from me for life; no less, and not one penny more." She had forgotten the malaria which, neglected, was to kill her within the next ten years.

Ah, if disappointed age could but understand, if youth could but explain.

Peterhead once more: the younger sister, unrecognisable now, Leader of the Brownies, pen friend of the pastor. Strong disapproval from the grandmother, but as compensation, conferences over cups of cocoa with the aunt, late at night, amid the antimacassars. She, too, had once skirted wedlock, and it was with twenty pounds from her savings plus two pounds from the maid's that the girl took the night train from Edinburgh to Bloomsbury.

"Excuse me," interrupted Rumbold, "but your acquaintances are yearning to sit down."

This was true. Fatigued by endless rumbas, the man Juan and the girl Inez had been circulating for some minutes near the table, their eyes beseeching, but the politeness of their race a bar to sitting down again unless invited. Of Mariano there was no sign.

"Let them sit at the next table," she said. "Juan," she called. "Drink the rest of this bottle and don't disturb us. We are busy. Unless," she said, turning to Rumbold who was laughing, "unless, of course, I am boring you?"

"Not in the least. I was only laughing at your feudal manner."

"It is the best way with ponces," she said drily. "Shall I continue?"

"Do! I enjoy a good autobiographical sketch. It reminds me of the Russian novels. Do you know what I mean . . . And so they told each other the story of Their Lives."

"The Russians come in at the right moment," she continued. "For it was on that first trip to the Great Metropolis that I discovered them."

"You were living where?" he said.

"Oh, in Earl's Court, of course, at first, until I discovered that chintz surroundings and two pieces of toast for breakfast make rather a big hole in tiny incomes! Then I moved to Camden Town: sordid, you know, but near the Zoo."

"And your game preserves?"

"Well . . . Charlotte Street, you know, and Zwemmers. A curious mixture, I suppose, of Bertorellis and ice skating rinks, of the Great Pretentious and the Great Untutored."

"You married, I suppose, about that time?"

"How did you guess?"

"Because the story is not new. What was he like?"

"Oh, good school, bone-idle; a mother's boy whose mother died before the completion of her work. For a living he played poker. When things got bad he sold a car or two. He was clever with his fingers, and made discs which he put into cigarette machines, so that smoking cost him nothing. It was a shot-gun wedding. His father sent five pounds, my mother ten. I remember we had a drink at Bailey's."

"And the child?"

"A boy. I loathed it from the first. Fortunately, we had an Irish girl called Eileen. 'Tay' she taught it to say . . . 'Tay'. The child nearly drove me mad with it, and it wasn't till months later that I learned that he meant 'Tea'. When Denis and I split up, he was adopted."

"And where is your husband now?"

"Where do you think? In Kenya, learning about sisal and knocking the 'niggers' about. In the war he became a major, I believe, but I don't think he ever heard a shot fired. Very few of these professional patriots ever do."

"You were then twenty."

"Yes," she said. "I was twenty. But now I'm thirty-two."

Twenty! Rumbold calculated. That meant 1934: a bad year; one in which the great slump was nearly over, but one in which the Hitlerian decade had also just begun. What a difference, he reflected, between those who were thirty to-day, and their juniors by ten years. What a difference, also, between those who were thirty and those who, twenty-five now, had sprung from the Latin primer to the Bren gun.

These thoughts, which Rumbold attributed to the influence of champagne, he put from him as others might a leper. His mind blank once more, he listened to the unfolding of her tale.

The marriage at an end, all contact with the family in Scotland had been severed. The aunt was ill, the grandmother was dying of some bowel disease; each weekly attack more serious than the last. Soon the vast gas-lit house, with its cargo of horrific but often priceless Victoriana, would pass to the priggish, but, it seemed, warm-hearted sister.

"She often lent me money. Here is her photograph. Do you notice any point in common?"

"She has more chin than you," he said. "A better brow. The eyes are her defect: too small."

And he wondered at the voyage or two, the infrequently expressed preference of a wilful mother that could transform persons of the same blood: one into the performer of good works, the other to a feather for each wind that blew.

Just enough money to stave off with an occasional good meal the pernicious anæmia threatened by late nights, not enough to smoke, as she wished to do incessantly; not enough to buy the clothes which would have enabled her to use the writing paper in the Berkeley. Two sides to this personality: one serious, *réflechie*, the relic of Lausanne, the student of philosophy; the second flighty, irresponsible, determined to enjoy each venial and some mortal sins before her ankles thickened and the first creases should appear upon her neck:

"But I was never much good with men," she said. "For it was not money that I wanted, but affection. Conversation, polite usage, the subtleties of erotic etiquette . . . all these defeated me. I had a girl-friend. We lived together. With business men from Bradford she could talk of worsted cloth; with Poonas home from India, of polo. Yet she knew nothing of these subjects: it is a talent, I suppose."

Values! One must have some, however tawdry, even if they be represented by the dictum that the first ten thousand is the hardest one to make. She had no values, and could not play bridge. Among her own class, still comfortable in the flourishing Chamberlain era, she was an outcast. With what she naïvely termed the "Lower Orders" she felt uncomfortable and guilty, suffering no doubt from that scrupulous malady of which the Jesuits complain. Artists, real artists of course, urged her to work: the counterfeit variety borrowed sixpences from her for half-pints of bitter.

By 1938 she was in Paris with an American photographer. This must have been the period of her greatest beauty. The photographer gave her the chance of work as mannequin to a *Grande Couturière*. She refused; not from sloth, but from lack of confidence:

"Clothes I loved indeed," she said, "but somehow could never wear them. Could never summon the energy to sit for an hour before a mirror, making slight alterations to my face. My style was the politely tatty, not the mink."

"Yet you seem feminine enough," he said.

"Too much so."

And now he divined the conflict, the long shadows of the Sunday School and John Knox, denied indeed, but still powerful.

"I suppose the next step was the Great Love," he said coarsely, pleased with his own perspicacity, and yet ashamed of it.

"Yes," she said. "It was. Nor do I regret it. You know St. Tropez. Several of us had gone down there. I met a fisherman. . . ."

"You don't surprise me. The confraternity exists to pleasure English ladies on the loose."

"Not this one. He knew I had no money. My friends went back to Paris, but I stayed on. I stayed, in all, for nearly twenty months."

Puritan to Puritan, birds of the same plumage cleave together. He stopped her from smoking (later an attack of whooping cough removed the craving altogether). He cut down her drinking to three or four apéritifs each day. At night they would go out in his boat, catching lobster, red mullet and the ingredients of some rich man's *bouillabaisse* . . . round the Cap Camaret to Cavalaire and Le Lavandou; lovely names and the surrounding pinewoods as lovely. It was upon the discarded foliage of those pines, brown, resilient, that they had made their mattress.

"Was he, then, so very handsome?" he enquired.

"Yes . . . in that peculiar, hawk-like Italian way. Naples has added something to the Southern French. I did not know, then, that he was a coward. . . ."

"And with you, of course, that mattered?" he said, with calculated irony.

"When the war came he was mobilised. This made him suffer from a *Crise de Conscience*. For the first time for many months he thought of his wife, his two curly-headed children. He *abjured* me. . . ."

"I like that word," said Rumbold. "It is most suitably ecclesiastic. And you, I suppose, were suitably annoyed?"

"Oh yes, but not in the way that you imagine. I made friends with his wife. I confessed all (hitherto she had worn her horns in ignorance). We presented a united front on the lines of the Lysistrata. You can imagine the effect of *that* upon a small-time

tyrant. He went to confession five times in as many days. He hit me
once or twice but I can kick. There is a devil in me somewhere."

The Neapolitan had not collected very much from the brief
French war, except a benign form of phthisis, and, in consequence,
a pension. Meanwhile she had fled.

"To Iviza, in the Balearics. I spent the six years of the deluge
there."

"You did not think of return to England . . . the Ats, the Waffs,
the various forms of slave labour in khaki?"

"Oh, the Consul was prodigal with advice, and even warnings, to be sure: 'Mrs. Lampeter, do you not wish to serve your
country?' . . . 'No,' I replied. 'My country will always avoid its just
retribution somehow.' Also, of course, my mother, nursing to the
last in confirmation of her 1914-18 form, had joined me promptly
at the fall of France, and just as promptly died. Her will made of
me an heiress; my sister received nothing except some Paraguayan
railway funds. But there was a catch: a typically maternal one.
When the son whom I renounced is twenty-one, he inherits, and I
am left without a penny."

"How did she die?" he said.

"Well, she had lately become a Spiritualist ('I see something
behind your chair', she would say to me in a restaurant). She also
claimed to be in telepathic communication with Mary, Queen of
Scots. She must have renewed her subscription to *Psychic News* just
before she died: anyway, I received it for a whole year afterwards.
She died at lunch, literally between two mouthfuls. I had never
seen a dead person before."

"And you were sorry?"

"What do you expect . . . the conventional parade of grief? She
had never meant anything to me, nor I to her. The most that I can
say in her favour is that she never tried to bully me. Like most of
these cranks she was a fatalist. 'You will come to a bad end,' she
used to tell me, 'it is in your palm. Nothing that I can do will save
you.' Poor mother! So much energy, and so very little brain."

The hour was now late. The band, tired but valiant, had reached
the end of its repertoire and recommenced *Sweet Sue*. Primed

by champagne, the Consuls, the American business men had captured the Christmas spirit, towards the promotion of which the fat proprietress was now passing from table to table with a supply of paper hats. At the bar the man Mariano had embarked upon what he no doubt firmly believed to be the conquest of the cabaret artiste who had fallen. His former companions, Juan and Inez, had not accepted the change of programme so philosophically. As Rumbold and the woman rose to dance, Juan rose in his turn.

"This lady is with us, I think," he said. "You have spoken with her long enough."

Brave words, reinforced by the clenched fist, the high heel poised in readiness: the space between the tables was small. Rumbold trod upon the tiny toes prepared to kick, and grasped the fist, as if in friendship.

"Who *are* you with?" he said pleasantly, to the woman.

"Oh, I think I am with you, you know," she said.

"Little boys should be in bed by this time . . . no?" said Rumbold. He reinforced his grip upon the fist. "No, don't kick," he said to Inez. "For little boys have brittle knuckles."

He released the fist. Juan, his face pale with pain, steadied himself against the table. The girl, her lips drooping, looked contemptuous. Together they watched the English couple join the dancers. Then they searched the still warm seat for cigarettes or fallen change; but of course Rumbold had left nothing.

Six

"COME in and have a drink," she said. He paid off the taxi. The night porter, summoned, illuminated a table lamp in the curtained, frowsty lounge, and went in search of whisky.

"We might get to know one another better," she began.

"But I leave for Lisbon in two days."

"Me too. I shall be spending Christmas at the Aviz. Then, like yourself, I go to England. We might join forces: that is my suggestion."

"You have chosen a queer enough time of year to make the trip," he said.

"I didn't choose at all. Question of money: I have to see solicitors and so forth about my inheritance."

Rumbold paid and tipped the porter. "Soda?" he said, and filled her glass. "I take it that your proposition is of a business nature," he said drily.

"Certainly. I have the income, you the strength of character and . . ."

"And a suitably murky background?" he supplied.

"Well, I don't wish to hurt your feelings, you know, but that about expresses it. I need a partner in a certain enterprise."

"What enterprise?" he said.

"Oh, that we shall keep, like the good wine, until a little later. First, as in every business contract, there must be a short period of probation."

"I am sure you do not mean to be insulting," he said, "but in case you do, let me reduce the matter to terms which you will understand. I, too, have money . . . and quite a lot of it."

"Yes," she said contemptuously. "You have what you made on the Black in Marseilles. But how long will that last? Where is your income, and what prospects have you?"

Rumbold sipped his whisky. He sipped in silence. A potted palm threw its long shadow across his face and shoulders.

"I apologise," she said. "I had forgotten your quite legitimate masculine vanity. Well . . . let it be said, then . . . you are very far from ugly, and I want you for reasons other than those I have advanced."

She paused, laying her hand upon his own. "But we are neither of us, I think, people to waste time in useless sentiment or in polite evasions. It was in that spirit that I spoke."

"Then I reply in the same spirit," he said. "You are damnably good-looking but women are not scarce. Is it a lover or a porter that you want?"

"Neither," she said. "I want a man who will stop at nothing and I think I've found him."

Habitually, Rumbold slept for eight, for nine, for sometimes even ten hours of a night. This sleep, deep and dreamless, he regarded as essential to his health, being in this respect something of a faddist. Nor, when finally awake, did he respond quickly to the renewed exigencies of life, and herein lay some part of the explanation of his failure in the banking world, of his complete inaptitude for all business conducted between fixed hours.

Upon that night . . . or in what remained of it when he returned to his hotel . . . Rumbold slept poorly. He awoke, plagued by a shaft of winter sunlight, and lay for some moments in meditation. Then he threw back the bedclothes and, after tasting the coffee brought up to him some hours before, crouched upon the icy floor in performance of certain exercises: ten press-ups, forty knee-bends, twenty oscillations of the trunk. He did not do this every morning, but when he did so the exercises never varied: strong biceps, stronger calves, a narrow waist-line . . . these were his requirements. In other attributes he was uninterested.

Shaved, dressed and bathed, he was about to pass the reception desk when the cashier, smirking, requested his attention:

"A young person has been enquiring for you, Señor. She is waiting in the lounge."

The lounge was empty of all residents. In a corner, upon Louis Quinze, sat the girl, Mañuela.

"Yes?" he said. "How did you find me?"

"I saw you going in. I have come to return you the two hundred pesetas which you very kindly lent me, because I am now able to do so."

"How is that?" he said. "What've you been up to?"

"It is not what you think," she said with dignity. "I have been so fortunate as to obtain a position as a parlour-maid. In a very good family, too: the uncle is a Bishop. I explained the position to my employer. He made me an advance upon my salary."

"The money," he said, "as you well know, was not a loan but a present. Therefore you don't need to pay it back, still less to come here and persecute me." He returned the money to her.

"I didn't mean to persecute you. I thought you might be pleased to see me."

"And I suppose to-day is your day off?" he added, brutally.
"Yes," she said. "It is."

They walked across the road to the Retiro.
"You like parks?" he said.
"I like the ducks and winter flowers," she said. "But not the swans. The swans are far too proud." She gazed at him obliquely.
But he glanced at his watch, then pointed to the Japanese bridge across the ornamental lake.
"I have to meet a lady there in twenty minutes," he said.
"An English lady?"
"Correct. First we shall have lunch, then we are going to the Prado. You shall come, too, if you like. There is no need to be frightened."
"I am not frightened," she said. "Only sad, because I am too young for you."
He was much struck by this remark. "You find me old, then?" he enquired.
"Old in sin," she said. "Yesterday I lit a candle for you."
"Do you like your work?" he said, to change the conversation. "Somehow, I don't see you carrying coffee trays."
"The trays are nothing. The trick is to be demure and look at no one. Much worse is to clean silver. My father had some silver, too, but not as much as these people. Rub . . . Rub . . . and then you polish till your fingers stiffen. The most dreadful are not the soup tureens, but the little angled things like milk jugs. The husband is a Falangist: he eats ham and eggs for breakfast, just like you do. Meanwhile, the Mother Superior at Saragossa is perhaps looking for me. I should like to go to Portugal with you."
"And how would you get there without a passport?"
"When we came near the frontier you would lock me in the lavatory and pretend to tie your shoe-lace just outside."
"You have worked it all out very nicely, haven't you! But I think you would do better to go under the seat, as usual."
"Because you are older that is no reason for you to mock me," she said.
"Come," he said, pointing to a seat. "Let us sit down here and wait."

And it was in this attitude of expectancy that Fiona found them.

"But this is charming!" she said in English. "Only two days here, and already you have a little friend. Why didn't you tell me?"

Rumbold explained the presence of Mañuela, and her history. The contrast between the two women amused him: the one dark, sedate, with malice in her eyes; the other fair, politely waspish, of good carriage. He rose and seated himself between them, at once their buffer and their butt. He made his fashion notes: Fiona wore a red turban, Mañuela a mantilla of the poorest quality. The girl's dress was black, her coat thin (no doubt her employer's summer cast-off). Beneath the turban Fiona wore a tailor-made, half hidden by opossum, with opossum gloves to match. Her shoes were shapely, the other's cracked and curving upwards like a Turk's.

"And so you met her in the train?" the Englishwoman was saying. Her voice was candid. Her attitude held nothing of the embarrassment for which he had been pleasantly prepared.

"Yes," he said. "Shall we go now and have lunch?"

"Ah, not so soon, my friend. You have been hiding your light under a bushel. I didn't suspect you of these generous impulses. Two hundred pesetas . . . just like that." She snapped her fingers, and turned to Mañuela: "Was he good about it?" she said. "Were there no conditions?"

"No," said Mañuela, with the placid but deadly insolence of her race. "He did good by stealth, as I have heard the English always do . . . with ostentation."

Rumbold inspected his feet, the rare blades of grass. The mutual recognition of check-mate he felt could not now be long delayed.

But he had reckoned without the feminine will-to-win, the search for any weapon, no matter how base and vulgar.

"And so you are now in domestic service?" began Fiona sweetly. This remark was greeted by a silence. The tactical error, the lapse into fishwifery, was evident. She perceived it herself: "I am sorry," she continued, "I should not have said that. I know you are a lawyer's daughter, and deserve better. The times are hard, but it is not my fault that I am exempt from their full horror."

"That is one error," interrupted Rumbold, "but another is your belief that this meeting was engineered in some way by myself. I had no appointment with this young person. She appeared, then followed me."

"Ah, thank you," said Mañuela. "Now at least I know what to do." She rose. He caught the tail of her coat as it swirled, and pulled her back upon the hard green seat.

"Don't go," he said, touched by a warning of his very bowels. "Don't go. We mean no harm. It is the desire to talk that is the enemy; the eighty thousand words a day, all of them waste of breath."

"Especially if they are couched like yours," said Fiona. "In the rounded periods of Macaulay."

"Let us go and have lunch," he said. "After all, it is nearly one."

"No oysters," said Fiona. "I don't care if there is an R in the month. I distrust oysters in Madrid."

"They come from Corunna, I expect," said Mañuela. "You can tell by the black markings on the shells."

"Pilaf for me," said Rumbold. "And you?"

Mañuela ordered a Paella; Fiona, Canalones, followed by a Tortilla. So that in the end nobody had oysters at all, and the waiter, who had given them one of the best tables in expectation of a heavy booking, expressed his displeasure by the extreme slowness of his service.

"Do you know," said Mañuela, "that I have not been in a restaurant nor eaten a chocolate cake since I was eleven years old."

Rumbold regarded the menu. "No cake," he said, "but there is a trifle made with rum. Would that do?"

"Oh yes! But first, if you please, I will go to the toilet."

"But you've just been," he said, surprised.

She explained. There was a three-way mirror in the Ladies-room. She had always wanted to look at herself in a three-way mirror, but on the previous visit there had been someone else in front of it, and she had not dared. Now the place was empty.

"Do you intend to persevere with this young person?" enquired Fiona, when Mañuela had departed.

"I don't know what you mean. To me the boot seems to be rather on the other foot."

"Don't you think that she is a little too coy and teeny-weeny to be true? Or perhaps it is your Christmas gesture of good will . . . though I should be careful: offences against minors are punishable."

"If she has her little act," he said, "I imagine it is a form of defence against your own."

"You don't think, then, that you look rather silly?"

"I think that any man sitting between two women looks rather silly."

"Your Canalones, Señora," said the waiter.

"Do you still wish to come with me to Portugal to-morrow?" she said.

"Certainly. I know which side my bread is buttered."

"Then it's time you knew that it can't be buttered upon both sides. If you attempt to bring that girl with us the deal is off."

"Listen," he said. "I've no interest in her, none at all, but she's got a passport, and with us to help she could bluff about her visas at the frontier. In Portugal they're very slack. Once there she'd have the chance she won't get here. You could pass her through quite easily as your maid."

"You went back to her last night, I suppose?"

"Jealous?" he said. "Are you really jealous? Well, this is fine. Meanwhile your meal is getting cold."

"Why didn't you stay with me?"

"I'm not a dog. I like acquaintances to ripen first."

Mañuela returned. "Do you know," she said, "that not only is there the mirror and one of those towels which roll for ever, but also the glass in the door is made in such a way that I could see out of it without being seen. I saw a man just behind you spill some macaroni down his shirt. He looked all round him furtively, and thought that nobody had spotted him. But I had . . . and made a face."

"Splendid," said Rumbold. "But won't anybody eat?" He poked at his pilaf which, none too warm in the first place, now resembled the viscous surface of some dead sea.

They munched, at varying speeds.

"It seems queer," said Fiona, "you want to go to the Prado yet I would never have imagined that you knew anything of painting."

"Oh, I've no technical pretensions," he said. "I've read Wilenski. As a matter of fact, I stole him from Foyle's. I was a kid then. I had a motor bike. On Saturday afternoons I used to go down to Dulwich. That's the gallery to see the Spaniards . . . especially Ribera. I used to like lost causes then. You'd never catch me looking at a Poussin: I followed old Gaspard Dughet, his brother-in-law. Such a tangle! I wouldn't care to walk through one of *his* woods. They say that Poussin put in the Pans and Shepherdesses for him, but I don't believe that."

"Me, I like Ribalta," said Mañuela. "And that Moor . . . what's his name . . . who was a pupil of Velazquez? But my father was old-fashioned. He liked Murillo. 'I never saw a beggar boy like that,' I said. 'No, nor you never will, but that's what a beggar boy *should* look like.' His favourite picture was the Assumption of the Virgin. 'That's heaven,' he said, 'the only glimpse you'll ever get of it.' It all looked very uncomfortable to me, like trapeze artists and only a cloud or two to sit down upon. I still think sometimes that my guardian angel must be a bird."

And, indeed, thought Rumbold, he might well have been. The luncheon had reached the coffee-brandy stage. Across the table he surveyed the two women whom, from curiosity as much as courtesy, he had caused to sit side by side upon the red plush of the *banquette*. They were talking. In the mirror immediately behind them he could see their necks, the one half hidden by a ragged bob, the other bared, the hair swept upwards and secured by unknown means within the russet mane upon her occiput.

Vice does not destroy the body corporeal, but pickles it. The fires of hell fan and mummify the soul long before the last breath is rendered. In appearance there was little to indicate that sixteen years separated these two women. Sisters in God, the facial creams of one did for her that which glandular secretions still provided for the other. Yet, between the child, already more than half a woman, at the outset of her life, and the woman, more than half a child, he yet discerned a most distinct affinity.

He desired to possess neither of them, and was bored by both. His own sensuality ran in darker corridors than these. Violence and sentimentality were his see-saw. Unpropped by principle, devoid of purpose, he was well prepared to link his destiny with that of Fiona, well aware that she required some service of him, the nature of which she did not yet possess sufficient confidence to formulate . . . but which he, already, had divined.

In compensation for this baseness (for even the apostate conscience does not slumber) he required payment in the one currency that never varies. Gratitude he must receive, and would extract it from this girl, by a disinterestedness and a devotion which—had he, as usual, probed a little deeper—he would have seen as affecting nothing but his purse.

The novelist must not cast his net too wide, lest he catch too many in its tangle. The good, the vile, those nuclear properties of "Eric", of "East Lynne", and "Middlemarch", *ça va toujours*. Yet the ridiculous—ingredient of half our lives—we instinctively avoid, as I have seen mares in a field avoid a rabbit which ran between their hooves, by rearing. Of the ridiculous there was certainly much in Rumbold, and still more of it in the woman whose name was to become so tragically associated with his own. Possessing neither point of departure nor lines of resistance prepared in advance; no bearings, no hope and no established rule of conduct, each was attracted by this girl who, fired with the certainty of youth, showed them what they themselves had been, half a generation earlier. And—inevitable corollary—each hoped to see her fail and crumble, to hear that whimper, birth-pang of the first wrinkle, herald of the first droop in her too generous mouth. Is it not so with all who have spoilt their lives?

Meanwhile Mañuela, the object of their varied interest, sat nibbling a macaroon, the which she dipped from time to time into her glass of Cognac. Particles of sugar, released from the sweetmeat, floated free and formed a sediment at the bottom of the glass.

"Taxi. . . . "
"We could all go to my hotel," suggested Fiona.

"Oh yes," he said. "I know that we could all go to your hotel but, none the less, we are going to the Prado."

He pushed them both inside the vehicle.

"The afternoon is lovely. Perhaps the Prado would be nicer," suggested Mañuela timidly.

"Here," said Rumbold roughly. "I've bought you some violets."

Fiona gave a rather high-pitched laugh. "But how funny," she said. "I thought I saw him talking to the head-waiter. I should have guessed, because I spoke to him myself. Here are some chocolates for you, child. The ones with silver paper are the soft ones."

"It only remains," said Rumbold, "to ask her which present she prefers."

"Oh," said Mañuela steadily, and without embarrassment, "I think that I prefer the violets."

The three passed through the turnstile, and immediately dissension arose. "The Flemings," suggested Fiona, but Rumbold wished to start with France. After some argument they compromised and agreed to begin with the miscellaneous rooms; strange galleries these, ill-lit, ill-hung and dusty, but which yet contain work of startling merit, made more startling by the element of contrast . . . the licentious Boilly, the vapid but graceful Lancret, the non-licentious and libellously named Sodoma, two Cranach virgins and a number of splendiferous bull-fighting scenes by Fortuny, a better tauromachian than Goya.

From his seat the guardian watched them, not quite asleep, but nodding. "A race apart, those fellows," remarked Rumbold. "I'm sure he wouldn't stir, even if I produced a saw, and you two a pair of chisels. They must ransack the furthest reaches of Philistinism to find them."

"Oh," said Fiona, "even diamonds must become dull if you sit staring at them for a living."

"I wonder if he has ever been in any other rooms but these?"

"Why not ask him?"

Rumbold did so. The man stared back at him aggressively. Yes, it transpired, he had once been with the Italian Primitives, but these had depressed him to such an extent that he had applied for and received a transfer. He had never been in any of the main Spanish rooms, but had helped to carry both the "Los Borrachos" of Velazquez and "The Forge of Vulcan" when these had been removed for cleaning. Every guardian had his preferences, and dislikes. For example in a roomful of Uccellos one had been driven to a nervous breakdown by the omnipresent foreshortening, from which he could not keep his eyes. The lascivious liked Boucher, of course, and Rubens, though they inclined to the view that these painters displayed their ladies' charms too freely, so that in the end one grew bored.

"Boilly is better," said the man. "Look over there. One always thinks her bodice is just going to burst . . . and yet it never does."

"That is certainly a point of view," said Rumbold.

They moved on, slicing across the centuries and through croco-diles of earnest schoolgirls who stared at Mañuela with mistrust. "And yet Fry," said Fiona, "maintained that one should not see more than ten pictures in a day."

"Fry was a fool," replied Rumbold. "The more you see, the more exalted you become, and in the end the deadweight counts, however undigested."

"Yet don't you think it is too like Church?" asked Mañuela. "I mean . . . I, who know so little, enjoy it too, but I don't enjoy the silence, and the way the floor creaks every time I take a step, and all the galleries ahead of me seen through the open door. And then the things one's expected to say: it's like the Stations of the Cross."

They were in the Bosch room now. Bosch, Geronimo, fifteen this to fifteen that. "And there, of course, you have it," said Rum-bold. "The man must have been a glass-blower. There is no other explanation."

"The horror of death," suggested Fiona.

Yet this, too, seemed inadequate to describe these panels, with their lambent hues, their technical mastery, and imaginative genius.

"You have to kneel down to see the best bits," said Rumbold. "Trust the gallery authorities for that."

The Last Judgment: Ruskin, albeit somewhat shocked, has described the work in terms denying imitation. Yet Ruskin missed

something: here was a painter to whom the appearance of evil
was as important as the sin itself. The weird Lilliputian figures,
naked as eggs and hairless, the Japanese garden background, the
quite fantastic attention to detail: here was no stolid Fleming but
a man illumined by the will of the Master, with a gift for unearth-
ing the intentions of the wicked and for portraying them, not as
one, but as a thousand awful warnings. It is said of French Marshal
Gouvion St. Cyr, when he saw this picture, that although a lifelong
atheist he proceeded immediately to Church.

At tea, which they took in one of the fashionable cafés on the
Puerta where warm brown dish-water serves the function of the
tannic beverage, Rumbold showed himself morose, Fiona not less
so, and it was left to Mañuela, her mouth half blocked by cake, to
sustain the flagging conversation.

"It's been a lovely, lovely, *lovely* day," she said. "And so secular!
You can't imagine what fun it is to be out without a nun in sight,
nor even a Soutane."

"*She* can't," said Rumbold, indicating the Englishwoman. "But I
can: the Jesuits held me captive for two years." His head hurt him,
as it often did, above the left temple, where a German had once
hit him with a rifle butt. The café was half empty. Three of the
waiters, for whom no other employment could be found, were
hanging up Christmas decorations.

"They nearly had me in a cloister for life," said Mañuela. "If
I hadn't run away perhaps they would have. The vocation must
be sought and not awaited: that was what they said. 'Look at St.
Ursula,' they said, 'and St. Philomena' . . . Oh, the saintly examples
were not lacking, I can tell you."

Signalling to one of the waiters Rumbold ordered chocolate
éclairs. Rushing, willing enough to do his bidding, the man forgot
that he held a paper garland in his hand, and tripped over it. Some
merriment was caused.

"We leave," said Rumbold, "to-morrow evening at 8.30."

"And so?" said Fiona.

"And so if she wishes to be at the station by that time, I will
book a ticket for her."

"Oh, of *course* I wish it," said Mañuela. "I wish nothing else. You are both so kind. I trust you absolutely. If there is any trouble . . . at the frontier for example . . . I shall know what to do. I shall take the blame."

"There will be no trouble," said Rumbold. "I am a dog who has been taught a trick or two in its time. Portuguese entry stamps are very poorly made. If you care to give me your passport now, I daresay that I can remedy the matter."

"You forget the exit permit," said Fiona drily.

"Carbon paper and a sharp pencil point will soon fix that," he said. "I have my own to copy. The trouble with these authoritarian régimes is that they spend too much upon their police, and too little upon the quality of their rubber stamps."

"Here is my passport," said Mañuela.

A waiter approached: "Señor Rumbold?"

"Yes?"

"You are wanted on the telephone."

"I think there must be some mistake."

"No mistake, Señor. I was given an exact description of you."

Rumbold rose. He entered the telephone booth and picked up the receiver. "Yes?" he said.

"How are you, Señor Rumbold?" said Aranjuez.

"You rang up to enquire about my health?"

"I rang up to enquire whether you were enjoying your tea."

"Also, I suppose, to take the credit from the spies you send to follow me about?"

"Come, come, Señor Rumbold, no bitterness. Tell me, how *is* your tea?"

"I can only say that it reveals the dreadful position of your country's imports."

Aranjuez chuckled. The sound of his chuckle came over the wire, slightly amplified. "And you leave us to-morrow?" he said. "I am sad."

"Yes," said Rumbold. "I leave to-morrow. You can provide a brass band for me at the station if you like."

"That would be out of office hours, I fear. Good luck, Señor Rumbold. Don't forget my little proposition to you."

Rumbold hung up. He returned to the tea-room. The table which he had occupied was empty: "Where are the two ladies?" he demanded of a waiter.

"The ladies have paid and gone, Señor."

"They did not say where they were going?"

"No, Señor." The waiter permitted himself a slight smile which vanished quickly as he intercepted Rumbold's scowl.

"Good," said the latter. He called for his coat and hat, and left. He called at Fiona's hotel, but they were not there. Nor were they at his own hotel, nor at the Escapada, which, at that hour was open for a *Thé Dansant*.

Rumbold called at both hotels, and at the night-club, several times throughout the evening, without result. In the intervals between these visits, he drank.

Seven

THE train had already started. The wheels ran slowly, and lurching, across the maze of points. They were sitting in a small private carriage with four seats. They were alone.

"Now," he said. "A little explanation, if you please."

"Why didn't you ask me when you met me on the platform?" said Fiona. She drew the travelling rug more tightly about her knees. She was a cold subject.

"You took every precaution, didn't you?" said Rumbold. "You even telephoned to have your baggage removed from the hotel so as to be quite sure of not meeting me."

"I wished to spare you trouble," she said, lighting a cigarette.

Rumbold snatched the cigarette from her and stamped it flat upon the floor. "Listen," he said. "Don't adopt that attitude or I'll not answer for the consequences."

"No?" she queried, mockingly.

"No," he said. He seized her hand and bent it backwards from the wrist.

"Ah, now you are becoming violent," she said. "I was not wrong when I guessed that there was something of the brute in you."

"Answer," he said. "What is she to you?"

"She is . . . or rather was, an impediment."

"You fixed that telephone call, I suppose?"

"Oh yes. I, too, know your friend Aranjuez. We have many memories in common."

"Where did you spend last night?" he said.

"I spent it with her . . . Oh, quite chastely, I assure you. She was rather drunk, I'm afraid. I had to hold her head above the toilet for an hour. This afternoon I took her home. Unfortunately, her employers didn't share my view of our little escapade. They sacked her."

"At which point, I suppose," said Rumbold, "you offered her some money?"

"Not only offered, but persuaded her to take it. You are too sentimental, my friend. The pure of heart are rarer than you think."

The train was now passing Illescas, swinging as it took the rising gradient of the Sierra, swinging to the right as it followed the bend of the still distant Tagus.

"I suppose you realise I still have her passport?" he said.

"She won't need it now. If she does, she can make another application. Honestly I acted for the best, even if my methods didn't please you."

"I shall never forgive you for this," he said.

"Ah, don't be silly. If you hadn't the firm intention of forgiving me you wouldn't have got on the train."

"You forget that you arrived two minutes before it left."

"That's right," she said. "Make yourself excuses. Square your very accommodating conscience: 'I wanted to give a girl a helping hand, to take her to Portugal, but a woman prevented me from doing so.' It sounds lovely, doesn't it? All right. This train stops at Talavera. Get off, go back, and find her."

But Rumbold was silent.

"*Donde una puerta se cierra, otre se abre,*" said Fiona. "When one door is shut another opens. Our friend Aranjuez was very fond of quoting that at one time. He likes Cervantes. A lot of these modern Torquemadas do."

"Where is she now?" said Rumbold.

"I left her in a *hôtel meublé* with five thousand pesetas in her purse. She was a little tearful, of course, because . . . you must forgive me . . . I had given her to believe that I had telephoned you without success: that you wanted no more to do with her. You see . . . I am quite frank. I might easily have said that she ran away from me."

"Hardly," he said, "for you know that she would have run straight towards the station."

"Not even that, I'm afraid, because we found that you had already taken the morning train."

A man, passing down the corridor on his way to the lavatory, looked in. Rumbold pulled down the blinds.

"We have six hours before we reach the frontier," he said. "We might use them to discuss certain matters."

"By all means," she said. "That was my intention, but you can see now that the discussion would not have gone as well *à trois*."

Stretching herself upon the full length of her seat, she wrapped the travelling rug and mink around her. "These railway pillows are not bad either," she said. "Why don't you try yours, and switch out the light. What we have to say can best be said in darkness."

Rumbold applied his finger to the switch. The small carriage, no bigger in area than a brake, was immersed in darkness . . . a darkness punctuated only by the distant lights of farm houses, three centuries old perhaps, the focal points of several dozen lives, the mortal habitation of several dozen more gone to the churchyard.

The weak radiance of lamps, three kilometres away above a cow-stall, shone now upon a stretch of fur, a lighted cigarette, a lock of hair, a thermos flask.

It is not good to travel too long by the railway, for the man seen with his scythe beside a pinewood, the girl seen hoeing, the commercial traveller with his brief case on a platform, are symbols of no solitude but your own.

Rumbold possessed no rug. He lay down and covered himself with his coat, doubling up his legs and breathing beneath the tweed to preserve the warmth. The carriage was very poorly heated.

"So you have met Aranjuez before?" he said.

"Yes. I met him in Minorca, at Ciudadelo."

"You worked for him?"

"Oh yes, from time to time. We sank a submarine or two together."

"What kind of submarines?"

"Italian. They used to lie up in the Santa Guldana creek below Ferrerias. That was the time of the Malta convoys. Yours was not the only parachute on the landing grounds, you know. There is a plateau there to-day, of course, but covered with fern and heather just like Surrey. I had nine visitors in all and distributed them in farms. I was, of course, above reproach . . . Aranjuez saw to that. On moonless nights our visitors used to swim out to the submarines and fix their limpet bombs, for the Italians were very cautious and wouldn't tie up alongside the quay."

"Weren't you discovered?"

"Well, of course there was some suspicion, but it was Spanish pride that saved me in the end. You see, the Italians were only there by courtesy, and by courtesy of the Government in Madrid at that. When they began to kick up a fuss the local authorities kicked up a fuss as well. Italians in a martial mood are not popular, you know. Spaniards prefer them when they sell hot chestnuts or ice-cream."

"You were paid for this work?"

"Oh, naturally. I should think so. Aranjuez, you must understand, was working both tickets at the time. He still is. For every submarine put out of action three hundred Frenchmen who had crossed the Pyrenees would be retained indefinitely in prison at Pamplona or Figueras . . . until the Allies provided petrol: one barrel for every Frenchman capable of fighting."

"How did the agents get away?"

"By fishing-boat to Gibraltar. All but one, that is. The ninth got drunk in a bar and hit a Carabinero. He was arrested. That was the last I heard of him."

"How much money did you get?"

"Three thousand pesetas for a drop. Only yesterday, Aranjuez was pestering me again to give him the receipts. He wants to prove himself a patriot, but of course London is a little shy about such matters. The war once over, the agent who has served his purpose comes up against the dead hand of Whitehall. You'll find that, too, when you return."

Rumbold stretched his feet. His feet were too long for the *banquette* but by screwing, twisting, he was able to insert their extremities between the cushion and the carriage wall, and thus to live in hope of body warmth retained. To complete his defensive dispositions he held the thermos flask, scalding inside with coffee, against his chest.

"Why did you do all this?" he said. "Not for England, I'll be sure."

"England," she said, "can sink beneath the sea for all I care. Indeed, I wish it would. Forty-six million people with the obligation to export their pots and pans and cutlery and coal, or die . . . is that a life, is that something to be proud of? As for their famous integrity, one saw something of that in the way of collaboration when the Channel Islands were occupied. If the Germans had got to Golders Green one might have seen a little more. England is the great anachronism, my friend: the Dodo who survived because twenty miles of sea protected it from a just retribution. No, wait," she said, for she had observed Rumbold raising himself for the *riposte*. "Wait! Of course we still have our culture, our ninety-nine ways of patting a ball about. If England sank, how should we send a Test Team to Australia? Nevertheless, I prefer that solution to the new war which will soon come because we must sell our hideous egg-cups in the Balkans."

From his hip pocket Rumbold pulled his brandy flask, and drank. "Your premises are excellent," he said. "Your conclusions too. I would agree with all of them if I didn't know that, seventeen years ago, some burly girls bruised you with cricket balls in the nets."

The train rolled on. At this moment, three kilometres before Talavera-de-la-Reina, it was crossing a bridge between the Tagus and one of that river's northern tributaries. Rumbold lowered the window and looked out: a bridge was, after all, a bridge, appurtenance of peace to-day but to-morrow perhaps once again the scene of conflict. His eyes met those of the sentry, a Moor, who had risen from a doze in his box to peer between the shutters of the sleeping cars. Inexplicably, and against his will—for so strong is the association of ideas caused by inanimate objects—Rumbold was reminded of another bridge between Dax and Toulouse, upon which, his buttocks outboard, his bowels creaking with dysentery, he had crouched beneath a German sentry, bearer of a Schmeisser.

He pulled down the outer curtains. "Now," he said, in the tone though without the manner of a man coming to a decision, "what is it that you want with me?"

"I want you to kill my child," she said.

"Why?"

"Because in eleven years, when he is twenty-one, he will inherit all my money."

"Is that a reason to kill him? How do you know he won't make you an allowance?"

"Why should he? He's never even seen me. Under the terms of his adoption, I'm not *allowed* to see him."

"Where is he now, then?"

"Somewhere in Devonshire . . . with a family called Vivian. I can easily find out where. He's taken their name. I don't suppose he even knows his true one."

"Yes . . . but *they* know, I suppose?" he said.

"Naturally. That's what makes it a little awkward."

"But," interrupted Rumbold, "you can't just go around killing children without suspicion being aroused. If a child is killed the police want to know why. They make enquiries. They find out who stands to benefit."

"I didn't suggest that you should *shoot* him," she said contemptuously. "In the country people die in many curious ways. They fall into ponds. They break their necks tripping over stiles. They even get lost in woods."

Rumbold grinned: "So you suggest that I lead him by his little hand into some deep, dark wood, do you? Believe me, you don't know much about children. I should hardly have gone ten yards before he caught me with something from his catapult. You can't kill a child as easily as a man. With a child you've got first to make acquaintance."

"Get to know him, then. Your expenses will be paid."

"And supposing I don't want to kill him . . . supposing I say that I have a moral objection?"

"Why should you have any objection? You have killed men often enough. In fact, it's the only profession you know."

"It seems appropriate to point out," said Rumbold, "that the men I killed were Germans. I was congratulated for doing so. I wouldn't receive any congratulations for killing an innocent child. More likely I should be tracked and caught by the police."

Fiona reached above her head and switched on the light. The light was uncomplimentary. It revealed her face; white, strained, the eyes brilliant. Rumbold understood. "Why should you wish to kill him?" he repeated. "He has done you no harm."

" 'Done me no harm' . . . 'Innocent' . . . Have you finished with your clichés yet or will you evoke the image of a curly head upon a pillow? The child stands in my way. He must be removed."

"Right," said Rumbold. "Since the sentimental approach is no use, look at the matter in terms of money. What is your income?"

"About three thousand a year."

"Which you will enjoy for almost a dozen years to come?"

"What of it? After that, if the child remains alive, I won't have a single penny."

"Take it this way: if I killed him you would have to give me quite a considerable sum to keep my mouth shut . . . a very considerable sum, perhaps. You're thirty-two now. Let's assume that you die at the age of fifty. A lot of people do that. What would you have gained in that case . . . seven years perhaps with the weight of a crime on your conscience? Wouldn't it be better to save money now, even if you have to live with a little less magnificence later on."

She looked at him steadily. "You don't want to do it, do you?" she said. "You're afraid, and your nasty little bourgeois conscience troubles you at the very thought."

"That's enough about my conscience," he said. "If I decide to do it, I'll do it. What are your terms?"

"A thousand down in cash."

"When it's over?"

"No . . . half before, half afterwards."

"It's not enough."

"Very well. I'll open a joint account for you at my bank. You can draw up to five hundred from it each year for three years."

"And if I use the joint account to draw out everything and skip?"

"You won't be able to because I don't control my capital. A certain amount comes in each year: that's all. Oh, believe me, I've thought of everything."

"You flatter yourself," he said. "I wonder if you have a heart to touch. Are you so very certain that I am capable of doing this?"

"You'll do it all right," she said. "Not for the money so much but because now I've put the idea into your head, you've *got* to do it. In the same way, if I said that you couldn't jump out of this train at thirty miles an hour you'd feel obliged to try."

"You're very penetrating," he said. "How do you imagine that we are going to get on together with this hanging over our heads?"

"It needn't hang for very long. When we get to England draw your cash . . . go off and do it."

"But how?"

"I leave that to you."

"And if I bungle it?"

"If you bungle it, you take the consequences. There will be nothing to connect you with me. The five hundred in your possession will have been paid in cash. For the joint account you will use another name. If you implicate me I shall deny everything except that I once met you here in Spain. They will set you down as some kind of a sexual maniac, and sentence you accordingly."

"In other words I am to end my days in Broadmoor, while you, perhaps, take a world cruise? Oh no, my fine lady. *Je ne marche pas.*"

"I am only trying to put things in the least favourable light, so that you will appreciate the risks."

"You want this to be a purely business arrangement, I take it," he said.

Fiona regarded him in a curious fashion. "Oh no," she said slowly. "For I need a husband, too."

Rumbold stood up. The motion of the train caused him to sway. He flexed his knees against it. "A husband?" he said. "Well that's an odd idea at your age and with your experience, isn't it? And why me rather than another, please?"

"Why not you?" she said. "You please me."

Rumbold sat down. The train had not stopped at Talavera, after all, but, with speed reduced, was passing through the suburbs of the town. Lights flecked the window curtains. A shunting engine passed, going in the opposite direction, with a hiss of ill-held steam.

"Either," he said, "you are a monster, or else, quite simply, you are mad."

"Neither," she said. "On the contrary, I am logical, I see clearly. There is something I have long wanted done. I meet a man whose past history suggests that he can do it. Since there is a tariff in these affairs I offer him an adequate reward. And since I like him, I offer him also something more."

"How do you think we could ever live together with that hanging over us?"

"Oh, you exaggerate! What does the removal of a small boy mean to two people who have never even seen him? To drop for a moment into your own kind of talk, the child needn't even 'suffer'. He can go straight to heaven." She laughed, but he shivered. "There is a blind spot in me somewhere," she said, "but also certain qualities of vision. You need me, Rumbold, as much as I need you, for you're weak . . . very weak. Once upon a time you worked: you'd hate to have to work again."

Rumbold poured out fresh coffee from the thermos. He added brandy to the mugs, and handed one mug to her. "Very well," he said. "Proceed."

Fiona took a small red notebook from her bag. She flicked the pages. "In Lisbon I'm staying at the Aviz, as you know," she said. "You'd better stay somewhere else . . . the Americano might do. My seat is booked on a Constellation for London on the 28th. Again, it might be better if we were not seen together. You could follow in a day or two and contact me, in London, at Brown's."

"And then?"

"You can go down to Devonshire. You'll need a few days to get your bearings, to make enquiries. The thing could take place in the second week of the New Year. He will still be on his holidays."

"And then?" Somewhere, thought Rumbold, a small boy was spending his last Christmas.

"By then I shall have taken a house somewhere . . . Sussex, perhaps, or even Scotland: it would be amusing to see Peterhead again. My sister could teach you knots and splices."

"I can't do it," he said. "I can't . . . I can't. It's just not in my nature."

"Yet how you wish it *were* . . . isn't that true?"

"Maybe."

"You want me to play Lady Macbeth, don't you . . . to push, and convince and advance you every kind of Jesuitical argument? I have too much respect for your intelligence. What does it matter? There's no risk . . . you don't fear the gallows, do you?"

"I fear them horribly," he said. "I'm not the man I once was." He bent his head, pressing the palm of his right hand against one eye. "And you," he said. "How can I trust you? I do the work: you benefit."

She hesitated. "Give me your penknife," she said.

"Why?"

"Give me your penknife all the same."

He handed it to her. Quickly she opened the blade and before he could resist, drew it sharply across his wrist and then her own. She pressed her hand to his. Their blood fell together to the floor.

"Where did you learn that schoolgirl trick?" he said.

"Blood," she said. "Blood is what counts, and mine is calling to yours. In blood and in experience shared we will make a new life together."

Rumbold withdrew his hand. "Let's get some sleep," he said roughly. He lay down, covering himself with his coat, but she sat long erect, watching the shadow of the lamp upon his forehead, his ruffled hair and his out-thrust feet.

The train continued its slow progress towards Portugal.

Eight

RUMBOLD began to fill in the form without which admission to the vast hinterland of the War Office was impossible. At the space devoted to the name of the person whom he wished to see, he hesitated. Observing this hesitation the attendant, who prided himself upon his ability to classify visitors, thought fit to prompt him:

"Room P. 56 perhaps?" he said.

"Exactly," said Rumbold. The attendant then begged him to sit down, which Rumbold did, between a Brigadier clutching a brief-case and a Subaltern in the Irish Guards, whose well cut battle-dress and walking stick revealed a certain conflict in the young man's mind between the *laisser-aller* of Montgomery and the correctitude of Alexander.

Presently, the Brigadier was called, his fingers twitching nervously, for he had ordered just one court-martial too many in Sumatra, and now faced an almost certain demotion. The Subaltern turned to Rumbold:

"Been in the Army?" he said.

"Oh yes," said Rumbold. "You, too, I see."

The Subaltern ignored the jest. "I couldn't help hearing the number of the room you're going to," he said. "You're one of those queer fellows, eh? What luck! It's not much fun when your call-up age coincides with the end of a war." He tapped with his stick in his embarrassment.

Rumbold was touched. "I shouldn't worry," he said. "Your chance will come."

"Have to worry," said the Subaltern. "No authority over the men. Yet know I'm as good as they are. Just haven't had the chance, that's all."

"You'll get it," said Rumbold. "There must be a hundred thousand just like you. Men will always fight to find out what quota of guts they possess. That's what makes it so easy for the Government." He stopped, conscious of being sententious.

"Mr. Rumbold." The attendant beckoned.

"Well . . . goodbye," said Rumbold.

"Goodbye, old man," said the Subaltern. "Shan't meet again, I suppose. I've volunteered for Palestine. Seems to be the only place there's something doing."

Preceded by his guide, Rumbold embarked upon the gloomy, ill-lit maze. Clop-clop, the four feet, unsynchronised, sounded on the stone. They turned right, they turned left, they turned right again, but this time a mistake had been made, for they found themselves in a blind alley where workmen were removing sandbags, the battle post of full Colonels in 1940.

Eventually they discovered the true direction. The attendant tapped loudly upon the door. "Room P. 56, sir," he said, impressively. Rumbold entered. A gas fire was lit. The floor was covered by an Aubusson. From behind a Remington, a young woman looked up.

"Rumbold?" she said. "Go in there, will you please." She indicated an annexe, glass-panelled upon all sides. Rumbold went in, as ordered. He sat down and began to read an ancient copy of the *Tatler*. On one page, in the margin of some racing pictures, someone had scrawled a statement of accounts . . . "to three double whiskies . . . to taxi, Tottenham Court Road to Maida Vale . . . to four hours wait outside house, West Cromwell Road . . . to tips concerning enquiries. Left Luggage Office, Charing Cross."

Cassell came in. "Well, Rumbold," he said. "You're back at last, I see."

"Cut out the *boniments*," said Rumbold. "You knew I was back the moment my plane touched down at Poole."

Cassell was a small, bird-like man. His voice was high-pitched, chirpy, not unlike a flute. He was always most immaculately dressed: generally, as to-day, in civilian clothes. There was nothing immediately sinister about him except his extreme gentleness.

"Don't be tough, Rumbold," he said. "I know it's part of your defensive mechanism but spare me the more purple passages."

"I'll spare you nothing," said Rumbold. "You were the Country

Section Officer. You took him on. You are responsible for the death of those nine men."

Cassell sat down. He flicked the pages of the *Tatler*.

"Not nine," he said. "Ninety-nine. Sluys is dead. He was shot at Hamburg last year. Nor, I'm afraid, did he die with courage. But now, Rumbold, we have to deal with *you*."

"Deal then."

"You are a deserter, Rumbold."

"Splendid. All right . . . court-martial me. Even in a military trial a few facts will come to light."

Cassell closed the *Tatler*. "I wish you wouldn't rush bull-headed at it always, Rumbold," he said. "A little deference, a certain sense of shame, and we might get on very well together . . . even now."

"I have nothing to retract," said Rumbold.

"Yet they tell me, Rumbold, that when you were in the Ardèche after that unfortunate affair, you refused to join the Resistance movement."

"I don't blow railway lines under the orders of incompetent peasants," said Rumbold. "I blow them by myself."

"And they tell me," pursued Cassell, "that you made a considerable amount of cash on the black market in Marseilles. They even tell me that when you were in Madrid, you saw my friend Aranjuez."

"What a lot of Government money must be wasted on following the activities of private individuals," said Rumbold.

Cassell explored his teeth with a silver toothpick, a mannerism which he had developed less in the interests of hygiene than because he knew that the rasp of metal against ivory set the nerves of visitors on edge.

"Where is all that money now?" he said pleasantly.

"Well, I don't ask you to believe me," said Rumbold, "but as a matter of fact it's in the heels of my shoes."

"Show," said Cassell.

Rumbold removed his shoes, and swung back the hinges. He had already secreted the gold and dollars in the chimney of his hotel bedroom, retaining only the pesetas, for which currency, exchange in England would be difficult.

"I must confiscate this," said Cassell.

"That's all right," said Rumbold. "I daresay you can put it to good use."

The two men stared at one another. "Rumbold," said Cassell, "do you know that I could send you to Scotland to cut wood for ten years?"

"Hardly," said Rumbold. "Remember that I'm not paid out of Army funds. The only contract you have with me is my signature on a piece of paper stating the penalties for infringement of the Official Secrets Act. You can't get me there because you know I've kept my mouth shut. Then . . . not being quite a fool . . . I've made a few enquiries since I came to London. I know the organisation has been broken up, for example."

"Not broken up but gone to ground," said Cassell. He surveyed Rumbold amicably, smiling his thin smile. Above Rumbold's head hung a view by Raoul Dufy of the garden in the Luxembourg. Cassell's gaze transferred itself to this picture, which he had bought quite cheaply from a Belgian banker who had felt the urgent need to square his conscience.

"I like to see you sitting there, Rumbold," he said. "It's as if a ghost had returned. Do you remember Antelme and Abazarian? You're one of the few of our early birds who have come through."

"*Ne cherchez pas à faire apitoyer*," said Rumbold. "I know quite well that they were hanged."

Cassell grinned. "If you were as hard as you like to pretend," he said, "I could cut you up for lighter flints, couldn't I? But you're not hard at all, are you, Rumbold . . . and you're worried. I wonder what you're worried about?"

"I should have thought it was pretty obvious," said Rumbold. "I have no desire to be court-martialled at this stage of the Peace."

"Now what put that idea into your head?" said Cassell. "We know you were wounded. We know that you made two attempts to get through Spain."

"You must be badly misinformed, then. The only attempt I made was the other day when I travelled in some comfort in various first-class carriages."

Cassell tapped with his toothpick upon an ash-tray, another

habit of his, and one which he knew to be as irritating as the first. "Don't be tiresome, Rumbold," he said. "Respect the official version, even if it may not be your own. You have a friend here in me, in a place where you don't count many friends. The point is . . . what are you going to do now? I suppose you know you're a Major: we promoted you on the day you dropped at Labouheyre."

"The Control Commission in Germany perhaps," said Rumbold. "I understand that most of the bottom of the bag go there. Up to what date do you intend to pay me?"

"Up till the Armistice. I can't go further without involving both of us in serious trouble."

"Oh, very handsome," said Rumbold. "In that case you can count the Control Commission out, for I am neither sufficiently ghoulish to search for traces of dead men, nor sufficiently venal to live on the proceeds of my sweet ration."

He rose as if to go.

"Wait a minute," said Cassell. "Your money is in the outer office. It will take some time to count it. Meanwhile what about Aranjuez?" He signalled to the girl behind the Remington.

"There is nothing between Aranjuez and me," said Rumbold. "No understanding and certainly no contract. I don't say it will always be the same. If you demobilise me I'm free."

"Oh *free*," said Cassell with fine irony. "Yet, as Jonson says: 'Apes are apes, though clothed in scarlet.' The reflection is not meant personally, I assure you, but I have been here sixteen years and more, Rumbold. Cast your mind back a bit . . . The disarmament conferences, the Peace Pledge, Ramsay Macdonald, and no stone left unturned; the Abyssinian fiasco, Munich, the phoney war and then the real one. In my position, with the facts before me, I have had an unrivalled insight into the curious workings of British hypocrisy. I *know* that within ten years Russian troops will replace the Germans between the Bidassoa and the North Cape. I *know* that doomed in any case we shall be less doomed if we preserve a foothold in the peninsula. Yet, upon Motions for the Adjournment, fools stand up inside the House of Commons to urge a break with Fascist Spain. What a pity, I sometimes think, that we were never invaded."

"Forgive me short-circuiting," said Rumbold, "but am I to understand that you would *like* me to work for Aranjuez? Am I to understand that that is the price you ask for ignoring my past behaviour? If so the joke is very rich."

"You could do much worse," said Cassell. "The life of an *Agent Double* is not unpleasant and—if you will forgive me saying so, Rumbold—you have never seemed to me exactly fitted for a civilian career. The Spanish Consulate is only a shilling taxi-ride from here and opposite there is a pub where, if you are at all polite, you might be served a *pastis*."

"Thank you for nothing," said Rumbold. "I'm too old now to serve as instrument to chairborne Mephistopheles. You taught me the trade. Now I intend to practise it alone."

"Not quite alone, surely," said Cassell. "The lady in whose room you spent last night will perhaps have some influence upon your projects?"

"The trouble with all you people," said Rumbold, "is that you're drowning in your own cleverness. You set a man to follow me. He sees me go into a public lavatory and a tobacconist's. A lot of bumf is wasted as he types the two hundred words required to describe these everyday activities. Then you take the credit . . . just as you take it when somebody tells you what Bevin said to Attlee at the Royal Garden Party. I do detest you 'knowledgeable' men. I positively abhor you. Let me go into the next room now and draw my screw. It's all I want."

"All right," said Cassell calmly. "Check each note as she pays out: I believe you've been taught the habit. And don't forget, Rumbold, that the section which I direct turned you from a dirty little bank-clerk into something like a man . . . and that you let us down . . . and that you're letting us down again now when the only appeal I can make to you is that of loyalty."

"Cut that," said Rumbold. "You used them. Let's not shed tears. Before they took the jump you gave them gold cuff-links . . . 'Please accept this little present, Rumbold, as a token of our respect.' I spit on your respect. I spit on all those who sent men to blow up factories in the name of freedom, but in reality to diminish post-war competition."

Cassell laid down his toothpick, and seized instead a dahlia from the flower-pot. "To the impure," he said, "all things are dirty. I'm sorry about you, Rumbold. Yours is the kind of case which we don't often meet, I'm glad to say. Because you once worked well, and because of some friends of yours who are dead now, I shall spare you the indignity of the trial you well deserve. Draw your money: go and get demobilised, and if there is a recommendation I can make to you, it's this . . . take your romanticism straight in future, not inverted."

The woman who had sat behind the Remington came in. She laid a folder on the desk.

"Pay Mr. Rumbold, will you?" said Cassell.

The insult lay like a Communion wafer in Rumbold's mouth. He tasted it, then swallowed.

"Don't you know me, Violet?" he said.

"I don't know deserters," said the woman.

The morning was very cold. On leaving the War Office Rumbold crossed Whitehall and stood for a few moments by the theatre. He inspected his fellow pedestrians and in particular a man with a bowler hat who had stopped to tie his shoe-lace some thirty yards down the street.

Rumbold moved on. He went through the Admiralty Archway and along towards Carlton Gardens, where the crowds were thinner. Arrived at the steps he ran up them quickly, and turned the corner by the Foreign Office annexe. The man with the bowler hat followed slowly.

There are elm trees in that cul-de-sac, and by one elm tree in particular a public telephone box. Rumbold stood behind this tree. As his pursuer came level with it, uncertain which direction to follow, Rumbold stepped forward, caught the man by his tie and dragged him inside the telephone booth.

"What the hell do you think you're doing?" said the man.

"You'll see," said Rumbold. He wedged the man against the glass, and retaining his grip upon the tie, dialled Cassell's number with his free hand.

"Listen," he said. "Call off your nark, will you, or get a better one."

"What nark?" said Cassell. "You must be seeing things."

"Oh no, I'm not. I have it here in the box with me if you'd care to hear it talk." He trod on the man's foot and jerked his head nearer to the mouthpiece. "Go on . . . talk," he said. "Say something to the great White Chief."

The man groaned with pain.

"He doesn't seem very happy," said Rumbold to Cassell. "Should I turn him loose, do you think?"

"It might be wiser," said Cassell.

Rumbold rang off, but did not release the man, whose bowler hat had fallen, revealing a bald head glistening with small beads of sweat.

"Now," said Rumbold. "Let's have it."

"Honest, Guvnor, I don't know what you're talking about."

"Ah, come on, let's have it," said Rumbold. He trod with all his weight upon the already damaged foot.

"Christ," said the man.

"Well?" said Rumbold.

"It was only the bank, Guvnor . . . just to follow you to the bank."

"What bank?"

"Any bank, Guvnor . . . just to see where you put your money."

"Anywhere else?"

"Just the Spanish Embassy or Consulate . . . to see if you went in there."

"And supposing I did?"

"I could knock off then, Guvnor."

"Good," said Rumbold. Having discovered what he wished to know, he released the man, handed him his bowler hat politely and watched him out of sight. Then he set off up the Haymarket, and along Swallow Street to the Twin pub, where Fiona was waiting for him.

"Well?" she said.

"Oh, nothing much," he said. "The pay-off and a few words of wisdom and reproach. The trouble with Cassell is that he thinks that Mata Hari was his mother." He explained about the scene inside the telephone booth.

"But isn't that bad? Supposing they follow you everywhere?"

"They haven't got the money or the time. The beautiful days when every agent had his shadow are over. When you're trying to discover other countries' trade secrets on a Government grant of a bare million a year, you stick to the essentials. As long as I don't step inside that Embassy I don't interest them."

"Well, I hope so," she said. "Aren't you drinking?"

"Yes. A gin, please. You look very pretty this morning."

"I've been working. I went to my solicitors and found out *all*. He's in Devon, as I said, between Kingsbridge and Salcombe. The village is called Mutterford. The farm is some distance out of it on the Salcombe road. I only brought up the subject casually so I couldn't press for details. But the first thing you're going to need is a car."

"No, thank you," said Rumbold. "What I do, I do on foot. Cars have number plates. Hikers are too humble to bother about. Have you got me the trains?"

"Yes. There's quite a good one at 10.15 in the morning. You change at South Brent. You can put up at either Kingsbridge or Salcombe, but Kingsbridge is better because it's a market town and more busy."

"Glendinnon,
"Peterhead,
"Aberdeen.
"December 29th, 1946.

"DEAR FIONA,—I heard quite by chance when I wrote to the Solicitors about Granny's estate that you were coming back and putting up at Brown's. It is such a long time since we met that I hope now to see something of you. Up here, life goes on much the same as usual. I have kept on the house though I am only using part of it. I daresay you heard that I was married during the war . . . to a Naval officer. He is now demobilised and has gone out to Ceylon as a tea-planter. I hope to join him next year but things are very difficult in more ways than one. I won't write much more now as you know I hate it, and also I want to be sure that you get my letter. If you are free at all and want to come north I shall be very glad to put you up, though of course it is bitterly cold at present, and not at all like Minorca.

"Your affectionate sister,

"Peggy."

The paper was blue, the writing rounded, childish, yet not devoid of character. The sting, it seemed, was in the final line.

"Well?" said Rumbold.

"Oh, I think I'll go. Why not? There's a good hotel, and if I leave to-morrow night I'll be in time for the grisly feast of hogmanay."

Rumbold fiddled with his glass of gin: "Scotland is certainly a long way from Devonshire," he said.

She laid her hand upon his arm. The suède of her gloves rubbed rough against the serge. "You're not going to start all that again, are you?" she said.

"I'm not starting anything," said Rumbold. "I'm just wondering how far this business is going to take us. I find it rather amusing that I should turn down respectable employment with both Aranjuez and Cassell in order to hire myself to you." He called the waiter. "Two more double pinks," he said.

"Hire," she said. "That's not a very pleasant word. I told you that you pleased me. I've proved it since."

"By lying on your back? Motor tyres wear out, my dear, and gramophones; but not the attribute which God has given women."

The waiter laid the glasses on the table. He had put in too much Angostura. Fiona searched for words: "Don't be horrid to me," she said. "For the present I can do no more than take you to my bank and cash your cheques, but one day you'll realise that there's more to it than that. I love you and I want affection."

"And perhaps another child as well? Nonsense. . . ."

"I'd bear your child with pleasure," she said. "That would be quite different."

"Diplomacy," he said. "Why don't you pack up and treat it as a business deal?"

"Tell me something," she said. "When you've done this will you despise me?"

"Certainly."

"I don't think you will," she said. "For though *you'll* do the work, the deed and thought are mine."

"You want me to admire you for them?"

"I want you to treat me with just a little fairness. Maybe my character's not strong, but just look at what my life has been. . . ."

"Don't come with that stale stuff," he said. "I've heard it in the mouth of every misfit since I wore long trousers. All right . . . I'll kill the boy and take the cash, but then we finish."

Fiona smiled: "It's very instructive to see you adopting the viewpoint of morality," she said. "You eat the various cakes, then have them. The Jesuits you speak about must have done you greater harm than I imagined. At one and the same time, you are the murderer and the censor. Yet aren't you as bad as me, and worse?"

"That's what you want, isn't it?" he said. "You *want* to drag me down. *All* of you want to drag me down . . . one offers money, one security and power. But the motive is the same: toads must have company beneath their stones or the slime begins to tickle them."

"If you could only know," she said, "only know what's in my heart. In yours there is so much bitterness. I could dissolve that bitterness, but first get rid of the idea that I want to bind you to me by what we are about to do. I ask nothing of you, although I need so much."

"You are certainly a refreshing change from the Borgias," he said. "I never heard that they discussed sentimental love and brotherhood with their various agents."

"Hard," she said. "Hard is what you are, and cruel . . . not I. Because one bad action is performed, does that mean that the person who performs it is incapable of any feeling, any kindness, any love? Yet that's the opinion which you are quite determined to have of me. And for why? Because you are afraid, Rumbold . . . because you're no good at people, and every contact frightens you."

"Have it any way you like," he said, and opening his pocket he showed the cheque which she had given him that morning. "*That's* what counts with me."

"You deceive yourself," she said. "Money, earned in that way

. . . the child . . . the drop by parachute . . . the tin-hat stories; these are proof that Rumbold is a man. And Rumbold, like many others, dearly wants to be a man, doesn't he?"

Nine

THE long passage entrance of the Monmouth Hotel stretched dark and fumed and webby towards a kind of clearing by the staircase where the aspidistras and warming pans were kept; the first squatting by right upon the oaken chests above a sea of hunting crops and visiting cards, the second suspended upon walls from which they would not be unhitched until next year's spring cleaning. An umbrella stand, some conch shells, a grandfather clock of solemn tick, a pervasive smell of mutton and a few prints from Jorrocks completed this Olde Worlde décor.

To its left lay the "office", with spy hole cunningly arranged between lace curtains; to the right the bars . . . saloon, smoking, and public . . . full now with the clamour of farmers in rude song and the exchange of fat stock prices. For this . . . as the long line of Ford Utility vans in the darkening street, as the sad plod of the odd bull off to the knackers yard, as the distant cackle of a thousand hens could testify . . . this was the evening of a market day.

From Start Point and from Bolt Head, the foghorns of which were too far distant to be heard, the griping fog crept inland from the Channel. The English, uninvaded, build their towns, not upon eminences, but in hollows, and presently, as the hour of closing struck and chemists rearranged the displays of cough mixture in their windows, Salcombe, Kingsbridge, Modbury and Aveton Gifford were swathed in mist both bronchial and icy.

Rumbold, recently arrived, tweeded as befitted the *ambiance*, and registered in the name of Gurney, descended the stairs after a wash during which he had discovered to his surprise that the hot tap ran hot. Arrived at the aspidistra clearing he hesitated, but the hour was as yet too early to consider dining. Accordingly he entered the saloon bar, and insinuating himself between two men in full discussion, ordered a dog's nose, with which, when delivered, he retired to a hard chair beneath a portrait of Gladstone, and at some distance from the fire.

He had not been sitting there for very long before two men, recently arrived, approached, bearing mugs of bitter, with the polite request that they might use the free chairs at his table. Rumbold agreed and, preoccupied by his drink and thoughts, paid, for the time being, no farther attention to them. The two men were discussing the difficulties in labour of a cow, apparently the property of one of them; the instruments employed in assisting its delivery and the injuries suffered by the head of the calf during the course of these operations. Rumbold knew nothing of the subject and ignored the conversation as far as was possible until his attention was aroused by the reference of one of the men to the other as "Vivian".

"So you are Vivian," he thought. "And I've come to kill the child you couldn't spawn yourself." He found the trivial coincidence amusing. Vivian was a large man, heavily built, with the promise of much future fat. He was dressed casually: only in the trim cut of his hair and the immaculate condition of his nails was it possible to find evidence of refinement. Otherwise, the face was doggy, the small moustache ill-tended, and the paunch that of a man too partial to his own farm produce.

His companion, lean of face, belegginged and bestocked, was quite evidently a cattle dealer. Rumbold, after some reflection, plunged for the main chance.

"Excuse me interrupting," he said during a pause in the conversation necessitated by the swallowing of beer, "but I'm staying down here for a few days and I wonder if you could tell me where I can get some rough shooting?"

A short silence ensued. It was clear that the question, demanding as it did an offer of assistance or a curt evasion, was far from well received. The man, Vivian, fingered his tie and looked away. It was left to the supposed cattle dealer, whose knowledge of polite usage was less extensive, to intervene.

"What is it you want?" he said. "Rabbits? There's bags of rabbits in these woods, but of course you've got to square the farmers first . . . Eh, Mr. Vivian?" and he slapped Vivian on the knee. Vivian looked acutely uncomfortable.

"Oh, I don't much care," continued Rumbold hastily, "Rabbits, rooks . . . sparrows, pigeon, I'll take anything that comes and don't guarantee to hit anything." He swallowed the last of his dog's nose. "I'm down here on sick leave as a matter of fact," he said in what he imagined to be a confidential tone. "Civil Service. The doctor told me the best thing for me is to hump about the hills in every kind of weather to get some exercise."

Vivian still looked uncomfortable, but it was evident that his interest was aroused. The desire to place the intruder socially, always the hobby of the middle classes, had overcome the first inclination to reply with a snub.

Rumbold observed this and determined to extend the slim beach-head of acquaintance by a move which would place the others, at least temporarily, in his power. "Look, what are you drinking?" he said. "Bitter, isn't it? I see your glasses are empty. No . . . don't get up," and before either man could rise, he had seized both tankards and moved with them to the bar.

"Two bitters, please," he said. "And put a slug of gin in each." Gin, if stirred, is difficult to detect, and mixed with beer, it talks.

Returning to the table he remarked with satisfaction that the two men sat silent and uneasy, evidently not having possessed the wit to make a brief consultation of opinion while his back was turned.

"Well, there we are," he said jovially, and laid the tankards down. From the glances exchanged between the pair he saw that neither knew the other's thoughts, and that, in consequence, the conventions must triumph.

"That's uncommonly civil of you," said Vivian, speaking for the first time. He had evidently decided to put a pleasant face upon the matter. Rumbold blessed the public school system which prevented gentlemen farmers from revealing their natural barbarism before mere cattle dealers.

"Cheers," he said, now in full attack. "I do hope you don't mind me interrupting your conversation, but I couldn't help overhearing it, and thought that you might give me a tip or two."

The cattle dealer drank, swilled, swallowed, cleared his throat. "Cartridges," he said. "That's the trouble. Any amount of guns round here but we just can't get the stuff to fire them."

"What a damned nuisance," said Rumbold, and of course it was because he had not thought of this impediment. Recovering quickly he assumed a look of such hangdog disappointment as he calculated might touch even the bovine Vivian.

Vivian was touched in fact. "Look here, Mr. . . . ."

"Gurney," said Rumbold.

"Look here, then, Mr. Gurney, I can't promise you unlimited ammunition but I've always got a few spare boxes lying about my gunroom. Vivian's the name. I live a couple of miles from here, near Mutterford. Verron Farm. You can't miss it. Big gates. Come out any time and you'll be doing me a favour if you keep the rooks off my crops."

"Well," said Rumbold. "It's damned decent of you, but I don't want to cause any inconvenience, you know."

"No inconvenience at all. I may be busy, but my two boys will show you round. Damned good shots both of them."

Both of them? Rumbold reflected. Had some mistake been made? He was certain that Fiona had described the couple as childless. Unable to make a direct enquiry he endured this uncertainty for several minutes, during which the conversation proceeded at molluscan cadence. Shooting in general, beer, and Devonshire were discussed, but, at length, when Vivian, having paid a further round, rose to go, he gave the clue:

"Well, goodbye. See you to-morrow perhaps. By the way, if you get lost don't ask for Vivian or you may land up in my brother's farm next door. Not that he'd care. You can shoot his land as well, but all the same keep an eye open for Verron Farm and you'll find me."

"Much obliged," said Rumbold. Hands were shaken. The cattle dealer, who evidently regarded himself as personally responsible for the happy outcome of the meeting, winked hugely at Rumbold as he left.

As soon as he was alone, Rumbold went upstairs to his room. He opened his map and spread it on the eiderdown. Verron Farm was near the sea, but Randolph Farm, next door, covered land which actually touched the cliffs.

And this was what Rumbold wanted.

He made his appearance at the farm shortly before ten o'clock upon the following morning. The day was cold and crisp. Ice hung from the hawthorns, and cars, turning the corners of the narrow lanes, manœuvred slowly for fear of skidding. The sun, as yet, lacked force.

The walk, about two miles in all, did Rumbold good. He breathed deeply, let his feet resound upon the tarmac, cut himself a crude walking stick from a pendant willow. Passing through the small village of Mutterford he observed the absence of a police station. Thus, any enquiries which might be made would have to come from Kingsbridge. Likewise, the ambulance; a fact which he had already checked discreetly in the hotel.

Rumbold hummed and threw a pebble at a robin. He was happy. At each side turning which led to the sea he halted and made examination of his map. The embranchments were all either cart-tracks or wide foot-paths, much used in summer no doubt, but at this season overgrown with tufted grass among which lay rabbit droppings. Between the main road to Salcombe and the sea, the land was private property. Witnesses need not be feared. Reflecting in the dark hours of the night before a last toothmug of brandy and a dreamless sleep, Rumbold had allowed himself three days for this job, four at the outside. On the fifth day, as well he knew, he would be obliged to produce his ration cards in the hotel, thus revealing that his name was other than the one written with such a flourish in the register.

"Verron Farm." The painting was ancient, but the castellated gates imposing, the drive neatly overlaid with pebbles above the rust-red Devon soil.

Somewhere, and not far away either, a pig was being killed. Rumbold advanced slowly and presently arrived at the scene of the assassination, which latter had already reached an advanced stage.

Perceiving Rumbold, Vivian detached himself from the group of farm-hands, and came forward to his encounter.

"Good morning," he said. "Sorry to have to greet you with such a harrowing scene." They shook hands.

Rumbold surveyed the pig, now dead. Much blood, slopped from buckets, stained the soil a deeper red, and from this blood and from the basins of hot water with which the carcase already was being washed, steam arose and the acid scent of death.

A senior farm-hand stood ready with sharpened knife waiting for the moment when the twitching trotters should point skyward: then the knife would plunge and hands, forearms, elbows, lever out the tripes.

"Wouldn't it be less noisy to put a bullet in his head?" asked Rumbold.

"By no means," said Vivian, scandalised. "The heart must go on beating as the blood runs out. Cruel, perhaps . . . but necessary if you want to eat good pork."

He led the way towards the house. "Come in," he said.

"I don't want to disturb you," said Rumbold.

"Nonsense. You must come in if you want to choose your gun. I'm not asking you to lunch."

Well, that's one awkward hurdle over, thought Rumbold. He hastened to explain that he carried a packet of sandwiches in his pocket. Lunch had bothered him because he realised that if he lingered too long upon the farm the owner might feel constrained to invite him. Conversation would ensue and with conversation a degree of intimacy which would enable the host to form an opinion of the guest. Rumbold did not want Vivian to form an opinion of him, did not want his table manners judged. He desired to leave behind him only the memory of some casual encounters and a half-forgotten face.

Meanwhile Vivian surprised him. In his own house the man seemed more confident, more jovial, a person to be reckoned with, and possessed of much authority. Twice, in the course of the few paces which separated the yard from the front-door, he halted in order to give instructions to employees. He demanded that Rumbold wipe his feet upon the mat. In the gunroom, while explaining the merits of various items in his armoury, he took good care to offer nothing better than a rook rifle.

"Sorry the Missus is out," he said. "I'll call the boys. Denis! Michael!" The cry resounded down a parquet passage full of gum boots, oilskins, baskets of eggs and wooden-shafted golf clubs. This—for it was bounded by doors marked "Private" or "Knock and wait; don't listen"—was evidently the utilitarian part of the building, the tribunal in which men were hired or sacked, the counting house of milk receipts and money.

Two boys appeared. They were aged about fourteen years and twelve. One carried a book, the other a massive air pistol shaped like a Colt.

"Boys," said Vivian, "this is Mr. Gurney. I want you to take him up to the oatfields by the wood. You ought to try the wood," he said to Rumbold. "Bags of pigeon if you wait for them." He moved off, muttering some excuse. The door marked "Private" closed. Rumbold had the impression that the first whisky of the day would presently be decanted.

"Right," he said. He was conscious of the boys' inspection: they were small boys for their age, but thickset, pugnacious in appearance, and deeply distrustful.

"Come along then," said the elder ungraciously. He flung his book aside and led the way. In the yard a man was rubbing down a pony. A Landgirl paused, with bucket raised, to stare. "Don't moon there, Mary. Get on with your work," said the elder boy.

Beneath the first gate, the recent rains and the constant passage of cows had transformed what had once been solid ground into a quagmire. A saloon-bar psychologist, Rumbold knew the value of first impressions upon the very young. Jumping from stone to stone set in the mud, he vaulted the gate nimbly with one hand. The boys followed more slowly, and by climbing. Wiping his gun clean, he could hear them muttering.

"Do you play Rugger?" said the small one suddenly.

"I used to," said Rumbold. "On the wing."

"Bet you can't race us to that tree over there."

Rumbold grinned. He saw the catch. The field was sloping, slippery. The boys knew the ground, he not, and on mud it is the heavy weight that falls. "Good," he said. "How much start?" for he had noticed a dry-cleaning shop in Kingsbridge and judged it worth while to accept the challenge. "Ten yards," said the elder boy. They set off. He followed, not running, as they had hoped, but bounding and choosing each foot-fall with great care.

Twenty yards from the tree he caught up with the smaller boy, picked him up, ran on. He caught the elder boy five yards from the winning post and passed it with both upon his back. All three stood panting. The steam of their breath sprang horizontal in the air.

"Gosh, sir, you can run," said the smaller boy. Rumbold noticed the term of deference with amusement. "That's a nice pistol you've got there," he said.

"It's a Christmas present."

"Like me to try it?"

"What you going to aim at?"

"How about that twig over there?" He took the pistol, steadied his hand, brought it round beneath his chest with eye, wrist and index finger all in line. He bent low and fired. The shot missed but the twig stirred. With his second shot Rumbold snapped the twig in two, then a second twig, and then a third.

"Why do you bend down like that?" asked the elder of the two.

"It's called the Battle Crouch. I learnt it in the war."

"But you didn't even aim."

"There isn't always time to aim, son." Rumbold grinned.

This was going well. He might have known the war would be sure thing with children of this age. He reviewed the various parlour tricks learnt years before at the Sabotage School in Scotland, rejecting the purely Scout accomplishments. He might teach them how to stalk and camouflage themselves. A couple of days of higher education and they would leave home and follow him. Rumbold grinned again: he had forgotten how exhilarating life with kids could be. A whole weight of sin dropped from him.

The path led downwards to the wood, where water dripped from the branches of the naked elms. They entered and stood concealed by bushes. Rumbold lit a cigarette and offered the packet to his companions. After some hesitation both accepted. They lit up; evidently not for the first time in their lives.

"No pigeons yet," said the elder.

"Oh, I don't mind waiting."

They withdrew and he could see and hear them whispering some yards away. Presently, the elder returned.

"We want to show you something," he said.

"What's that?"

"It's our hide-out. You mustn't tell. Nobody's ever seen it but us."

They beckoned him to follow. In the dark interior, the wood rose in terraces of rabbit warrens and all the sadness of wet leaves. The undergrowth was thick.

"Can you spot it?" said the elder boy.

"No," said Rumbold, though in point of fact he could.

They laughed in triumph. "Come on," they said, and seizing his hand, led him towards a clump of bushes even thicker than the rest. An uprooted rhododendron shrub swung free and Rumbold could see steps leading downwards.

"Very choice," he said. "Very choice, indeed. How long did it take you to do that?"

"Two whole holidays and part of these. But wait a sec.: you've seen nothing yet. Come down. It's not dark inside. We've made kind of windows, and there're three rooms . . . with doors too."

Stooping, Rumbold followed. At the bottom of the steps, about six feet below the surface of the ground, a circular chamber had been excavated, ten or twelve feet in diameter. Shafts cut in the roof provided light; the fall of leaves and the rain being prevented by plates of glass inset at ground level. Two doors, evidently the by-product of a plundered greenhouse frame, pointed the way to other and more secret chambers, for which this was but an annexe.

"Well?" said the elder boy. "What do you think of it?"

"I'm amazed at the way you've got rid of all the earth," said Rumbold. "I can't see a trace of it outside."

"That was the awkward part. We dumped it in buckets in the stream. The furniture's good, too, isn't it? That storm lantern came from a cow stall: Dad still doesn't know he's lost it. We pinched the stools and most of the other stuff from the storeroom."

A poster of the type hung in troop canteens throughout the war had been tacked against the wall. The poster showed the uniforms of the late German and Italian Empires. Rumbold smiled. He picked up an American tin helmet. "And what are you to-day?" he said.

"To-day we're German Werewolves in Bavaria. Sometimes we're Russians fighting Yanks but that's not much fun because it hasn't happened yet. Usually we're Jews in Palestine. We've blown up the farm . . . I mean the H.Q. . . . a dozen times."

They gazed at him with great seriousness, anxious for approbation. "Is it as good as the real war?" asked the younger one. "I mean . . . since you were in it, you can tell us."

"It's much better," said Rumbold. He sat down upon a stool. The dimensions of the cave were not designed to accommodate a grown man, standing. "But there're a couple of points you want to watch," he continued. "I didn't like to hurt your feelings outside but I caught on at once because of the path your feet have worn in coming here. You want to approach it always from a different direction. Then there's the rhododendron bush, too. You shouldn't uproot it or it withers. Plant another and clip away the leaves so that you can wriggle through."

They listened intently, but with evident chagrin. War, Sex and Travel are the only major subjects upon which children accept the opinion of adults. "Come and look at the other rooms," said the elder boy, hiding his shame. He pulled open a door. "We haven't finished this one yet," he said. "Just a kind of hammock we've rigged up . . . *hullo! what're you doing there, you little squit? Get out of our hide-out at once. . . .*"

Rumbold, who had been following behind, heard first these words, spoken in a tone of furious anger, then a scuffle, then a squeal of pain.

A small boy . . . smaller than either of the others . . . was led into the central chamber between two outraged gaolers.

"It's our cousin, Desmond," said the oldest boy disgustedly. "I don't know how he got here. He's not supposed to even know we built it."

"I found it weeks ago," said the newcomer, reassured perhaps by the protective presence of a stranger. "I often come here when you're out with uncle."

The eldest boy, his fist clenched, hit his cousin hard upon the chin. "Well, you bloody well won't come here any more," he said.

"Here . . . steady on," said Rumbold.

He examined the child. The resemblance to Fiona was striking: the same green eyes, the same fair hair, the same wide mouth and pallor, but with these primary features of heredity others which had certainly not come from the mother . . . spindle shanks, a tall, domed forehead, an almost complete absence of that muscular development associated with the first decade of life, when trees are climbed and balls thrown and caught with vigour.

The eldest boy must have seen sufficient in Rumbold's stare to justify a continuance of his baiting tactics. "He collects flowers," he said. "Collects flowers on the cliffs and presses them."

"Do you?" asked Rumbold.

The small victim said nothing.

"Don't be afraid," said Rumbold.

"I'm not afraid," he said. "They won't play with me, so I play by myself. *And* I've got better games than they have, I can tell you."

"I shouldn't be at all surprised. I'll come and play with you myself one day, but cut along now or you'll be late for your lunch." He smiled, not so much at the boy as at the schoolroom jargon he had employed in addressing him. How the years slipped off one's shoulders!

"But I don't want to go," the boy said. "I want to stay and watch you shoot."

This reply appeared to delight the two cousins. Joining hands, they danced round the cave, chanting: *"Dirty, dirty Dessy . . . his pants are always messy,"* a taunt which was evidently not without some foundation, for the boy blushed deeply and began to snivel.

"All right," he said. "But you just wait. I'll pay you out. Wait and see."

And he ran up the steps and disappeared, pausing only to fling a stone which struck the wet wall of the cave with a dull sound.

"You see," said the eldest boy contemptuously. "You see what a funk he is. He won't fight with us. He won't even wrestle when I tie one hand behind my back."

"You're a good bit older," observed Rumbold.

"*Michael* isn't much older. He could wrestle with Michael, couldn't he? But he's always been like that, always funking. When we showed him our tame ferrets he was sick. He's like a bloody girl."

"What's his father like?" said Rumbold.

"Oh, Uncle Jim's not bad, but he can't farm like Dad. You just look at his land and ours and you see the difference. As for Auntie Mary . . . that's Desmond's mother . . . she's been in bed for two years. Two years! Just imagine that, and Dad says there's nothing wrong with her at all. Sheer laziness, he says, hypo . . . hypo. . . ."

"Hypochondria?" suggested Rumbold.

"Yes, that's it . . . hypochondria. Listen, we'd better go and shoot now or Dad will tan us. He gets mad when we don't bring back a pigeon. He thinks we're idling because he doesn't know about this place."

They ascended the steps. The two boys pulled up a fresh rhododendron bush and planted it in the place of the one to which Rumbold had taken exception. In half an hour Rumbold shot two pigeons and a rook and explained to his companions, upon their demand, the principles of childbirth and the composition of high explosive.

"Shall I see you to-morrow?" he said when, looking at his watch, he saw that the time was past mid-day.

"Not to-morrow. We've got to go to a beastly Point-to-Point at Okehampton. But the day after if you like. We'll take you ferreting. Magnus . . . that's our biggest one . . . is a real terror. He drinks neat whisky."

They walked slowly towards the farm. At a gate leading to the main road Rumbold paused. "Well, goodbye," he said. "Goodbye," they replied, but seemed embarrassed. They were not very articulate children. "It's been jolly good fun, sir," burst out the elder one. "You won't split about the hide-out, will you?" "No fear," said Rumbold, and to prove it gave them his penknife, receiving in return a priceless conker which had remained unbeaten throughout the winter term at school.

He walked back to his hotel. A letter awaited him. Over his luncheon mutton and two veg. he read it. "I am here," wrote Fiona, *"en pleine pudibonderie bourgeoise.* How goes it with you and shall I see you by Saturday?" Peterhead, it seemed, had not changed for the better. The house was still gas-lit but might serve them as a haven for the remaining winter months. "We are married now," he read. "I am afraid that this is quite essential as Scottish betrothals do not run their course beneath a single roof. We were married, for your information, in Barcelona. . . ."

Of the sister, not a word. In length the letter reached six pages, the last three of which were devoted to the expression of sentiments more tender: "Darling, forgive all that I said to you in the pub. You have given a new meaning to my horrid life. I know we can be happy, and all that I have to give is yours."

When he had finished his lunch, Rumbold took the letter upstairs and copied it out upon a writing pad. After about an hour he had achieved a fair imitation of Fiona's hand. With practise, he knew that he would do still better.

Ten

THE sand was soft. In places the prevailing south-west winds had stacked up drifts, and here the foot sank in to the ankle and caused small crabs busy building nests to scurry. Several times Rumbold was obliged to halt and shake the ballast from his shoes.

He made his way beneath the cliffs. He was searching for a path. At length he found one, treacherous, twisting, along which some band of hardy trippers had perhaps slithered on their bottoms in the summer, but of which few could ever have attempted the ascent. Down upon his hands and knees went Rumbold. Allez . . . oop, and with fingers clawing for the grass, and calf muscles tensed he left sea-level. Dislodged at every redeployment of his feet, pebbles and even more formidable fragments of England's heritage fell, bounding and rebounding to the rocks beneath. Pausing to regain breath he saw the beach below him, blank and melancholy, its only inhabitants a school of sea-gulls grouped like pontoon players round a broken barrel.

At the summit of the path the sea-bound breeze, beating

offshore from the relatively warmer land, caught him in the face
with stinging insistence. He rested for a moment, concealed by
bracken, checking his position. To his right, a mile inland, lay
Verron Farm, hidden from where he sat by the wood in which he
had shot the previous day. To his left, but only slightly, and much
nearer—the uncle's farm, the home of little Desmond, whom
he could see some distance off, playing a solitary game upon the
extreme edge of the cliffs.

Rumbold stood up: in this rolling and uncultivated downland
no great need for concealment. At most, the two farmers turned
loose their flocks of scraggy sheep upon it, and on Sundays, perhaps, a horse recuperating with a bellyful of heather from the
labours of the plough. The fertile land, the acres which paid the
income tax and the trips to race-meetings lay far distant from this
salt-blown scrub. If farm-hands passed here they came with a purpose: to shoot a rabbit, not to admire the view.

Rumbold approached the boy. His feet made no sound upon
the turf. The boy held a cricket bat. He stood in the correct stance,
his eyes fixed upon a ghostly bowler or surveying the placing of
equally ghostly fieldsmen. At intervals he played a stroke, sometimes defensive, sometimes a cut or a drive through the covers.
When this happened he would call out "four" or "two", or pat the
turf in front of him with the flat part of his bat.

"Hullo," said Rumbold.

Startled, the boy turned round. He seemed both resentful and
ashamed. "Hullo," he said.

"What are you playing cricket for in winter?" said Rumbold.

"We're on tour," said the boy.

"Ah, England in Australia . . . is it?"

"No," said the boy. "I told you I had better games than they had.
I'm Liberia. . . ."

Rumbold sat down. He lit a cigarette. "Tell me about Liberia,"
he said.

The boy hesitated. "I can't stop now," he said. "We're 342 for six.
I'm in the middle of an over." He looked about him as if, already,
he saw the protests of the fieldsmen, the outraged umpires.

"Why not pretend it's the tea interval?" suggested Rumbold. He stretched his legs and sucked a blade of grass. Green juice in his mouth, the grey of the tobacco smoke which had rinsed his lungs: it tasted good. The boy sat down. He made a note in pencil upon a pad. "I have to remember the score," he said seriously.

And so it came out; with hesitancy at first, then with a rush of which there was no holding. God alone knew where the boy had got the idea . . . perhaps in some geography lesson when, bored by temperate climes, his eyes had strayed downwards to the torrid coasts of Africa. To others, Liberia was a Negro republic, inaugurated and preserved by Yankee philanthropists: to him it was an independent and somewhat bellicose state populated by a clean-limbed race of predominantly Irish origin. Sport ruled here, but not only sport, for while other children lived their dream-world piecemeal, this one had fitted his within an all-embracing framework. Now a monarchy, now republic . . . each change of regime providing the excuse for positional warfare on the cliff-tops . . . governed by a multiplicity of political parties in the Gallic style (constant elections) with an aristocracy (here he did not seem inventive) whose names were constantly repeated in the National rugby and cricket teams; with stamps, with coinage (pennies treated by electrolysis in the lab. at school), with civil and criminal laws (every decent British murder was at once repeated in Monrovia, the capital); with a spirit of Imperialism as obstinate and pedantic as that of the Mother Country in her palmy days.

For, though Britain knew it not, Sierra Leone and Gambia had quite recently changed hands. The future of Portuguese West Africa hung in the balance. Rumbold was shown the campaign maps, hidden in a grubby pocket-book. The Supreme Commander, whose description he obtained, possessed a perhaps entirely fortuitous resemblance to Montgomery.

"With Britain we want only a just peace," said the boy (his terminology perhaps borrowed from his father's *Times*), "but with Portugal it is different . . . their Queen has refused the marriage offer of our King."

"But there is no Queen of Portugal," said Rumbold.

The boy waved this aside. Eventualities arose which justified some tampering with history.

"But doesn't Liberia ever lose?"

"Oh, yes, sometimes." His eyes lit up. "Then we have a revolution" . . . generally, it seemed, conducted by some popular cricket professional who, gaining power, abolished all sports other than his own. Thus, he was always sure to be supplanted when the football season started.

And King Rudolph; safe, on and off, upon his throne until the boy heard of Mayerling (the monarch had, of course, following a distinguished example, indulged in several Morganatic unions). And the cricketers; browned, tanned simple souls, juggling with the bat and ball, unaware that in a few years, with the discovery of Keats, they would have suffered a cruel metamorphosis and become poets. And the gallant soldiers, whose future, had they but known it, would have been the firing squad for refusal to sign the first Peace Manifesto, when the boy caught that virus at fourteen. And the gradual transformation of this manly, Spartan State into a gynæcocracy as its creator, wrestling with puberty, learnt to wriggle beneath the sheets, a page from mother's *Vogue* in his right hand.

Yes, Rumbold was glad that it lay within his power to save Liberia. He felt no compunction, no regret. A blinding pain, a broken head, a body lying multiply contused among the rocks. One push, a simple shove, and fifty years were snatched away, a decimal point altered in demographical statistics.

The boy rose. The tea interval, it seemed, was over. Rumbold watched him at his miming. Wickets were falling quickly. "All out," he announced presently. "And Bradman made a duck."

Rumbold lay back. He placed his hands behind his neck. The grey clouds scudded overhead. Ceiling three thousand feet. "Where is your father?" he asked. "I saw a car coming out of your drive when I was on the road."

"They've gone to Newton Abbot for the day. I'm to have a picnic lunch in the kitchen."

"You'll taste better food when your head is in the rock pools," said Rumbold to himself. "Go on . . . why don't you play?"

"I *am* playing," said the boy. "You don't have to run about to play. I'm making an election speech inside my head."

"Supposing," said Rumbold, sitting up. "Supposing that I were to kill you."

"It depends how you did it," said the boy, intrigued.

"All right . . . supposing I were to hit you on the head?"

"There's only the bat to do it with. You couldn't do much with that."

"Well, never mind. Supposing I *did* do it. What would happen then?"

The boy considered the question. "A farm-hand did something very like that to a little girl not long ago," he said. "They're hanging him at Dorchester to-morrow."

"I could strangle you," said Rumbold.

The boy sketched parallel lines with his bat in the sandy soil: trenches perhaps: a pitched battle in his war against the Portuguese. "No good," he said. "For then I'd scratch and the police would find fragments of cloth between my finger nails. They'd catch you easily."

"Not so easily as that," said Rumbold. "Look at it my way. I told them in the hotel this morning that I'd have my lunch in Salcombe. The way I've come by the cliffs is a short cut. If I killed you now I could be drinking a pint in Salcombe inside twenty minutes."

"And supposing I screamed?" said the boy.

"No one would hear you," said Rumbold. "Only the sea-gulls."

The boy made a wry mouth: "I don't really like this story," he said. "Tell me a nicer one."

Rumbold looked at his watch. The time was a quarter past eleven. "What shall I tell you?" he said. "Shall I tell you about myself? Once upon a time there was a little boy who lived in a back street in a town near London. . . ."

"How old?"

"About your age, but with this difference that his mother made him wear short trousers till he was twelve because she hadn't enough money to buy him long ones."

"But trousers are not very expensive," said the boy.

"Everything seems expensive when your father's saving up to have five pounds a week at sixty and a brass-plated coffin for his funeral. The boy cottoned on to that right away, so he did his best to rectify matters. He stole. . . ."

"What did he steal?"

"Sweets at first: he used to open the lockers of the other boys when they were in the playground. It wasn't a good school like yours . . . only ten pounds a term and a guinea extra for music lessons. The Masters lived in: that was what first gave the boy the idea of stealing money. He used to go up to their rooms in the break. He always took something with him, an exercise book or a hockey list, so that if he was found there he would have an excuse. The nicest Master was also the most stupid: he always left his drawer open, so naturally it was he who lost most."

Rumbold's turn now to draw pictures in the sand. He sat cross-legged, sucking the grit from behind his finger nail. "Of course at that time," he said, "the boy's needs were modest. He only wanted a Meccano set or an air pistol like the one your cousin has. The money meant nothing to him except as a means to these ends. But as he grew older and wanted a motor-bike or wanted to take girls to the pictures he began to see that money was important in itself."

He paused, surveying the boy, who watched him, rapt and attentive. "And it *is*, too, you know," he said, "unless I've made a dreadful mistake."

"Go on," said the boy. "I've pinched things myself."

Rumbold lit another cigarette. "Well as soon as this boy realised *that*," he said, "he stopped stealing from necessity, and began to steal partly from sheer pleasure and partly to have a reserve to fall back upon if times got bad."

"But wasn't he ever caught?" asked the child.

"Never. Mind you, there were some pretty close shaves, and once there were police in the house. The boy blubbed a lot in the lavatory that day, but he stuck to his story because he knew that if he admitted one thing the whole of the rest would come out. It's quite easy to steal if your parents are respectable. This boy's parents were eminently respectable. His father belonged to the Rotary Club. He wanted his son to work in a bank." Rumbold laughed. "That was a good joke, wasn't it?"

"But you can't steal money from a bank," said the child. "I've heard my own Dad say so."

"Oh, when I say 'steal' you mustn't take me literally," said Rumbold. "My young man was long past simple pilfering by this time. Naturally, you can't take hard cash from a bank but you can sell the clients' secrets to people who are interested in them. And it's surprising what interest is taken in the monthly rise and fall of a big account. One thing leads to another in that game. The position of the intelligent bank clerk is ideally suited for blackmail. . . ."

He paused. "Especially abroad," he said. He paused again, staring at the sand, but seeing instead the Place du Théâtre Français in Paris, the clock across the street, the red and yellow awnings of the Régence. It was there in the embrasure used by lovers that he had met Montenotte, once a week, usually after lunch.

"The only trouble about having more money than your circumstances make plausible," he said, "is that you can't carry it about with you in office hours. A lot of people get caught that way. They simply invite investigation. But not this young man. When he played poker he took very good care to do so in carefully chosen company. All crooks are exhibitionists, but this one kept his good suits and his gold cigarette case for the evenings. Immunity from danger had not, in his case, bred over-confidence."

He stopped talking. "Do you know why I'm telling you all this?" he said. "It's because you won't tell anybody else."

"Oh, I wouldn't dream of sneaking," said the child.

Rumbold laughed. "That's about all," he said. "I won't tire you with my tin-hat stories. I'll keep them for your cousins. Let's talk of something else, shall we? . . . I met your mother not so long ago."

"But she's in bed. How could you have seen her?"

"Not that one. Not the pale invalid who can't conceive. I'm talking of your real mother now. You didn't know you had one, did you?"

"Yes," said the child surprisingly. "I did. Our gardener told me on my birthday, when I was seven. He's the only one who remembers me coming here as a baby. He said it was a shame for me to grow up not knowing it. But he made me promise not to tell anybody else."

"Well, *isn't* it a shame?" said Rumbold. "Don't you sometimes lie awake at night and think about it? Don't you wonder what your real name is, and where you were born, and why they got rid of you like that . . . never coming to see you, never writing, not even caring whether you're still alive or not?"

He had expected tears, but no tears came. The boy sat looking downwards, his fingers plucking at the grass.

"No, I don't," he said. "If they sent me away they must have had a reason, and I bet it was a horrid one. I'm quite happy here and I don't have to love Denis and Michael, either, now that I know they're not my real cousins."

"Your mother's very beautiful," said Rumbold. "Would you like to see a picture of her?" From his wallet he took snapshot a fortnight old: Fiona on the steps of the Aviz in Lisbon.

"Look," he said. "See how like you she is."

"No," said the boy. "No, I don't want to." He thrust away the hand which held the photograph, but Rumbold seized him by the shoulders, forcing him to look.

"You can pretend she's the Queen of Portugal," he said. "I promise you she's just as fickle."

"Leave go," said the boy. "You're hurting me."

"No leaving go now my little one. No more little games, no more pretending. We're face to face with reality now . . . both of us, and both for the very first time."

Again he looked at his watch. The time was now well after twelve.

"Come," he said rising.

"No."

"Come."

The boy began to run, but Rumbold, sprinting, caught him and swung the frail body upwards in his arms.

"What do you want?" said the boy. "What are you trying to do? I'll tell my father."

"There's only God the Father now," said Rumbold. "I'm sorry it had to happen this way. I'm sorry I had to frighten you, when with a single push. . . ."

He stopped. The boy had scratched his face.

"Ah, *tu deviens méchant*," he said. He pressed the boy's body closer so that he could scratch no more.

"No, please stop screaming," he said. "I tell you that's the way it was ordained. In matters of this kind I have to drive myself to a point where only the chosen solution remains. You can see that, can't you? Don't be afraid of death. It's nothing . . . nothing at all. I've half a mind to join you. Come now . . . let's get it over. Then I'll pray."

The boy screamed only once again, this time as he fell, but the sound of that scream still echoed among the cavities of the lonely cliffs when his body lay inert among the rocks.

Rumbold picked up the cricket bat, and smoothed over the traces of his footsteps and of the struggle. Then he set off at a brisk pace towards Salcombe. From time to time he dabbed with his handkerchief at his face.

Shortly after he had gone, another man began to make his way from the cliffs towards the Salcombe road.

Eleven

"PARDON."

What . . . going to the toilet again? This was the second time within an hour. The woman must be suffering from colic. He was about to push open the sliding door for her when she trod on his toe. Leaning back in the obscurity he pretended to be asleep. Never take a seat adjoining the corridor.

The carriage was obscurely lit. The train rolled somewhere in the desert between Exeter and Reading. The fug was appalling: why did English people never think of opening a window nowadays? An aftermath of the war, no doubt . . . *Pull the blinds down . . . Mind the black-out.* The black-out had gone, but the closed window which had been part of it remained. It was the same with everything. Bloody sheep! Rumbold scowled at a sleeping major who, with Sam Browne unhitched and tie awry, snored placidly against a patch of ginny moisture on the glass. Strip them all naked, that was what he would like to do . . . strip them to the buff and watch them fight for the two fig-leaves which he would place upon the luggage rack.

He opened his flask and drank, then lit a cigarette. Things had not gone badly, though he wouldn't care to pass a second afternoon like that one in the hotel lounge; fidgeting, fingering then setting down the China shepherdesses, flicking the pages of dog-eared magazines, speckling the fire-grate with a score of cigarette butts. "Not going out this afternoon, Mr. Gurney?" "No, I don't think so. I have a slight cold." The telephone call had not come until after five o'clock, when, in desperation, he had already ordered tea. "Hullo . . . is that you, Gurney? Vivian this end. Look here, old man, I'm sorry but I can't ask you to come up shooting to-morrow. There's been a dreadful accident. My nephew's been killed."

Killed? A fist had closed round Rumbold's heart at that word. But no! It was just the man's unfortunate way of expressing himself. Everything was quite in order. Boys will be boys remained the official explanation. Decorous expressions of sympathy on Rumbold's part. Would they be seeing him again at Vivian's? . . . it would be quite all right after the funeral, especially as he seemed to have made a big hit with the boys. Well, no, he was damned sorry but he had to get up to town within forty-eight hours. One of those sudden recalls. Back to the old office desk. Perhaps next time. . . .

Next time, indeed! Grinning and light of heart, he had made discreet enquiries in the town. Yes, the ambulance had been sent out as soon as the news came through at two o'clock. A farm-hand had discovered the body and rigged up some kind of contraption of pulley and ropes with which to hoist it to the summit of the cliffs. The remains now lay, snug and be-sheeted, in the municipal mortuary. There would be an inquest, of course, but what was the good of that with the poor little lad a shapeless mass upon a cold stone slab? There were no two ways about it, declared public opinion: the father was mean. Ten pounds it would have cost him to put barbed wire along the cliff top. Now he must spend three times that amount in black ties and crepe and coffins. Rumbold's informant, an ironmonger, showed him a stack of the barbed wire in question, with gloomy satisfaction.

"Pardon." Ah, the bitch had finished, and suffering, no doubt, from night blindness, trampled at random among the out-flung feet. A sudden lurch of the train sent her into Rumbold's lap. Suspender belt too low, he thought. "Pardon," she said again. "Don't mention it," said Rumbold. Opposite, the major, whose ideas upon the amenities to be expected from first-class carriages were sound, had got his feet up. Blanket drill. The major was enjoying his kip enormously, oblivious of the fact that he had swiped the lady's seat. "Do you mind if I sit here?" she whispered. "Not at all," he said. Her profile, against the light, was charming, the clothes somewhat dowdy. A clergyman's daughter, perhaps? Good Works, in any case, but willing. Her thigh was closer than need be to his own.

He drank. "Like a little?" he said. "I'm sorry I've no cup." She looked at him doubtfully while the others slept. "Go on," he urged. "It's whisky . . . very warming." He extended the flask, and touched her hand, playing clever-clumsy. He watched her tilt it back, noticing with amusement the movement which she made, then checked, to wipe the orifice. In that class, the dread of syphilis is inborn.

And the trip made by taxi to the farm. Never content to leave well alone, that was him. "I know all this is most irregular, but I just had to come." The embarrassment of Vivian, the plum cake baked before the tragedy and now cut in slices thin as Communion wafers in honour of it. The mistress of the house was absent once again; this time decanting bromide at the bedside of the bereaved mother. The boys, clad in their best suits, were forbidden the exit to the dung-strewn farmyard.

"No shooting for at least a week," said Denis, when his father had gone to take a leak. "I always knew he'd fall over," said Michael. "Silly little fool."

Yet in his eyes Rumbold read a new respect for the victim. To slip, to fall eighty feet and bash one's brains out . . . after all, there was much more in that than swopping conkers. "And he might have got his colours at hockey next term," said the elder boy, who, to Rumbold's surprise, proved the more emotionally susceptible of the two.

Ah! The world of childhood, the conventions of the adult superimposed by force and Eton collars upon the instincts of the savage. "Making mud pies! It's so charming to see them playing with sand," but if mother knew that the little mind was playing with s—t, she might have very different ideas.

"Come back," the elder boys had said. "Please come back next hols." No possibility of doubt in that appeal. Children, not having reached the tax-paying age, remain upon the side of the lawless.

And, of course, he had said that he would, but now he stretched his right hand sideways . . . inch by inch, touching a button on the upholstery provided by the Great Western Railway, then a complicated pattern in relief, then the material of a jacket, then a rib felt through this jacket. Cautious, diffident, always ready to retire, Rumbold's fingers slipped further. The woman made no movement. Well aware of the proprieties, he left the possibilities of refusal with her. His hand now encircled the waist, climbed, crawled through some lace, made about turn and descended the one-in-three slope of the right breast.

What now? A triumph indeed, but an empty one. Rumbold's fingers descended further, touched a fold of flesh above the stomach, then became tangled in a hook of some sort designed to maintain the midriff. His flesh was ripped: he felt the blood drop and the woman shiver.

"No," she said. "No," and with some reason, for if the light had brightened even slightly, her situation would have been far from enviable.

Rumbold obeyed her. Withdrawing his hand he transferred his attention to her legs which, crossing, stiffening, she attempted to deny him.

These fun and games continued for a certain time; through half of Wilts, through a part of Berks. Presently, however, Rumbold discovered amusement more subtle. He withdrew his hand. He sat back. The gloom was such that the woman could not see his face, and yet he knew she peered, could sense the questing forehead, the fingers on the purse. Rumbold lay back, doggo, his neck against the carriage corner. He breathed quietly, listening for the breathing of the woman, which came now sharp and short and charged with anger. "Ah! *tu es mécontente, ma fille? Tu n'aimes pas qu'on te pelote rien que pour te laisser tomber. . . ."* On the seat something was moving. It was her hand advancing in conditional surrender. Rumbold lifted the hand, and replaced it firmly in the owner's lap. At this moment the train, slackening speed, began to enter the labyrinthine approaches to Reading. Lights flashed. A soldier in the corridor raised his kit-bag. The major, groaning, thrashing with his feet, kicked the old lady in the corner. The senile smile of peace upon the face of the old lady changed to a look of righteous indignation. Her umbrella fell . . . could it have been done deliberately? . . . and roused the gentleman with the appearance of a senior civil servant sitting opposite. In a moment the whole carriage was awake. The cruel unshaded light above an extinct book-stall revealed the clot of sleep in the eyes of the major, the intermediate position of the old lady's denture. Venomous glances were exchanged as the passengers, dreaming of spring beds, returned to grips with muggy reality.

But none more venomous than that directed against Rumbold by the young woman who sat beside him. Watching her covertly, he saw her rise and take her bag. She left the compartment. He followed, leaning out of the corridor window, so that he might the better survey the platform. But no! Reading was not her station. A woman's pride demanded the last word.

"Not far to London now," the major said. It was the type of fatuous remark for which the old lady had been waiting. She sniffed.

And crossing London. . . .

Rumbold took the Inner Circle, a circuit loaded at that hour of the morning with night porters, workmen from the power stations and charwomen on their way to scrub an office step. At Waterloo he queued for his scalding cup of tea, and surveyed the indicator. "Alas, Posthumus, the flying years glide by . . ." Six of them since he had last stood on these platforms, with home his destination. He entered the Post Office and sent his telegram: *"It is done. I shall be with you Saturday."* He captured a fleeing porter, and had his bag taken to the Guildford train.

Woking, Guildford, Haslemere, then Hampshire. Memories of half-crowns pressed into his hands by uncles and of not over-successful excursions to Christmas pantomines . . . memories of other boys, their holidays over, taking these same trains while he, with satchel filled, trudged to the grammar school, two hundred yards away from home . . . memories of rugger matches upon a sloping pitch with tangential uprights . . . Haslemere 2nd XV versus Linchmere . . . the day the scrum-half kicked him in the crutch and he had lain gasping, retching on the touchline. Memories of a little boy, of a chunky and aggressive youth, of a bank employee with a *Daily Telegraph* and a fifty-shilling suit . . . memories which had nothing and yet, at the same time, everything to do with the bag-eyed, long-chinned man sitting opposite the workman in blue overalls who travelled first-class because he knew that the ticket-inspector did not come on duty until eight o'clock.

At Guildford Rumbold disembarked. White-toothed, pyjamaed, the advertisement for a dentifrice pursued him; its manner and spirit very different from that of the black-coat workers piling in the train upon the other platform. The ticket-collector spat, was surly . . . no recognition here, though Rumbold had known the man since he had been an apprentice rolling milk churns.

He traversed the clammy tunnel, emerged, whistled to the single taxi on the rank.

"Fourteen, Acacia Road," he said. The taxi chugged to life, glided past the first blank shop-fronts.

Beyond the High Street, the first suburbs. "Take it easy," he said to the taxi-driver. "Don't go right up. You can drop me at the end of the road." By a pillar-box the driver halted. Rumbold got out, paid, watched the taxi crawl away. From somewhere, a smell of burnt sausages came as a reminder that he was hungry. The road was deserted. This was the hour of breakfast: the exodus of office workers bound for the 8.11 would not take place for another thirty minutes.

Two-storied houses, semi-detached, stuccoed, then overlaid with a brownish gravel substance. Twenty yards of garden front-age; thirty more fenced in at the back among the chicken runs, the rabbit hutches and the Dig-for-Victory plots. The trees which lined the avenue were not acacias as the name implied. They were elms. No acacias had been available at the time of the inauguration of the estate.

Fifty-two houses on either side, £400 down in 1928, the balance by easy stages. The last man, a Mr. Tyrell, in number six, had paid his whack in 1937. Mr. Tyrell, whose residence was sub-titled "The Moorings", favoured crazy paving. Nor was he alone in this, though many of his neighbours preferred roses, trellis-work or sun-dials, with a background of small ornamental gnomes from whose eyes the twinkle had long faded and upon whose once-red caps snails and spiders pursued their devious endeavours. Some residents had succeeded in offering all of these amenities in the small space at their disposal, while others—more eccentric—had sunk goldfish ponds, in the waters of which, inimical to piscine life but kind to tadpoles, the green and slimy pancake leaves of lilies floated.

Number two; the Robinsons . . . fishcakes this morning, apparently . . . number four, the Godbys; a small boy, picking his nose upon the doorstep, looked up indifferently before continuing his dissection of a cockroach . . . number six, the Benhams; four bottles of milk now inside the porch indicating the continued virility of the owner . . . number eight, the Hodges (she was said to bully him and, indeed, even at this early hour the lawn mower, the hedge clippers lay in waiting on the path) . . . number ten, the Lockwoods, whose radio, springing to life at dawn, functioned without pause until the midnight anthem.

Five yards from his father's gate, Rumbold hesitated. Impossible to make his approach by stealth, for all was public here, and already Mrs. Lennard, in number twelve, clutching her dressing-gown, patting hair curlers, had peered between the chintz.

Rumbold lifted the gate latch softly, tiptoed up the path. So far, so good. His parents sat at breakfast, their backs turned to him. He knocked, then rang, then cleared his throat. They would think it was the postman.

A flurry of movement, the framework of an argument. . . . "You go." . . . "No, go yourself" . . . the pad of feet in bedroom slippers: his mother, white-haired, a smear of bacon fat across her cheek, a piece of marmalade toast in her hand.

"Eric!" Difficult, however, to embrace him because of the toast. He took it from her, and munched as the arms enfolded him.

"It's been so long, boy." She seemed to have grown smaller but perhaps this was an illusion caused by her slippers. The arms hugged his splaying ribs yet could not meet about the backbone. Tears followed. Meanwhile his father, forewarned by the scuffling in the passage, had made his appearance at the dining-room door. "Good God! Come in; have you had breakfast?" Already they seemed ill at ease in his presence.

An egg fried in frantic haste, still mucous, the bacon, on the contrary, overdone. He stirred his coffee, surveyed ironically the photograph of himself when eight.

"You staying long?" enquired Dad.

"Two days, if you'll have me."

"Your room's still there. We've waited for you." Dad was on his dignity but Mother, oblivious of her own and the long lapse in correspondence, fawned about the room. She was not unlike her son: he had her features and his father's bulk, made more malleable in his case by years of exercise.

"Fellow called here the other day, asking for you," said Dad. He scraped the last of the butter from its saucer, then remembering that he had left none for his son, replaced some.

"What kind of fellow?" said Rumbold.

"Little fellow. Brown shoes, umbrella. Didn't give his name. Just said he'd like to see you."

"He told *me* that he came on behalf of Colonel Cassell," said Mum. She unplugged the electric kettle, refilled the coffee pot. "Oh, Eric . . . why did you never write?" she said.

"You should ask your friend Cassell that," said Rumbold, unmoved. "I understand he's kept you informed. He's very good at it. He makes a speciality of bereaved relations."

Dad ate his buttered toast. He had forgotten to add marmalade. "Four years without a word," he said.

"Three of them knowing you were alive. Don't you think that was a bit hard on your mother, lad?"

Rumbold grinned. "I don't pretend to be a model son," he said, and rising, he laid his arm about his mother's shoulders. Her cheek touched his hand, rubbing against it. "Leave him be," she said, at which Rumbold laughed. "It's no use, Dad," he said. "You'd better drop it. The charm still works."

"Aye," said his father grimly. "But bedazzling foolish women is one thing, and deceiving me another. I've heard tales about you, lad, and they don't make pleasant hearing. For two pins I'd shut the front door on you . . . and that's straight."

"Leave him be," repeated the old woman. She wept. "Five minutes here and already you're quarreling."

"A very ancient antagonism, isn't it, Dad?" said Rumbold. He began to range the greasy plates upon the breakfast tray. "But never mind," he said. "I'll be a good boy while I'm here."

The father rose, a Patriarch on his rococo hearth. "I don't care what you've done, lad," he said. "There's still some things that make me proud of you. But don't worry your Mum while you're here. That's all I ask, and you can't say it's very much."

He passed outside into the hall, took his frayed coat from its peg, his bowler hat, his brief-case. Rumbold followed. "Listen, Dad . . ." he said. The old man surveyed him intently, then stepped forward. "Ah, God damn you for a wheedling swindler," he said. He threw down his brief-case, put his arms about his son. "God damn you," he kept saying. "God damn you. . . ."

"Why, you old ruffian," said Rumbold, delighted. "Tears in your stupid old eyes too! Who'd have thought of such a thing." He dropped back a step, assumed a boxing stance. "Remember when you used to teach me fighting with one hand?" he said. With his left fist he jabbed tentatively and hit a watch-chain. The old man seized his Sunday walking stick, mimed as if to strike, then recollected himself.

"That's enough horse-play for now," he said. "We'll have a talk this evening. Some people have got to work even if others think it waste of time."

"Why don't you retire, you old hypocrite?" said Rumbold.

"I shall next year," the old man said. "And what do you think we're going to buy, your Mum and I?"

"A pub?" said Rumbold.

"No . . . a seed nursery. For twenty years I've grown every

cabbage, every leek back there in my plot from Carters. I've nothing against Carters . . . I just want to have my own. You know me. I don't follow the instructions, and for why? Because out there, by using my nut I've had Cocozelle marrows, aubergines, even Michaelmas daisies twice as big and twice as beautiful as any that spring up from a packet."

"Well, don't leave the business to me, I beg you," said Rumbold. He escorted his father to the door. "Nice azaleas you have there," he said pointing.

"Ah, get away with you. You don't know a daisy from a daffodil." Ten steps, the creaking of a gate latch, left turn, and father joined the happy throng now debouching from every house towards the station. Rumbold shut the door. His mother knelt, a brush in hand, gathering up the crumbs from father's table.

A bed, a crucifix above it on the wall, a marble wash-stand with a china bowl upon which roses bloomed; a wicker chair, a wardrobe, a tripartite scent of Jeyes fluid, of furniture polish and of dust. The old people received few visitors: it was likely that the room had lain untenanted for many months.

Rumbold unpacked, flung his sponge-bag in the washbowl, slid the folded pyjamas beneath the pillow. Then he opened the wardrobe: some clothes of his hung there garlanded with moth-balls . . . the pin-stripe for the bank, the dark grey flannel purchased by dint of saving seven shillings every week. Rumbold barely touched them. His thoughts flew, not to these almost adult levels, but to the drawers beneath, where lay the miscellania of a childhood more remote.

Tug . . . the drawer came easily, revealing first a football jersey, then a group of pipes, then a note-book. Ah! The scientific and intellectual period! So much scribbling, and to what end?

"In 1889, Nietsche was attacked by brain fever in Turin. He thought himself first God, then the Prince Eugene of Savoy, arrived in that city to attend his (Nietsche's funeral.) Nietsche, however, did not die until 1900."

Well, that was information at least, and here, on page twenty-three, was something better; a hint, almost, of futurity: *"During the Great War captured spies were executed in many different ways. The French and Germans shot them. The British hung them. The Austrians strangled them on a post. . . ."*

Rumbold rummaged further. He threw aside the note-books, the salacious postcards. The flotsam of adolescence does not seem funny once the thirties are approached. Rumbold rummaged further. Papers . . . *Papers* . . . here a bunch of letters from a girl and here financial jottings, largely on the debit; evidence of some long-forgotten attempt to float an interim budget.

Searching, Rumbold's fingers encountered straw. He pulled the object forth. It was a doll; flat, painted, cotton-covered. Its name was "Puck" and, crumpled, unresponsive, increasingly discoloured, it had lain, first in his cradle, then in his cot, then in his grown boy's bed throughout ten years of his life.

He held it up. The head dropped. The arms lay lax. "Puck," he said, "Puck." A quick glance round, but no one was watching. He stooped and kissed the painted face.

His mother never knocked on doors. She entered suddenly. "Do come and help me peel potatoes, there's a dear boy," she said. "I've *so* much work to do."

She made no remark about the doll. Very likely, she had not noticed it at all.

In the chicken run the birds ran forward as they did every evening at this time; for food.

Oh, sad illusion!

"Take the one that limps," his father said. "I meant to put her in the pot at Christmas."

"Come, my little beauty," murmured Rumbold. He extended his hand as if to offer grain. Can a chicken tell? This one could. With a shrill clamour and pageantry of outspread wings the bird made for the safety of its roosting place.

Too late! Already cruel fingers closed about the neck, tightened, twisted, wrenched. Thirty minutes later the trussed and empty carcase lay on the kitchen table.

"Believe me or not," said Rumbold, "but I was once taught how to mesmerise these birds. It's a great help, too, because it enables you to kill them without noise or fuss. You do it in the same way as with trout . . . by tickling . . . here, in the gullet." He demonstrated with the severed head, then flung it to the family cat.

"I didn't know you could cook," said father. Mother, who stood by, said not a word; more used to treacle tart and vegetables boiled into a pulp than *Poulet Ratatouille*.

"I didn't know myself until I tried," said Rumbold.

He watched the fat spit in the saucepan, sliced up the onion and the salsify, added his bouillon, rosemary and thyme, tossed in four cubes of bacon lard, then legs, wings, rib system of the dismembered bird.

"Right," he said. "Let her simmer for two hours. Remind me to strain the grease from the sauce. Grease in a *sauce piquante* is fatal."

In the sitting-room, the fire burned cheerfully. Father sank into his Sunday chair, raised slippered feet towards a footstool. Mother, darning socks, watched the sole fruit of her womb uncork a bottle.

"Now, son," said father when primed with Black and White, "it's time to tell us something of your plans."

"Plans," said Rumbold turning. "I have no plans. I live upon my wits. You know that." From his pocket he took an envelope and laid it on the mantelpiece. "Just a portion of the loot," he said. "Your cut. . . ."

The mother swallowed and—unprecedented gesture—laid down her handiwork. "Two days," she said. "It's such a little time. Be kind. Be nice to us. Your father's too obstinate to speak. He'll let things go with a drink or two and a good dinner. And so I must speak to you myself."

But Rumbold, busy with the preparation of his sauce, paid no attention, so that she was obliged to rise, to cross the room, to seize him by the shoulders.

They knelt together by the fireplace.

"Son," she said. "Son . . . speak to me."

But something closed inside his heart and he could not.

Twelve

THE small local train puffed away along the culvert: bound God knew whither, but very probably towards Elgin, Nairn and other places in the bleak and unpopulated north. To the right the sea; shallow, yellow, dismal, non-stop to the Skager Rak. To the left the moors, the exclusive property of deer-shooting gentlemen from London.

"Oh, gie me the lass that has acres of charms.
"Oh, gie me the lass with the weel-stockit farms."

Fiona let in the clutch, then laid her hand upon Rumbold's as the car gained motion.

"Have a good journey?" she said, conversationally.

"Yes," he said. "On the whole."

"Did you stay long in London?"

"I didn't stay in London. I stayed with my parents."

"Your parents?" She turned towards him in surprise. "I didn't know you had any."

"They're not very grand," he said. "That's why I'm obliged to neglect them for long periods."

The first dinner had gone off well, with the bird cooked to a turn, the wine, the whisky; but for the second, and his last beneath the paternal roof, Mother had insisted upon her rights.

"You shall have meringues . . . meringues and Dover sole with chips."

Useless to protest: in extreme youth he had liked meringues, therefore he must like them now. It was the same with lollipops, of which she had produced two on the first day after lunch. It was the same also with certain household tasks.

"Here's the table polish. I always remember how you love to make it shine."

—And polishing father's shoes (once his first task of the day: now elevated to a rite, of which it seemed that he had been the initiator).

—And crossword puzzles! At the age of twelve he had spent much time

in this pursuit. Now she presented him with a sheaf of them extracted from all the daily papers and from several weeklies.

"*I know you like them, dear. I went specially to buy the papers.*"

Invincible, not to be gainsaid . . . the Mother. *Crafty, pertinacious, clinging, with a preference for those remote periods of which her child could have no memory.*

"*You were a dreadful wetter, Eric. Every night, two nappies. And such howls . . . Your father had to walk you up and down the room.*"

The adult Rumbold (twelve stone ten; six foot two inches) had listened gloomily. He had heard it all before and knew better than to attempt a defence. Mother is no novelty in the world. Her family raised, her house in order, her daily shopping courses smoothly organised, she has no interest more empirical than the bedevilment of her children. And, the more these stray, the more unscrupulous her methods.

On that last evening, guests had been invited for a sherry. Rather silent . . . Rumbold; in fact, definitely morose. In face of which situation, Mother to the rescue:

"*Do you remember, Eric darling?*" *Pause, and then* adagio, "*how when you first began to walk you emptied your pot into the flower vase?*"

Recognising defeat, he had escaped in darkness, without waiting for breakfast, without saying goodbye.

Sometimes he wondered how much his mother knew.

And this other; at ease now in her tweeds, her brogues, who had contrived with him in crime?

"No," he said, "I don't often see my parents."

Whirr—whirr, up the hill and past the Presbyterian church and the fried fish shop: the little car ran smoothly. "Yours?" he said.

"No, just one more family retainer. You'll be meeting several by and by."

"This marriage business," he said. "To what extent have you committed me?"

"To the hilt, darling, I'm afraid, so far as Peterhead's concerned. I warned you they were rather stuffy here."

"I see," said Rumbold. Then: "Do you intend to stay the entire winter in this dump?"

"Well," she said. "I thought we might find it moderately amusing for two months. You don't want to go abroad again immediately, do you?"

"No," he said. "No, not immediately."

"*Meet me in the saloon bar across the street.*" *Thus the Third Secretary when Rumbold, telephoning, had expressed his disinclination to enter the Embassy openly.*

A pale young man, a too hearty handshake, and, "Waiter, two double whiskies please." Then, "Yes, Mr. Rumbold, we know all about you," and "Yes, Mr. Rumbold, we have instructions to give you every facility should you wish to re-enter Spain."

Dear old Aranjuez: like Cassell, always one to keep in touch.

"I might need the protection of a diplomatic passport and a Spanish plane." He was cautious now, playing it deep and bold and tricky. But the Secretary had jumped immediately for the bait: "How so, Mr. Rumbold? You have a passport of your own. Surely you could leave quite normally with that?"

"I think not. You forget that I have certain old associates in this country. They might not be too pleased to see me depart again for foreign parts."

"Ah!" the Secretary had said. "Ah yes, I see your point there. But I shall have to consult Madrid about it. Clandestine passengers with false papers are rather further than we normally care to go."

"Consult them, then," said Rumbold. "For myself, I say quite bluntly that I regard the matter as a test of your good faith. If the reply is favourable I shall have no further qualms. Incidentally, you might do worse than quote my exact words to your boss."

Two more double whiskies, a pause for half-time and five minutes of conversation with respect to Murcia, the young gentleman's home town.

Then: "And when exactly would you propose to leave, Mr. Rumbold?"

"Let us say mid-March. I have a few affairs to settle first."

The car climbed steadily on a gradient one in six. Beside a small pine wood Fiona slackened speed, stopped, applied the brake, lay back.

"I thought we might have our little chat here," she said. "There is so much we have to say."

"You live outside the town then?" said he.

"Yes. Just far enough to make life bearable." She smoothed her hair, then looked at him. "Did he suffer much?" she said.

Rumbold considered. "At the end," he said, "probably not at all. But before that I was foolish."

"How?" she said.

"I told him."

"Ah! That was not very nice of you, was it?"

"'Niceness' is a word which I find difficult to employ in this connection, though in a sense you're right. I meant to do it swiftly, without fuss. I swear to God that that was in my mind. Unfortunately I'd forgotten my extreme moral cowardice. I was obliged to clinch the matter by talking out of turn. Once that was done I *had* to kill him. Every line of retreat was out."

"Yes," she said. "I can see that. I can almost see it happening."

"Who's sorry now?" he said. "Don't forget your brave words in the train."

She stared at him again, the tragic eyes peeping between the white snowdrifts of her cheeks. "I'm not sorry," she said. "It is you who are sorry. You are not the man I should have asked to do it."

"Let's drive on," he said. "I just can't wait to meet your family." But she laid her hand upon his own. A moonstone ring she wore, and the heavy setting lay flat against his knuckles. "Do you know what day it is?" she said.

"I'm not much good at dates."

"Three weeks ago we met. It was a Saturday. I can see you sitting there at your table when the dancer fell." She paused, glanced at him sideways, then spoke almost in a whisper. "A woman cannot live alone."

"No, indeed." He laughed, but she, ignoring the coarse sound, continued. "You have something against me besides the affair at Kingsbridge, haven't you . . . something physical?" And, half jesting, because she feared to know the truth, she asked him if it was not the smallness of her bosom which repelled him?

"Oh, as to that," he laughed again. "One is nearer to the heart when the chest is flat. No, it is not your breasts, nor your legs, which are shapely, nor halitosis or any other disease of the advertising columns, nor even your age, for you are certainly one of those women who reach their best in the third decade of life. It is none of these things but something much more complicated."

"All I want is affection," she said. "You must admit that my demands are humble."

"Precisely . . . humility is the key word. All your life you have been bitchy. Now you feel the need to make amends. The recent murder . . . notice that I call it murder and by no other name . . . was to be your swan song in the world of wickedness. And with good reason, too, for now that the obstacle to your happiness has been abolished you can wait for the first twinges of rheumatism without a qualm. The winter in Scotland, the summer at Cannes or in the Antilles! A lovely prospect, isn't it? Three thousand a year and your baggage always labelled, ready for embarkation towards some new and as yet unvisited Cythera. But of course, there's one small snag. Life, as you know well, is not quite so simple as the travel brochures pretend. Life is real, and very, *very* earnest. And so one needs an anchor, something rather solid, which one carries about from port to port and lets slip in the estuary mud. *I'm* to be that anchor, aren't I? . . . the object of faint amusement in Casinos and of cupped hands behind which old women whisper: 'He's *so* kind . . . what a lucky girl she is to have him'."

"Not kind now," she said, "but cruel and shameful."

"Shameful perhaps, for like the policeman's, the gigolo's life is not a happy one. Though please don't mistake my meaning. I know that your intentions are entirely honourable. Corner-boys won't do now, will they, nor glamorous fishermen nor even artists on the staff of *Vogue*? You want a husband . . . a *husband*." He slapped his knee from merriment and stared out at the silent pine-trees.

She was crying now. The tears fell softly. She made no effort to staunch their lukewarm trickle. "How could you," she said, "how could you speak to me like that?"

"Why, easily, but let's go back a little, shall we? Let's take a look at you in the *Escapada*, in Madrid. The idea comes suddenly, prompted by champagne and the exchange of autobiographical data. It could be done, you think . . . two birds and the single stone retained for further use. What better than a man bound to you by the remembrance of a deed too dark for publication in a drawing-room? On such a soil love may grow, if not, perhaps, esteem."

"Yes," she said simply. "I had hoped it might, but although mine the Scottish upbringing it is you the Puritan . . . a dreadful, twisted Puritan who hates me because I made him hate himself."

"Ah," he said. "Ah, so you can hit back, can you? There is still some malice in the floods of sweetness and light," and seizing her arm, he pinched and twisted it.

"Now you are behaving like a barbarian," she said, freeing herself with difficulty.

"A barbarian? But naturally. What else can you expect? Wasn't it for my vices that you chose me? Panthers won't pull a milk-cart, you must understand. When they've caught one, hunters watch their step."

The tears had ceased now. "I don't think that's a very apt analogy," she said. "If you were the strong character you claim to be, you wouldn't make this fuss. I love you. You find that incomprehensible but all the same it is a fact. I love you for your weaknesses, not for your strength. I think that we are more alike than you imagine . . . certainly more alike than I shall ever get you to admit. What we have done . . ." She paused, seeing his hand raised, ready to interrupt. "All right, what *you* have done was perhaps not very pretty, but why dwell on it, why torture yourself unnecessarily? Believe me, I know the itch that's in you because I once possessed it in a high degree myself. *Bang . . . crash . . .* no sooner do you have the edifice of happiness than you set about destroying it."

She paused again and turned to him appealingly. From a corner of one eyelash the blue tinge of her mascara ran. "Don't you think," he said, "don't you think we have exchanged enough aphorisms for one morning? There is a more current one which goes: 'Don't bite the hand which feeds you,' and that, in the last resort is what you really mean."

"Listen," she said. "I'm indulgent . . . too indulgent even, but I can't let you have it every way. If the whole thing has been so repulsive to you, why did you come up here when it was over?"

"To collect," he said and, because that was his game, his line of strategy, he bent down and kissed her. The bucket seat slipped backwards on its rails.

"I want you so much," she whispered. "I need you. Don't be cruel to me any more."

Annually, tourists emplane for the sands of Egypt and marvel at the symmetry of pyramids erected by a hundred thousand slaves, but weight is only relative and the sands of Egypt flat. The Lairds of Dear Old Scotland, kilted, caber-tossing against a background of heather-covered hills, have, as their draughty, massive homes reveal, more exigence than any Pharaoh.

Slab upon granite slab, the house revealed itself as the car descended the winding road into the dip. The effect—and she stopped to let him look at it—was undeniably impressive. A mausoleum, but one of great solidity . . . rather in the style, with its gables and polyangular, jutting windows, of those illustrations on brick sets which children find beside their beds at Christmas-time.

"It was built," she said, "in 1862. That was before the Prince Consort's death, if you remember . . . long before John Brown. Balmoral, though not far away, was not yet a rival to Nice in the smart world. My grandfather took a chance."

"But why Peterhead?" he said. "Why not Dundee, or St. Andrews or the railway junctions with the unpronounceable names—Leuchars and Cupar?"

"Dundee was too vulgar for Victorians," she replied. "Sacking cloth, you know. St. Andrews was too genteel, and then, of course, there was no golf course then."

A high wall surrounded the property, for the Scots keep even the bitterns and the wild-cats out. Behind the wall a kitchen garden full of rotting brussels-sprouts and, spaced between these sprouts, fir trees with that curvature of the spine and umber-coloured foliage which are the consequence of unequal battle against a single and prevailing wind . . . the wind from Norway.

"*Eh bien, je t'en félicite,*" he said.

"Don't speak too soon," said she. "Behind the house it's comparatively sunny. In a good year the figs ripen. Even in a bad one they have peaches."

Four acres: certainly not more. An estate agent's pebble-toss from the North-South road, the same estate agent's stone-throw from the town. Gas-light of varying pressure and window corners letting in a constant stream of air.

The gate was open. They drove in past a lodge.

"And who lives there?" he said.

"Oh, just a kind of ghillie," said she. "The tenancy stays in the family. We don't bother them overmuch. He works for Ferguson up the hill. During the war he shot pellets at Commandos on the Mountain Warfare course. Now he reaps the benefit . . . every rabbit is his own because he saved the deer."

A gravel drive, a circular flower bed without benefit of blossoms, a face peering rapidly from an upstairs window; then as rapidly withdrawn.

"This is the moment," said Fiona. "Brace up. Prepare your little speech."

For the speech there was, however, no need, because the front door opened at once, silhouetting a young woman with thick legs.

"Peggy, this is Eric," said Fiona, disembarking with rucked skirt.

"How do you do?" said Rumbold, and he bowed slightly from the waist. His manners, when he thought the occasion warranted their display, were always very Olde-Worlde.

"How do you do?" said Peggy; then relinquishing his hand shouted in a loud voice for "Martha".

"It's no use," said Fiona. "She's out of harm's way by now. She saw us from the window."

"I'm so sorry," said Peggy. "About your bag, I mean."

"Oh, that's all right," said Rumbold and, seizing it, ran lightly up the steps to show that he was both athletic and good-natured. But alas! the hall was dark, so that even if it had been his intention he could have gone no further.

A stuffed mallard in a case stared down at him unwinking. The bird, for the death of which, a century earlier, some ancestor had no doubt been responsible, must have seen the come and go of many.

As Rumbold's eyes became accustomed to the light, half a cargo of Masefield's Dirty British Coaster introduced itself: ancient opalescent vases, amphoræ from Cyprus, beaten brass trays from

Benares. To the right of the mallard, who, although secure within his airtight case, seemed to resent their presence, a pair of antlers hung.

"Won't you come upstairs?" sister Peggy said.

They followed . . . pad-pad; cut-price carpets everywhere, for, as Rumbold recollected, Grandpapa had been a Consul in the Middle East. Twenty yards of Turkey, then a touch of Kurdistan, then a tapis from the Azerbaijan. Finally, the banisters, thicker than a flagpole and very much more knobbly.

"Fiona sleeps in the nursery," said Peggy, mounting. "I had a second bed put in this morning. I take it that you don't occupy separate rooms?"

"No," said Rumbold, somewhat disconcerted by this direct attack and by the hostility which it implied.

"There are sweet peas on the wall-paper," put in Fiona. "Unfortunately, they're peeling. Also little rhymes . . . Jack and Jill, you know, with a pikky of the bucket and the hill. But the bucket's peeling, too," she added.

The landing . . . several doors, before one of which they halted. "Well," said Peggy awkwardly, "I daresay you'd like a wash."

"Oh, yes, I would indeed," said Rumbold promptly. But since she seemed to linger, uncertain when or how to go, he added, "We'll be downstairs in a moment," and watched her trail away.

"And the water?" he said, when the door was closed. "Where is it?"

Fiona peeled off laddered stockings, revealed a cut of white-wash thigh. "You're in Scotland now," she said. "Not Barcelona. Walk down the passage to the bathroom. Light the geyser, but hold yourself well back . . . it's just a little temperamental." She unfolded nylons from a drawer. "And what do you think of sister Anne?" she said, not looking at him.

"Do you know, I don't know what to say. I scarcely saw her."

"Yes, that's her line: the three-quarter profile. I'm not speaking nastily, you know. She's shy. You must remember that, at thirty, she's been twice to London and perhaps ten times to Edinburgh."

"What a formidable chin she has," he said. "I noticed that at least," and off he went to the bathroom to wash his hands in rusty water and to speculate, like Hans Castorp, concerning the difference between children from the same sire and dam.

When he returned Fiona was lying on the bed, pads of wet cotton-wool above her eyelids. "Do you mind?" she said. "I've such a headache. I'd rather not come down till lunch-time. . . ."

"All right," he said, for the prospect of exploring the house alone was not unpleasant to him.

Fiona removed a plummet of wet wool and squinted. "Take my advice and try the library," she said. "First on the left at the bottom of the stairs. The rest I leave to your fieldcraft and sense of danger. Sister Peggy's probably in the kitchen, stirring soup."

"Just one thing," he said, "before I go. When do you expect your solicitors to tell you that the boy is dead?"

"Oh, not for weeks yet. There are so many six and eight pences to be plucked from an untimely death. The news will be shuttle-cockled between London and Australia. The letter with black margins may not reach me until March. I suppose you *did* kill him," she said suddenly, sitting up.

"Look and see," said Rumbold. From his wallet he removed and laid upon the counterpane a cutting from the *Western Morning News*.

"'Schoolboy's Tragic Fall,'" he said. "I had hoped it might be that. The report is very circumstantial, for, of course, such accidents happen every day."

Along the landing, down the stairs on tip-toe he went, every muscle tensed; but in the hall there was no sound other than the tick of the grandfather clock, though among the lower regions pots were being scraped.

Rumbold entered the library. This was a large room, measuring some forty feet by twenty even with the omission of several alcoves from the count. In the centre and no doubt the place of honour, a billiard table stood; besheeted now in white, the chink of its snooker balls a distant memory. At the far end, a fireplace with an open hearth of stone; this same fireplace laden with bellows, tongs, griddle-irons and other curved and twisted iron horrors. Above, upon the mantelpiece, the family picture gallery, *just* a little dusty . . . Fiona, *jeune fille*, very serious with her Russian

cheek-bones and wide eyes . . . Sister Peggy, improbable in Girl
Guide garb, clutching a lanyard and a whistle . . . then others, quite
easily identifiable . . . Mama, terrifically Edwardian, with breasts
like broken pears enclosed in court dress, and a young man with
the Black Watch headgear and short-clipped moustache; quite
obviously the daddy who had died on barbed wire in First Arras.

But for the remainder, who were not displayed so prominently,
Rumbold was obliged to employ rather his sense of period than
such slender knowledge of the family tree as he possessed. This
old Tartuffe, with mutton-chops and Gladstone collar, enclosed
within an oval of daguerreotype tint . . . ah, the famous Consul,
naturally, and the lady with the fringe and acid smile next door, his
wife; who had died (if Fiona was to be believed) in Davos.

These photographs of the second rank were all in some degree
sub-actionable but none more so than the two old ladies who,
hands upon their laps and fingers intertwined, stared upon the
world above single lines of pearls from the boom days of 1928.
The granny and the auntie! Rumbold was not conscious of having
said these words, but when he turned, hearing a step behind him,
Peggy proceeded with his thought.

"Yes," she said, "that's them. Granny's dead, but auntie's still
alive, though bedridden. We do what we can for her. She sleeps
upstairs in the blue-room next to yours."

"Why do you submit to 'Peggy'?" he said. "I can't bear these
diminutives. Isn't Margaret good enough?"

"One has these things from birth," she said. "There's no way
out. At school, there was a girl called Hortense. Are you really
married to Fiona?" she added.

"Yes," he said, surprised at her audacity, then countered quickly.
"And your husband in Ceylon . . . have you your marriage lines?"

"Fiona has all the luck," she said, ignoring this. "She always had
it. She was mother's favourite."

"And so you hate her?"

"No, certainly not," she said. "How could I hate my sister?"

Rumbold did not reply, but instead moved over towards the
bookcases.

The Children's Encyclopædia, the *Illustrated London News*, calf-bound; *Punch*, also calf bound (circa 1890), the complete *Charlotte M. Yonge* in red leather, the lives of *Sir Redvers Buller* and of *Mrs. Beeton*, whose own major work lay no doubt in the kitchen; the collected sermons of Dean Farrar, with those of Laurence Sterne in uneasy proximity; the daring modernity of Compton Mackenzie and Michael Arlen, and nudging their last volumes, Shakespeare and Shelley, from whose summits Rumbold blew the dust.

There was one French book, and it was, of course, *Tartarin of Tarascon*.

"Any further evidence of culture?" said Rumbold. "Mind you, I'm dead against it personally but one likes to know."

Peggy said nothing, but his eyes, following her, picked out the evidence she indicated.

"Ah, Virginia Woolf . . . now that shows *genuine* courage: and the sunflowers of Van Gogh upon the wall." Well! Well! He stared at them. "But why does no one ever buy the chair?" he said.

"I have it in my room."

"Then persevere. In twenty years you'll buy your first print of Matisse."

She asked him if he would like some coffee. He said "No, no coffee thanks" and, wandering about the room, was presently attracted by a cupboard containing many little ivory elephants, snuff boxes, spoons and several rows of spindled wine glasses.

"But this is drawing-room stuff," he said. "Why do you keep it here?"

"Because the drawing-room is locked. We never use it." She did not seem to resent his questions and made no protest when he removed a glass and tapped it with his index finger.

"Ting," he said, "ting," imitating the noise. "There is such pathos in that sound, don't you agree?"

She looked at him doubtfully, aware that he was clowning. Then she sat down, smoothed her woollen skirt, and laid her hands gently in her lap, so that for the first time he was obliged to look at her full-face.

"Do you know," she said, "that Fiona talks in her sleep?"

"Does she?" he said, much startled.

"Yes . . . or at any rate she does now. The other night she made a fearful row. I got up because I thought she was in pain."

"Ah?" He studied her well-modulated but unemphatic features, the small blue eyes, the facial down and the incongruous jutting chin.

"I'm glad you've come," she said. "With you here, she may keep quiet."

Thirteen

"BUT I assure you," protested Rumbold, and he clutched his spade more tightly, "I assure you that I *like* digging."

The gardener replied, in his barely comprehensible dialect, that in that case it would be better if the gentleman were to dig elsewhere than across the only bed of asparagus in the grounds.

"Well, I'm sorry about that," said Rumbold. He indicated his trench, the product of an hour's hard work. "I just thought I'd plant a few potatoes," he said.

The gardener said that this was not the time of year to plant potatoes.

"Cabbage, then . . . or salsify or cardoons."

The gardener said that, as the gentleman could see for himself, there was enough cabbage already in to feed the whole of Peterhead. As for the other plants mentioned, he had no knowledge of them and doubted their ability to grow in this poor soil.

"Yes," said Rumbold, "the soil is poor. I'm with you there at any rate."

The gardener said that the poverty of the soil was merely relative. In proper hands it gave as good a yield as any in this part of Scotland.

"Misther Eric . . . Misther Eric! Will ye come and eat your lunch."

The situation was saved by the appearance of Martha on the kitchen steps. Smiling, Rumbold relinquished his spade and made off along the path. When he turned, the gardener had already begun to fill in the trench.

"Dirty boots! Dirty boots!" said Martha. "Wipe your feet now, there's a good man."

Rumbold rubbed. Sectioned by the scraper the mud fell away off in chocolate sausages. "I'm still saying my novena for your cooking, Martha," he said.

"Ach, Misther Eric. Don't blaspheme . . . and you a Catholic, too."

"The only blasphemy's that dreadful soup of yours, you old rip," said Rumbold, and sportively he slapped her bottom. It had taken him no longer than a single day to complete the conquest of this old woman, once the children's nurse, and now the cook; but if the task had been an easy one, it had been none the less essential to his plans. Rumbold desired no enemy within the gates, and Martha, who had watched menfolk come and go in thirty-four years of service here, might well have been a more dangerous antagonist than her mistress.

Holy Mother Church had worked the trick . . . Holy Mother Church together with a rapid consultation in the library of Brebdon's *Saints of Ireland and Abroad*. Martha, in fact, made a cult of those young Amazons, the two Teresas, the three Catherines and the many Bridgets who had laid down their lives in early youth for the furtherance of the faith and the glory of its doctrines. To the ecstasies of St. Francis of Assisi she gave little credence, to the mental pyrotechnics of Loyola none at all; but the devout excesses of well-bred maidens . . . the fastings, the auto-flagellations, the trances, the massaging of dropsies and the wipings of pus from dreadful wounds . . . the recital of these deeds aroused her to the very highest pitch of religious exaltation and one which she could now share with a fellow member of the faith.

Born in 1878, in Connemara, in the historical lull between the Fenians and the ascendance of Parnell, Martha had been the seventh of nine daughters in one of those Irish families which, by right of economic plight and long-established custom, sail annually from Galway to pull up spuds in Scotland. How she had reached Peterhead and in what circumstances the grandmother had engaged her not even Peggy, usually well documented in family history, knew. In those happy days the house had teemed with servants who had scrubbed, polished, even slept in the dank, dark *oubliettes* beneath the stairs . . . skivvies, tweenies, cook, assistant-cook and parlour-maids; a whole female hierarchy, in fact, leavened and kept in order by the grooms.

Martha had very probably been a tweeny, for to the Papish Irish were the lowest tasks assigned. Soon, however, when the babies came, chance or some natural aptitude had elevated her, first to the honorary, then to the definite, position of their nurse. This, at any rate, was the official story, in so far as it was ever mentioned, but Fiona, enlightened by youthful conversation with the gardener (not the present incumbent, but his dad) thought that she knew better. It had been as a *wet*-nurse, she declared, that Martha had gained promotion. Some glorious evening in a hedge beneath a ditch had borne its just reward.

Be that as it might be, Martha, at close on seventy, was the sole survivor of the extinct domestic race, though in the matter of authority the fact profited her but little, for nowadays there came beneath her orders only a single, sullen kitchen-maid. Martha was paid one pound a week and was reputed to possess not less than three hundred of the same denomination inside a certain tea-cosy in her closet. Yet she was not miserly and half a crown travelled every Sunday from her purse into the offertory plate at Mass. This, together with the purchase of votive cards and saintly candles, was, to-day, her sole expenditure. She was not even called upon to send money back to Galway to her family, for this latter, like the domestic servants of her generation, was now extinct, or within religious cloisters, or long since emigrated to America.

Martha's position in the household was that, familiar to novel readers, of "the old servant who knows all". It remains but to make passing reference to her mode of speech, since samples of it must presently be rendered. Upon the broad vowels of the Gaeltacht, Scotland had imposed its throaty burr, only to yield with the course of time to the language of the gentry; first aped, then studied seriously, then finally acquired with some few native streaks to lend it pungency.

A brief wash, a briefer combing of the hair, and Rumbold passed from the ablutionary offices, along the passage hung with assegais and halberds, and into the dining-room, where the two sisters had not waited for his presence to attack their steaming plates of kedgeree.

"Sorry I'm so late," he said. "The fact is I was gardening."

"Yes," said Fiona. "Aitchison has just bellowed the first communiqué on your efforts through the window. It seems that, quite apart from the asparagus, you have also put a raspberry bush beyond repair."

Peggy said nothing. Discreetly, she was watching Rumbold's scoffing irons. Sure enough—though innocently—he took not the fish-knife, but the other, laid beside him for the second course of cheese. Observing his mistake and the slight smile which greeted it, Rumbold first blushed, then glared. He was well aware that his antagonist had chosen the terrain best suited to her in the secret, bitter battle engaged now between them for three days. In the field of etiquette, good manners and polite usage, she had him at her mercy.

"Well," he said, deliberately vulgar, and to add to the effect lifting a heavy load of kedgeree towards his mouth, "well, and what do you two *girls* propose to do this afternoon?"

"We thought we might drive into town," said Peggy coldly. "Fiona has to get a prescription renewed at the doctor's." The blow, this time, was more oblique, exploratory; for though Rumbold well knew that his mistress swallowed sleeping draughts, having tucked her up in bed himself, he also knew that Peggy could only surmise the extent to which her sister was to narcotic drugs attached.

"Very good," he said. "Very good," reaching for the cheese before the sullen maid had removed his plate. "Very good," he repeated. "In that case, I will first smoke a cigar, then wander round the house," for he knew well from the locked drawers and *secrétaires* discovered upon previous prowlings that it was just this procedure that Peggy had determined to prevent. In particular did she wish to keep him out of Auntie's room.

"Don't go and see Auntie again," she now said baldly. "You know that in the afternoon she takes her little nap."

"We'll see," he said, "we'll see." The tone was condescending, for in this household of three women, one of whom—the servant—was his by use of guile, and one, the mistress, his in circumstances more immutable than fate, the futility of the other's opposition to his will was obvious. The gardener was hers, and this was true . . . but the gardener lived three hundred yards away and had other things to occupy him.

And no other form of succour, save air-mail to Ceylon . . . except, perhaps, solicitors in Edinburgh.

The kedgeree disposed of, a glaucous treacle tart was served, followed by coffee as bitter as the dottle in an ancient pipe. Luncheon over, Rumbold repaired to the library, where, lying in an easy chair with heels upon a foot-rest, he was presently joined by Fiona in fur coat and gloves.

"Don't be horrid to poor Peggy," she pleaded, with furred fingers on his sleeve.

"I am not horrid to your sister," he replied, and after some other post-prandial by-play involving the unbuttoning of her jacket, permitted her to leave.

The library was warm. A turf fire in the grate supplemented the collywobbles of the central-heating pipes. Rising, Rumbold sought the drawer in which lay the box of Simon Bolivars. . . .

Who had left them there? The cigars were dry and peeling, perhaps a generation old, but still good. Reclining, Rumbold squinted as he puffed: his vision embracing a red glow, an inch of pendant ash, a portion of armorial fire-place and a glimpse of rain-soaked lawn. Half an hour later, the cigar stub abandoned, he was upstairs, padding the bedroom corridors, soft-toed.

Rustle . . . the noise was unmistakable: a page had just been turned. Then crease and pleat and rustle once again as the paper was folded to permit of closer scrutiny. Rumbold flung open the door, without benefit of knocking, and caught the old lady in full endeavour to stuff the *Sporting Times* beneath her pillow.

"It's only me, Auntie," he said soothingly.

"Ah," she said, her night-cap all awry. "I feared that it was Peggy. She comes in like a cat."

Rumbold sat down upon the counterpane, felt the hot water-bottle yield beneath his buttocks.

"Gazala for to-morrow," he said. "Take my advice. You can't go wrong. How much do you want on it?"

"Just a pound, Eric dear," she said. "I mustn't always risk a fiver."

"Ach," he said. "You've no nerve, no nerve at all. With your knowledge of form you should be tripling your income instead of frittering it away."

Neck buried in her feather pillow, the old lady gazed at him much as a rabbit at the stoat. "But the girls," she said. "I'm sure they know you're helping me. In the old days Peggy used to cut off my subscription to the paper almost every month. I had to get them to send it to me in a *Church Times* wrapper in the end."

"Never mind about the girls," he said. "Enjoy yourself. That's what I'm here to see," and pulling the fallen eiderdown about her neck he offered her an Egyptian cigarette from a packet bought that morning in the town.

"Should I?" she said. "Should I really? Doctor MacAllister says they're so bad for my heart," but the bony hand sneaked forth none the less, shuffled the silver paper and carried the deadly nicotine to her mouth.

"There you are," he said. "At eighty-one you still know what's good for you."

The room smelt of must and unswilled chamber-pots and gripe water; a sour smell, fit accompaniment to the leaden-footed afternoon. Plumb against the centre of the southern wall the bed, and in the centre of the bed, Auntie; a tiny figure, seven stone, well wrapped up in Paisley shawls and well on, too, in the interminable evening of her life. A static angina exacerbated by chronic asthma was the doctor's diagnosis, and once a month, as regularly as the lunar periods which had long since ceased to have significance for her shrivelled womb, the attacks overpowered her, so that the room, silent normally, would be full of the flapping of wet towels and the panic-laden rush of running women.

"I don't," said Rumbold, "wish to put my foot in it but I should be glad to hear the true circumstances of the death of the girls' grandfather."

Wizened, beady-eyed, and as fluffy-faced as any Kinkajou, the old lady replied craftily: "Simon didn't want to know."

"Simon," replied Rumbold, "is, from what I hear, somewhat lacking in imagination." (We are talking now, you must understand, of Peggy's husband, in Ceylon.)

"Simon," Rumbold added, "would probably not *want* to know even if he had guessed."

Across the coverlet his thick fingers making advance entwined in their moist grip those of the invalid. The stoat and rabbit relationship was re-established.

"I have never told this to anybody . . ." she began.

"Oh, naturally not, and I commend you for it. But you'll tell it to me, won't you, because I have a very special reason for asking." The thick fingers renewed their moist and sympathetic pressure.

"He cut his throat," she said. "Cut it with a Wilkinson razor two months before the girls' father was born. My sister, whose character was firm, as you can now perhaps appreciate, heard a curious noise, rushed in, and found him lying on the tiles beside the bathroom door. . . ."

"And the verdict . . . ?" he said.

She hesitated, blanching now, two generations later, with the memory. "It was death by misadventure," she replied at last. "My sister, whose character, as I have told you, was firm, lifted the body and thrust it through the lower pane of glass which formed the window. The jury, who were chosen well, assumed that he had fainted . . . and fainting fallen. The razor had been previously removed."

She puffed at her cigarette, inexpertly, yet indeed not without a certain charm; like some old relation abandoned by theatre-going relatives in a tatlered alcove of the Ladies' Lyceum Club.

"Why," he said, "did she never let you marry?"

"Yes, it's true," she said. "There was a clergyman. She thought him vulgar." A faint giggle. "He was a bit High Church, I must say. But she was so much more beautiful than I. . . ."

"So that, all your life, you have stayed here."

"Oh, not *all*. Once I went to Jamaica as a governess. But she got me back double quick. The job was, of course, a little *infra dig.*"

"Was she really so beautiful?" he said.

"Oh yes, exceedingly. You can have no idea. Even in middle age men turned to *stare*. And so kind too. Believe me, this is no old woman's fancy. She could be kind . . . upon occasion."

"How is it then," he said, "that she got on so badly with the children's mother?"

The invalid rearranged her shawl. "Bah!" she said, "a mere fish-packer's daughter at one genteel remove. Sylvia saw through her . . . saw through her at once."

"Which did not prevent her," he suggested, "from accepting the odd hundred for an educational excursion to Salzburg or Milan. . . . ?"

"Why not?" she said. "She had a household to keep. She fed them. Their mother was a gadabout. Her cheques always came late."

Rumbold extended a saucer, clipped off the grey curve of ash which leaned towards a fall.

"Yet," he said, "it was in your room . . . *this* room . . . that Fiona sometimes cried."

"Yes," she said listlessly. "Here or with Martha. It depended. Of course Peggy never cried at all."

Her head was drooping (no excitement; absolutely no emotional disturbances, the doctor had prescribed). The cigarette slipped from her fingers, charred the sheet. Rumbold rescued it, then taking the old lady by the shoulders laid her once more within the ravine of the pillows.

"Now you just lie quiet and have a little snooze," he said, and added: "I'll bring you cream cakes for your tea, and ones with pink icing too, and little blobs of marzipan."

But she only grunted; already in her happy Land of Nod.

He tip-toed from the room, hesitated in the passage, then tip-toed farther down towards Peggy's room.

The door was locked.

Rumbold smiled, crossed the passage, returned with the bath-room key, which slid and turned without hindrance in the latch. It was funny how they never realised that duplicity is the near relative of cunning. He entered the room, locking the door behind him. On the desk a half-finished pencil-written letter lay. Rumbold skipped the stilted references to the weather and the church bazaar, his eye descending with sure instinct to the third paragraph.

"As for Eric, I cannot make him out as yet, but I dislike and distrust him very deeply. . . ."

Such rounded periods for a schoolgirl hand! For a moment Rumbold was tempted to draw a little picture of a heart pierced by an arrow, where the letter ended. Resisting this impulse, he commenced to search the drawers.

The clothes drawers to begin with: two pairs of unworn Christmas nylons, many more of sober lisle much scarred by darning. Three handbags, the first two quite empty, but the third containing an old dance card dated 1939.

"Jim" . . . "Basil" . . . "Jim" again . . . then a long blank, the rest silence. Could she possibly have sat all that long period out, or had she been borne away to supper by some backwoods laird? Rumbold shut the drawer, proceeded further, fingering the heavy tweeds, ruffling the underclothes.

From the mantelpiece the husband, bristly of moustache and growing bald, stared down at the intruder.

"Ah," said Rumbold, catching the cuckold eye. "You don't like it, eh? Just go and plant some tea, there's a good fellow. I'll deal with you immediately."

With a burglar's extra and time-saving sense he continued with his search. The bills . . . dull, unambitious, and for the most part meaningless to him; the picture postcards . . . Gleneagles, Isle of Skye and technicolour view of Dundee docks; . . . some chemist's receipts, dating back for several years and indicative of hard winters overcome by the judicious sipping of cough mixture and lung syrup. Bored, Rumbold was about to search for more amusing treasure when he came upon a last receipt of quite especial interest.

"Chesterton and Queen, Prince's Street, Edinburgh . . . To Miss M. Macleod. 1 lb. Ars: Oxide, 11 June 1935."

"How very, very queer," he thought. "Can it be that the gift runs in the family?" and because it was not his way to abandon evidence which might later prove of use he tucked the receipt away in his pocket.

Now for the husband! The letters, chastely secured by much blue ribbon, were voluminous and prosy in the extreme:

"*Such a sunset as we had this evening, old girl* ..." and there followed two pages of blank verse in which Longfellow and Walt Whitman made uneasy marriage. What a pedagogic planter it was, what a windbag, with its chatter of "burnished skins" and "lush vegetation yearning towards the monsoon ridden sky". A breath of the Mysterious East in every line there was intended ... and sure enough Rumbold could visualise a humid, lamp-lit room, the whisky in a toothmug by the bed, the oppressive drape of the mosquito net and the unhappy man scribbling with fountain pen to conjure the first sex-charged watches of the night.

"*I don't know how you feel, old thing, but I wish that I had you between these sheets, I can tell you.*"

Bah! Rumbold returned the letter to its envelope, tied the blue ribbon, closed the drawer. A last quick glance round the room, ten seconds of listening behind the door and then off down the passage, still soft of toe, to pass a quiet half-hour with his homework.

He was in his own room now. He filled the fountain pen, drew the blank sheet of paper towards him and began:

"*Fiona Lampeter ... Fiona Lampeter ... Fiona Lampeter.*" Her signature, the serifed "F", the rolling uplands of the consonants were child's play. He had long since mastered that.

"*Please be so good as to cash the enclosed ... Please be so good ... This is my last will and ... is my last ... I declare ... is my last ... testament.*"

From a folder he took her bank statement. To credit: £7,318 ... To E. Rumbold, £1,000. The income was received quarterly, tax already deducted in Australia. There had been a payment shortly before Christmas. There would be another at the end of March. She had not yet kept her promise to make the account a joint one with his name beside her own. Perhaps she was waiting until they should go to London together? While his own plans remained uncertain, he was unwilling to broach this subject.

What to do? The letter from the Embassy, received that morning, lay before him.

"DEAR MR. RUMBOLD,—With reference to our recent conversation I am happy to inform you that I have now received instruc-

tions to facilitate your passage. If my memory serves me well you
mentioned mid-March as the date most suitable to yourself. This
would also suit us, we shall have a courier plane leaving Lyneham
on the 9th of that same month. Consequently, if you will come to
London some days beforehand, contacting me by the usual means,
I will provide you with an escort and the necessary papers."

Quite so . . . very amiable, very civil . . . *but what to do?* The
great adventure, or the smaller and more niggling one? He could
forge a cheque, of course, and skip, but that was dangerous: enquiries might be made, telephone calls exchanged. He would have to
pack his bag, leaving neither good suit nor favourite tie behind.
Then he would have to travel with her to the station, flank against
her flank, himself lying glibly:

"You promise that you'll be back by Monday?"

"Oh, certainly . . . Monday at the latest."

Better . . . oh, far better, cleaner, safer and more bold to kill her
. . . to send the bitch to join the boy upon the seaweed-laden rocks.
The will should not be difficult to fabricate.

"I bequeath. . . ."

They sold them, printed, nowadays in stationer's; tenpence for a
copy. Sufficient to imitate her hand, and to procure two witnesses,
these latter to be found in any pub.

"So sorry to trouble you. I have a somewhat unusual request to
make. A will, you know. I'm going East. That's the position, but I
don't want my family to be alarmed. . . ."

The strangers, beset suddenly by visions of beri-beri, Tsetse-fly,
pellagra, sign with alacrity, not noticing that blotting paper covers
the terms of the last testament, the testator's name.

Then towards the deed itself . . . but here no use denying that
affection had begun to sap the original resolve . . . no use to deny
either that "be kind to me" and "you're so cruel" had both had
their effect upon his resolve.

She employed, within the circle of her friends, a special terminology: the language of the nursery adopted to an adult end.
Cats she loved and called them Putta-Woos. Affection mentioned
by name above, and displayed by holding hands in cinemas, by a
leg thrust crossways in the bed in search of warmth, was "feck".

Sexual relations, the twisting of moist hands and the pummeling of chests together was called "seck". There were also distortions of the vowels—rahney, pahney, trahney: substituted, as no doubt the reader guesses, for rain and pain and train. But this was but the *ordinaire* of her conversation—which many a Britannic imitator of the Jewish Kafka might have envied.

Childish? Ah, but pardon me, who does not pray when the whistle of the bomb is heard . . . what smooth scoundrel skirting Long Acre, what business man within view of Cheapside but does not go down upon his pallid sun-forgotten knees? The safety of the womb is very much regretted; and that of the cradle with its rubber underblanket not much less so.

"I should like," she had once said to him, "to lie in bed all day with lots and lots of lovely drinkies by my side and glossy magazines upon the counterpane. I can't cope with life: I never wanted to. . . ."

"Anybody can cope with life upon your income."

"Ah no, how wrong you are! When Rockefeller grew rich did he face existence with any more enthusiasm than I do at the moment? When he was young his strong adrenaline secretions kept him going, but when the money bags were filled, he had to turn to charity . . . had to find some other outlet for all that energy."

"Well, I daresay he died happy. These dollar millionaires have curious powers of self-deception."

"Exactly . . . but I have none. I don't yearn for a better world, any more than I believe in the prospect of its achievement. Nor do the pleasures of materialist civilisation really tempt me very much. Of course I want my bed but I should like to have it on a magic mountain . . . not in horrid, bourgeois Switzerland, but in the Caucasus. Indeed, I often wished I *were* consumptive. I suppose that's my shortage of adrenaline again."

"All these clinicalities," he said. "You ought to hold a kidney dish while talking. There's only one solution and that's to be an outright bastard."

"Yes, but even bastards have their party line. I've often seen you stop to check on it, and you're such a *pious* bastard, too. Believe me, you'll not go as far as you intend."

A slight noise, the turning of a door handle. Quickly Rumbold removed his homework and bent down again, as if about to write a letter.

His visitor was Martha: "I have some tay for you," she said.

"Well, where is it?"

"Ach, you wouldn't want to drink it in this cold room, now would you? Come down to the kitchen, there's a dear man."

"All right," he said, then, pulling a Burns, Oates and Washbourne envelope from his pocket, handed her a votive card.

"St. Raymond of Penafort," he said. "Very rare. You just can't get them nowadays."

"Ah, the sweet fellow," said Martha. "And what did *he* do now?"

"Well," said Rumbold. "Opinions vary about that, but at any rate he was Confessor to the King of Aragon, and this King, who had some business there, took him on a trip to Majorca. Unfortunately the monarch had a mistress, a sin for which St. Raymond found it necessary to rebuke him publicly. The King was furious. He forbade his ships to re-embark the Saint. But that didn't worry Raymond: he just stretched his sheepskin cloak upon the sea and returned to Barcelona by himself."

"The angels must have blown the fair breeze behind him," remarked Martha.

"Yes, I suppose they did." Rumbold sipped his tea (for they were now in the kitchen). "The angels had a lot of work to do in those days. Here's St. Agnes for you and St. Louis de Gonzaque, too. Both took the vow of chastity at the age of nine. Wicked people wanted to do all sorts of things to them, but the angels came and stopped it just in time."

"Fancy that," said Martha.

"I don't fancy it at all," he said, and watched her tuck the three cards in her missal.

Beneath the picture of the Sacred Heart upon the wall, the crucifix, and beneath the crucifix . . . which had been stained a rich brown by the fumes of countless soups . . . the stove; massive, knobbly, shining, hissing with a plenitude of Nicholson's best ovoids. So large was this stove that the visitor, seeing it for the first time, would turn towards the doorway, wondering how it could ever have entered through an aperture so small. Perhaps the house had been built round it? No one knew and no one would ever know. Three fur-coated Russians might have stretched at ease upon that stove. Such aids to cooking are not built in our day.

And calendars of yester-year, and flour bins, bread bins, coal bins, jars of ginger. And rows of tomato chutney, sombre of colour, and pumpkins in a corner; and copper pans to boil or baste a brace of turkeys, and strings of bald and crinkled onions come from Brittany.

The kitchen was not modern. It was warm. Friendly, you might even call it, with the jammy finger-prints of long sacked tweenies still upon the wall and the boldly etched initials of grooms and butlers in the soft wood of the table . . . D. H. . . . H. J., and beneath that, a crudely incised heart.

Rumbold drew up an easy chair, leant forward, toasted toes and hands. Martha stood just beside him. She was boiling milk with which to make a tapioca pudding, her favourite, which she would eat at dusk.

"And why, please, Mr. Stay-At-Home, don't you go out with the girls?"

"Because the girls are shopping," he said briefly.

"Never a man I've known like you to laze about the house. Look at Peggy's Simon now. . . ."

"All right," he said, smiling. "Let's look at him," and because she did not answer, tugged her skirt. "Well?" he said, insisting.

"Ah, the poor creature," she conceded.

"When did the old lady die?"

"The Mistress? 1935, I think, or may be thirty-four. No matter . . . it was in September. The figs were picked, the pears were in the jars. Then, one day, she was taken badly. She never left her bed again until I took her up to wash her cold, dead body. 'Martha,' she used to say. 'Take heed. You're spending far too much on eggs.'"

"And the doctors, what did *they* say . . . enteritis? . . . tummy trouble?"

"Gastric 'flu, they declared it and her fair moaning with the pain, poor woman. One night she called me: 'I wish I had your faith, Martha,' she said. 'I wish you had it, too, Madam,' I told her.

'Do you think there's any hope for me?' she said then. 'Not much,'
I said, for never were there any lies between us. 'I've been a bad
woman, Martha dear,' she said. 'Hush!' I said, and what with hot
coffee and little petting I soon get the poor thing to sleep. But what
she let out there was true enough: strict in the home she was, religious in herself, but no churchgoer."

"And Peggy? How did she take the thing?"

"Take it! The poor girl was in a dreadful state. 'You stay here,'
I said. 'Don't go to the funeral, or I'll not answer for the consequences.' But she went, and fainted as they sent the coffin down."

"Tell me," he said, "what were they like as children?"

"Quiet."

"Always quiet?"

"Very nearly always, too. The one . . . Fiona . . . with the books;
Silas Marner she made me read her, and the other with her paints
and plants and rabbits. Oh, there was not much trouble, very little
mess. They were stu . . ."

"Studious?"

"Studious. Yes, that's the word I mean. Quiet, studious little
girls. . . ."

Fourteen

FOR some time now, although more than half asleep, he had been
conscious of intense cold. Curious dreams assailed him. One, in
particular, concerned a flat in which he had lived in Paris, in the
Rue Dombasle. Lacking money for his rent, he had been obliged
to leave this flat, departing by moonlight, down the fire-escape.
Several journeys had been necessary but the Concierge, normally
as watchful as a lynx, must have been at the cinema that evening.
Nor, later, had the estate agents succeeded in tracing him.

In his dream, which ran in serial form (for, half-conscious, he
made deliberate efforts to prolong it), he was back in clandestine
occupation of this flat, approaching it nightly along the flat roof
and entering through the skylight. The floors were dusty, in the
kitchen, plates on which he had eaten a dozen surreptitious meals

remained uncleaned. And behind the outer door the Concierge stood. He knew that she was there, could hear her breathing. Only the thickness of a plywood panel separated his own ear from hers. He flung open the door. The Concierge had gone. An icy blast of air swept past him and . . . sure enough . . . in this room, in Peterhead, years afterwards, the window had blown up as the night wind from Norway freshened.

How tiresome, dreams; how inescapably moral the never slumbering subconscious, laying down like fine wine in a cellar each small deceit and each ignoble action, to bring them forth hoary and encrusted with their shame, in the maturity of its time.

Utter darkness. Rumbold sat up; cold, and doubly cold because he never wore pyjamas. As usual, Fiona, with her rolling and her turning, had captured all the sheets, while with deft footwork she had sent the blankets to the floor. Mechanically, Rumbold fumbled for a cigarette, found it, lit it and watched the glow reflected on her linen-covered buttocks.

Her turn now? This was not certain. The Nembutol had done its work. Her sleep was very deep. Rumbold retrieved the fallen blankets, draped them Arab-wise about his shoulders, watched. Twenty minutes after three, the period of the night when the heart beats at its slowest.

All snore, but she snored like a dog; a sound half whistle, half complaint. On her cheeks the cold cream lay shiny; on the pillow a grey stain. Her fine, russet hair, which she so rarely troubled to brush smooth, lay now in coils, rats' tails and clusters on her neck.

She stirred . . . yes, the nightly séance was beginning. With quickening pulse, Rumbold took his torch, focusing its beam upon the mumbling lips.

"Don't . . . Don't do it . . . Please don't do it . . . please."

Don't do what? Well, that, of course, was her secret: the performance seldom varied, never became any the less equivocal. She writhed now like some poor wild thing, the cloth of her pyjamas quite damp with perspiration.

Gently, he turned her over on her back. The torch showed tears; fat, limpid tears zigzagging from beneath closed eyelids to the corners of her nose. Unbuttoning her jacket he laid his head

against her heart, the stroke of which was like that of some distant
rustic water pump.

"I can't bear it . . . I can't bear it any more."

Oftentimes, in spoken dreams, the words are unintelligible.
Not so with hers: each syllable was clearly enunciated with great
pathos.

To be awake alone, in these middle watches of the night, was
insupportable to Rumbold. Maliciously, he pinched her arm. She
groaned, then opened her eyes. Meanwhile, he had switched on
the light.

"What is it?" she said.

"You were dreaming. You dream every night now. Also, you've
taken every single blanket."

"I'm sorry. . . ."

"What were you dreaming about?"

"Nothing . . . I don't know . . . something horrible, I suppose."
Fully awake now, she roused herself, employing her elbows as
leverage, and reaching for a cigarette.

"Get me some water, will you . . . please?" she said. "I'm so
thirsty."

"Naturally you're thirsty," he said, leaning above her, bully-
ing, his eyes small and hard and hateful. "Naturally you're thirsty.
Whisky and Nembutol don't mix."

Not for the first time she had forgotten to place the carafe on
the closet chest beside her: the quantities of water which she was
able to drink in a single night were prodigious . . . three pints at
the least. When lucid, she filled wine bottles as a kind of reserve
catchment by the bed.

"All right," he said. "I'll get you some, but I'll have to go downstairs."

"You could get it from the bathroom."

"Certainly, I could," he said. "But I'm hungry. I want to make
myself a sandwich. You can wait five minutes, can't you?" The need
which he felt for spitefulness was surprising. He *loathed* her and . . .
in consequence . . . there was urgent need to loathe himself.

"Or are you afraid, perhaps, to be alone? Don't worry. Leave the
light on. Read a book."

She looked at him piteously. "You don't love me, do you? You don't really care at all."

"*Cherchez pas à faire apitoyer*," he said, and fastening his dressing gown, tucking toes in bedroom slippers, left the room.

But on the landing, in the fustian darkness, above the death-watch-beetle tick of the grandfather clock, he heard a noise as of a metal tray being pushed across a wooden surface.

"Now where could that be coming from?" he thought and, quick with instinct, entered the bathroom, filled the carafe, then nipped back into his bedroom.

"Here's your water," he said, and watched her drink. "Now I'm going down to make my sandwich. I may be twenty minutes even. It takes time to cut the ham."

"Bring me some, too," she said, dry-eyed, and then bent closer to her book. The *Concluding Unscientific Postscript* of Kierkegaard it was. Like many with a dislocated mind she had a philosophic turn.

Rumbold padded down the stairs, the banister his guide. Without mishap or even need to light his torch, he reached the kitchen, heard the noise renewed within.

He opened the door. Peggy, warm inside a thick blue flannel dressing gown, with blonde pigtails for a contrast, stared at him from just above a coffee percolator.

"That won't make you sleep any better," he said. He said this slowly.

"No," she said. "Nor you, it seems. . . ."

"Perhaps this is the better drug?" he said and advancing, his purpose manifest, suddenly enfolded her within his arms, bent back her head and kissed her lips until these yielded and his tongue sought hers.

"Dreams are very curious things," he continued. "Supposing that you commit murder . . . then you will be quite certain to dream about the bulls-eyes that you stole from the locker of your friend at school. There is a censor in the subconscious who would like us to be better than we are."

"Is there?" she said; this with faint irony.

"Oh, not in your case," he continued. "Nor in your sister's

either. You both dream *direct*. You must find it tiresome to repeat the same experience almost every night."

"Well," she replied. "I daresay I would if I had the faintest idea what you were talking about." The upper section of the percolator was now empty of all liquid. She removed it. "Won't you have some coffee?" she said.

"Thank you. I will," he said, and watched her opening the cupboard, fetching the sugar basin and the cups. As she moved, the loose nether of her dressing gown swung. She wore pyjamas. He laid his hand upon them.

"Where is Fiona?" she said.

"Fiona is reading. We're a very wakeful household, aren't we? Don't worry. She'll not come down, because she dreads the darkness. We can therefore have our little talk in peace."

Around the greater perimeter of the table there were stools. The coffee poured, she drew one up beside his own, stirred, blew across the steaming surface like a little girl, and sipped.

"And when do you propose to leave?" she said, ignoring the investigations of his wandering hand.

"I don't know that I propose to leave at all."

"I should leave if I were you," she said. "You see, I know that you're not married. I wrote to the British Consulate at Barcelona and they say that they have no record of such a marriage."

"Ah," he said, his turn now to sip at coffee. "So you are not only sharp: you are also clever. But supposing that I don't *want* to leave . . . supposing it's my intention to remain here, in this house?"

"Take your hand away," she said.

"Why should I when you help to keep it warm? Besides, we're comrades, you and I . . . behind those pigtails and that modest dressing-gown there lies something of which I could willingly see more."

"I hate you," she said.

"No, not hate . . . fear is the word you mean, for our characters are really not much different. I think the time has come to talk about your dreams."

"You prey upon women, don't you?" she said. "That's your profession because you are a coward. But don't prey *here* because, a hundred yards away, I have a gardener who doesn't like you very much. It would give him great pleasure to chuck your suitcase on the road."

"I don't think, somehow, that he will ever do that."

"No?"

"No. As I was saying, let's talk about your dreams. Ten years is a long time, isn't it: more than twice the number of the Arabian nights. Your mouldering Granny must have tickled your scruples quite a bit within that period."

From his own dressing-gown he drew the chemist's receipt from Edinburgh, laid it on the table, smoothed it.

"One really should not keep such things, should one?" he said. "Do you know . . . although I must condemn your negligence . . . I feel sincerely sorry for you. If there hadn't been a prying mind like mine, you might have been safe to-day."

"I don't know what you mean," she said, unsteadily.

"Listen," he said, and took the opportunity of looking at the kitchen clock. "We have approximately fifteen minutes now. After that, Fiona will brave the terrors of the landing and come down. It's important that we should understand each other. *Why did you kill your grandmother?*"

Slowly, very slowly, the colour began to leave her face: pink became white, white grey, and grey a fluorescent green. The features lost cohesion. Even the formidable and jutting chin broke loose from its anchorage.

"What makes you think that?" she whispered.

"What . . . no attempt at denial, no protests, no signs of outraged modesty? The Public Prosecutor would be shocked." Leaning forward, he touched her hand, but she shrank from the contact.

"I asked you what makes you think that?"

For answer he pointed to the piece of paper on the table.

"That proves nothing," she said more calmly.

"No, in itself, it proves nothing, as you say. I see you are regaining confidence. In a moment, when you think I am not looking, you'll stretch out your tiny fingers and tear that piece of paper up, won't you?"

And, indeed, already she had sketched a gesture which might have had that intention as its object.

"Go on," he urged. "Why don't you do it? I shan't have you charged. My kingdom is not of the law courts, but in this house. Quite sufficient for my purpose that you know I hold the secret. . . ."

"I don't think," she said, "that I've ever met a man as truly wicked as you are."

"Oh, come now, not too many claims to virtue. We're all murderers in this household, you know; all equal in the sight of Martha's God. Yes . . . even Fiona is an only too easily indictable accessory. Didn't you know, or did you perhaps guess? The other day I knocked off her little curly-headed boy."

Swiftly she slipped from her seat and sped towards the door, but he moved more swiftly still. "Not so fast," he said, and seizing the fastening of her dressing-gown he tore the garment from her shoulders, then flung it in a corner.

"That's better," he said. "What . . . shivering already? This won't do at all. You must get used to walking about in your nightie. Come . . . sit on my knee. It's very much more cosy."

"Murderer," she said.

He grinned. "No pot and kettle stuff please. We're both black. Let's make the best of it."

He had her cornered now, between the dresser and the bread bin. Swooping, he placed his left arm behind her knees; his right behind her shoulders. He carried her towards Martha's easy chair, beside the dying fire. She struggled.

"Right," he said. "Now tell uncle all about it. In what way did poor granny offend her little girl? Incidentally I notice you haven't got rid of auntie yet. Can the packet be empty so soon?"

"I shall tell you nothing . . . *nothing*."

"I've heard braver people than you say that, my dear. The only ones who were ever able to say it *afterwards* were those for whom the entertainments provided had been too *mild* . . . if you take my meaning."

He placed his hands about her wrist, gripped hard, then twisted each hand in a different direction as cruel schoolboys sometimes do.

"You're hurting," she said. "Please leave me go."

"Then lay your head on uncle's chest and speak, my darling."

She ceased to struggle, and looking at him, showed more curiosity than fear. "Do you know," she said, "I honestly believe you're mad."

"Mad?" He set her down. "Mad?" he repeated. "Oh, not at all, I promise you. I'm quite a natural phenomenon. For example, I always wanted several women. There must be something of the Pasha in me. And these too," he touched several of the kitchen utensils and the stove, the cupboards and the table. "All mine now. I like the sense of power that gives. It's another of my failings."

"One denunciation will bring the second," she said slowly. "Surely you can't help but realise that."

"Naturally," he said. "And, once again, allow me to compliment you. No tears for the little nephew lost for ever, no prevarication, no useless arguments. You go straight towards the point. I told you we had much in common. There's the same hard streak in both of us, whereas sister Fiona has rather too many virtuous impulses . . . don't you agree?"

"Perhaps," and standing before the stove, half smiling she said, "May I put my dressing-gown on now?"

"As you wish," he said indifferently, but when she crossed the room he leapt up, followed, seized her in his arms again.

"Who do you belong to now?" he said thickly.

"Not to you in any case." She shook him off, returned towards the stove.

He resumed his seat upon the stool, leant forward, elbows on his knees. "How did you do it?" he said. There was admiration in his stare.

She paused, with one arm inserted in her dressing-gown. The scene had undergone a curious transformation: it seemed to be no longer he, but she, who led the debates.

"You really want to know?" she said, almost scornfully.

"Yes, I want to know."

"It would be a mistake to think you can draw any profit from it. The evidence is very old now and rather patchy. Besides, in Scotland, exhumations are not popular."

"Reassure yourself," he said. "At ten years distance very likely nothing would be found except her bones and three or four assorted salts, none of which would be the ones that you administered."

"I put it in her lemon toddy," she said, "last thing at night. I was lucky. Even slaves have their compensations. Before she went to sleep she used to hold a private prayer meeting; with me kneeling by the bed—I daresay you can imagine that. Anyway, it gave me an opportunity to bring her the drink, although in principle she disliked a night-cap. The first night I put in far too much. She was already ill, with a chill or something, but the next day she was almost in extremis. I was badly frightened and went much more carefully afterwards. I don't know any physics. I had to work by trial and error. That's why the whole job took me something like three months. . . .

"And at the end she guessed," she added.

"She guessed? You mean she really knew?"

"I think she did. Sometimes she would look at me . . . wondering, I expect, whether it was me, or Martha or even poor old auntie: we all had cause to hate her. Sometimes I used to wonder, too, why she didn't break the glass or refuse the broth she had at lunchtime. I was very ignorant at that time. Since then I've read a lot. I've read that that . . . stuff saps the will-power a great deal. . . ."

"Besides," she continued, this time with more animation, "those old pharisees are all the same. I sometimes think they're like a man who's placed a bet involving all his fortune. When they see death near, it must be dreadful for them. So much to lose and, with their black hearts, nothing gained for certain. Believe me, she had obsessions much more powerful than the question 'who was poisoning her?' She often muttered to herself, I noticed. She was having arguments with God when she did that."

"I see," he said. "And she died peacefully?"

"No. I'm glad to say in agony."

"I see." He considered, holding the cup of cold coffee in his hand. Then: "May I ask about one small detail?" he said. "One tiny, teeny-weeny thing."

"Well?" she said.

"Why did you do it?"

"That will be for another time," she said. "Believe me, I had good reason," and moving from the stove, which scorched her back, she blew her nose upon one of those minuscule, embroidered handkerchiefs which women carry in their bags. "And you?" she said. "Why did you do it, since you ask the question?"

"For money," he replied. "Perhaps also as a prop to failing self-reliance. A cliff, a push, and all was over. You'll agree the method is less harrowing."

She did not reply for a moment, but instead stretched her handkerchief upon the stove to dry; by this gesture presenting herself to him in three-quarter profile. Her chest was abnormally flat, her hips wide but also angular; not gently curved as are those of child-bearing women. Rumbold was reminded of the photographs of famous Rugby players, taken just before the match begins. In these photographs the hands are always proudly thrust within the pockets. The trousers bell out, achieving the dashing and desired effect of jodhpurs.

"And don't you run any risk?" she said, turning to observe the reason for his silence.

"None that I know of," he replied drily. "I took the necessary precautions." A continuance of the conversation presented little further interest to him. He experienced a pressing need to digest what had transpired, and to reflect in solitude. Had she said all she might have said, had he been wise to. . . .

But even as he formulated this last thought, he knew it to be inappropriate. She had begun to talk again. From now on, she would never cease to talk.

"Then you're very lucky," she was saying. "I suppose that old gossip Martha's told you how I fainted by the grave-side. That wasn't remorse . . . it was sheer fear. She tried to persuade me not to go, but I *had* to go. I was convinced the doctor knew, absolutely certain of it. When they were lowering the coffin . . . oh, I admit that I was overwrought . . . I saw something in his eyes which made me shiver."

"Oh, and what was that?" Rumbold now felt completely at

his ease. To prove this, he crossed his legs with uncomfortable abandon and lit another cigarette.

"Not what you think," she said. "He made his pass a few days later. Imagine it . . . a medical man, with a girl still in her teens."

Her indignation was undoubtedly genuine.

"I can imagine it very well," said Rumbold. "And was he handsome, the devoted family medico?"

"Not a bit . . . an old whiskered paterfamilias with bad breath and a truss. You can't imagine what I went through. I sometimes wonder how I was able to bring myself to marry."

"Yet he knew?"

"No, he didn't know at all. I must have been mad to imagine that he did. But, of course, by the time I was certain, it was too late."

"And how long did this charming affair continue?"

"Don't laugh at me," she said, sharply.

"I'm not laughing, but you can't blame me if I find it funny."

"Every Wednesday and Saturday, weather permitting, in the summer-house for four years. I couldn't break it off because I was never *absolutely* sure. Then he died. That was just before the war."

"By whose hand?" he interposed.

"Oh, not mine, I promise you, though I wouldn't put it past his wife. Our affair was not exactly known . . . but, shall I say, surmised. There was quite a bit of gossip at the time."

A long silence. Rumbold regarded the last, faint, red coals inside the stove.

"What was that?" said Peggy suddenly.

"I heard nothing," he said lazily.

"There was a step. I'm sure of it."

"It's probably Fiona. Half an hour alone gives her courage for almost anything."

Carefully, he deposited his cigarette ash in the coffee saucer, then rising, gripped her elbows.

"You and I . . ." he said.

She gazed at him, as if conscious for the first time now of all that had been confessed within that brief half hour.

"I'm certain that I heard a step," she said. "God help us if it's Martha."

"Don't worry," he said. He said this almost soothingly. His hands were now beneath her armpits. "Don't worry. To talk at last, after ten years silence, must be a great relief. Don't worry: the cad can also be a gentleman."

"Come in, Fiona," he shouted, and receiving no response, opened the door.

Fiona stood behind it.

"Why do you stand there?" he said. "There's no need of knocking for admission . . . Your sister and I have been discussing murders . . . her own and ours. From what I hear, her own was very much more wily. She knocked off her granny, don't you see . . . you, your child."

But Fiona still stood there on the threshold, pale, immobile, and in certain other respects also like a ghost.

Fifteen

THE wind from Norway blew no longer. For five, for ten, for fifteen thousand feet above the earth the air was almost still. The feeble sun described its daily arc in seven hours, rising like some blood-stained conspirator who loiters in his course from lack of strength, then collapsing in a second bath of gore.

The cold, throughout the final days of January, was intense, its origin marine and Arctic. Successive ridges of high barometric pressure, situated above the Grampians, drifted slowly southward to the lowlands and disintegration. Snow fell at steady intervals. On hill farms the sheep, their life already made unendurable by the snap and bark of irritable collies, began to starve because they lacked the sense to burrow for the saving grass. Iceland, Orkney, Shetland, Peterhead: all four were one in this great refrigeration, and in Morocco the swallows, warned by some instinct beyond the ken of ornithologists, would now quite certainly postpone the homeward trip until April.

Inside the house, behind the double windows and the granite

slabs, comparative warmth obtained. Peat fires burnt in every bedroom, the glowing maw of Martha's stove gorged itself on anthracite ovoids and diamond cubes. Alone among the rooms the library was locked: it was no longer possible to heat it satisfactorily.

Since the midnight *conversazione* reported in the previous chapter, a change had taken place within the household . . . a change involving the relationship between the man and the two sisters. The servant, the bedridden aunt, the gardener remained in apparent ignorance of this change.

Fiona now spent, from choice perhaps as well as circumstance, much time alone. Subject by nature to all the ailments which cold weather brings in its train, to frozen toes, to the first jagged premonitions of sciatica, to chilblains, she would sit for half the day before the downstairs fire, her shin-bones red from the reflection of its heat. For books she had her Kierkegaards and with this esoteric Danish dwarf she seemed almost, as it were, in love. Notebooks, copiously filled, littered the floor at her feet, and once, when Rumbold stooped to pick one up, she ordered him almost sharply to leave it be.

At night, soon after dinner, she would go to bed with three hot water bottles. Rumbold seldom joined her. His honeymoon was in full swing.

Peggy had grown thin. Her eyes seemed wider, but they were without expression unless it were a gleam of hate. He had observed that gleam for the first time when he had taken her that night. As he had stepped into the lighted bedroom from the dark corridor their eyes had met, clashing in unblinking stare for five seconds, and perhaps more. Then he had thrown aside the sheets, lain down beside her. She had made no gesture of resistance— none at all.

That night he had returned to his own bedroom, but, on the second, Fiona, believing perhaps that he was still in the sitting-room, had come into her sister's bedroom without knocking, while the light still burned.

"Oh," she had said. "I beg your pardon," and had retired, had softly closed the door again and gone, even as Rumbold began to lift his head.

"Speak," he had said a little later to his partner. "For Christ's sake say something, can't you?"

"What is there to say?" she had replied with truth, for, as he well knew, their struggle was too evenly matched for points to be risked in incautious speech.

Yet in the daytime, she would follow him about. Polishing his shoes in what had once been the gun-room, he would lift his eyes from the brown and greasy brush to see her standing near him, silent but observant.

"What is it that you want?" he had said, not once, but many times. Never had she replied, but shortly afterwards muttering of saints with Martha by the sizzling kitchen stove, he would find her there again.

Did she wish, perhaps, to signify that his triumph was only in the flesh? A log of wood she may once have been, immobile and unresponsive, but he had sawed the log and made it quicken at his slightest touch. For this he claimed no credit. A clumsy husband and a vicious and half-impotent medico could hardly have enlarged her small horizon. No! Deeper, and far deeper, lay the motives for her open-legged silence. Her womb, impenetrable and sterile, pursued other ends than those for which nature had intended it.

It was not until some days later that they talked. *Désœuvré*, tired of the house, the frozen garden and Fiona's constant and neat nips of Haig and Haig (a half bottle was now always by her chair-side), Rumbold, with memories of the Polytechnic Art School, had undertaken to decorate the summer-house. A box of auntie's paints provided his material.

He wrapped up well: thick under-pants, two jerseys and an overcoat rather spoiled the waist-line which his morning exercises were designed to keep within the middle twenties. The summer-house was bare, except for a few cane chairs, a rejected dartboard and the green drum of an old lawn-mower. This was such a building of Birmingham Japanese design as one sees quite frequently in the gardens of provincial gentry, and it somehow happens—does it not—when one passes, whether it be upon the top deck of a bus, or as a mere trespasser on foot, that the oak trees are always dripping with a recent rain, that their leaves lie sodden and heavy on the paths and that the only sign of life is the spectacle of a startled cat diving for shelter among the rhododendrons.

The walls of this summer-house had once been distempered white. This white had now peeled and flaked, the sometime victim of rots both damp and dry. Having chipped and rubbed the surface smooth, Rumbold began to paint upon it. He painted a sailor with a French pom-pom cap; a bollard, a length of a steel hawser, and a portion of a harbour, coloured Hessian blue. It was while he was engaged upon the lighthouse in the background of this harbour that Peggy came in and stood, one arm upon her hip and watching. He did not notice her until she spoke.

"Rather night-club stuff, isn't it?" she said.

"No . . . bathing lido," he replied. "I haven't any talent, really, but I enjoy it."

She sat down in one of the ancient wicker chairs. She had brought an oil stove with her from the house, and now placed it between them.

"Ah, yes," he said. "This is where you used to meet the lascivious medico, isn't it? But surely . . ." and he gazed meaningly at the few poor sticks of furniture.

"Don't concern yourself unduly," she replied. "There was a divan in those days. It's since been burnt for firewood."

He laid down his paints, and stood before her with arms folded and head held slightly forward.

"There is a story you were going to tell me, isn't there?"

"You mean about my grandmother." She stared at him with what Fiona called her church-mouse face. "I can't imagine why you want to hear it."

He lit a cigarette. "No?" he said. "You mean you *really* can't see why? You must be most obtuse then. A true member of the lower middle class, I suffer from ancestor worship at one remove. My own ancestors were mostly plumbers, so naturally I can't worship them. Therefore I go mainly for the Anglo-Indians and the landed gentry, whose totem symbol, the running fox, has always seemed to me most suitable. Within those perimeters where crumpets are still served at teatime, I make my explorations. In brief, I probe. You will think, perhaps, that I am searching to incriminate you still further or to obtain some piece of knowledge which might serve me well. But that's not so at all. You poisoned granny; and granny is of great interest to me . . . because she is a kind of symbol which makes me feel much less of a bastard each time that I consult my heart."

"So be it," she replied. "You want granny. You shall have her. She's not a pretty sight. When a baby is very young it soils and wets its nappies, kicks out, cries when contradicted, howls the roof off if left alone. But that baby at least is innocent. You can't blame it. I only wish that I had had one. Granny was just such a baby once upon a time. I'm no scientist. I know nothing of the genes and hormones you're always speaking of. I only want to know how it can be that a woman, who must have had some generous impulses at one time, could have turned into the hateful tyrant of her last years."

"John Knox," he said immediately. "Or, if you prefer it . . . Pio Nono. Anyway both eunuchs. When I was aged seven I made my first communion and was positive that there was an angel hovering just above my shoulder. I remember mentioning it to my mother. She made no reply, for, after all, infant saints are not unknown . . . people might even have gone to Guildford instead of Lourdes.

"But," and he paused, looking at her, as they say, between the eyes. "If you've got to have that nonsense . . . if it's as essential as oil to motor to keep you going, then I'd rather have my own church than yours. At least, we offer the best insurance policy and don't bleat Jewish psalms on Sunday nights."

"We were talking," she said slowly, "about my grandmother."

"And so?" Silent, he waited for her to continue, but this she did not do at once. He saw that she was staring at a corner, where once, perhaps, the sofa had reposed.

"Imagine," she then began, "imagine a childhood absolutely without laughter. At six o'clock, winter, summer, rain or snow— the children must be up. By half past six they must have washed and said their prayers. And for lunch, three days a week . . . tapioca pudding. Once, when I was browsing through the big family dictionary I came upon that pretty word 'Chatelaine' . . . a word which I had always loved. But I didn't love it any more then, for I saw that it described *her*, with her keys, and lace fichu and uncanny way of creeping up behind me without making any noise."

"Oh, come now," he protested. "She can't have been a monster all of a single piece. Begin with the extenuating circumstances."

"Very well. She was beautiful, by which I mean beautifully proportioned. Besides her everybody seemed clumsy . . . all hands red, all ankles thick. Even when old, she had the face of a girl, quite unlined. And her eyes! Well, none seemed franker or more innocent. They were a rather pretty violet colour."

He examined her own hands which, just then, she laid upon the stove in search of warmth. They were large, the fingers stubby.

"You have heard," she said, "about her husband, our grandfather. What you have not heard is about her son, my father. He wore his hair in ringlets until he was fourteen, and never played with nasty village boys. I don't think he ever went to school either . . . or if he did he soon came back again. I believe she had a tutor to teach him his vulgar fractions. The tutor must have taught him one too many, for as soon as father could grow his own moustache he went out and married mother on the sly. That was disappointment number two . . . or number three, really, if you include poor auntie."

"Yes," he said. "I thought that we should come to auntie presently."

"Have you ever read," she said, "about those old sea-fights where one ship aims at the other's sails and rigging, and the second replies by raking its opponent's decks . . . then both sheer off, with honour satisfied? That was how it was between mother and granny. They were far too well matched to dream of really mortal combat. Mother had the money: granny the home and what she would sometimes describe as the 'position'. In the end they made their bargain: Fiona, though temporarily housed here remained mother's property, while I was transferred to granny, to do with as she pleased."

She paused: "*To do with as she pleased*," she repeated. "I killed her," she said, "because she was killing me. I don't say that I wouldn't also have killed my mother had I ever had the opportunity. Indeed, I know that I would have."

"And Fiona?" he said softly.

"I've no grudge against Fiona, though once . . . Oh God, how I used to envy her. But when I look at her to-day I realise that there's something to be said for the matriarchal education, after all," and she smiled at him wanly.

He rose. "Come inside," he said. "It's too cold here."

Three days later, on the tenth of February to be exact, Rumbold returned by train from a brief visit to Aberdeen.

He had the impression that he was being followed.

In Aberdeen he had obtained without difficulty the signatures of witnesses to Fiona's false will. Two teashop waitresses had obliged him . . . Irish girls whom he had chosen expressly, though by chance, because he had heard them say that they were returning shortly to their own country.

After a stomach-curdling luncheon, Rumbold had proceeded to the Central Post Office, from which building he had attempted to telephone the Spanish Embassy in London. In this enterprise he had been unsuccessful. The line, at first apparently engaged, had proved at the second and third attempts to be completely out of order. It had been on leaving the Post Office premises that Rumbold had received the strange impression that he was being followed.

His first action had been to buy a newspaper. Then, leaving the crowded shopping centre but at the same time walking slowly, he had turned down a deserted side-street which led towards the docks . . . a street of warehouses this, with blind windows, empty hawking carts, and many stationary lorries. Half-way down this street Rumbold had quickened his pace considerably, had almost broken into a run, in fact. Once around the corner, he had stopped, opened his newspaper and pretended to read it, with an air of nonchalance.

He did not have to wait very long . . . a patter of running feet, a sound of heavy breathing and a man turned the corner, barging into him.

"Do look where you're going . . . please," said Rumbold petulantly. He had managed to administer a smart kick in the scrimmage and now watched gleefully as his antagonist moved off after rubbing his shin . . . moved off down the long, long road towards the gasworks which the man was obliged to follow since he had appeared to be in such a hurry to embark upon it.

Grinning, Rumbold walked off in the opposite direction, towards the station. He did not know the man.

Rumbold returned to the house, having travelled on foot from the station, towards five o'clock. The sky was already dark, so that, once inside the drive and beneath the oak trees, he was obliged to use his torch. Something suspect stirring at the frontier of its feeble arc, Rumbold turned the lamp beam on the adjacent shrubberies. He saw the gardener.

"Mighty cold to be out," he said somewhat sharply. "Why don't you go and have your tea, man?"

"I don't need muckle tay," the gardener replied.

Rumbold continued up the drive, the light from his torch crisscrossing on the broken stones unloaded here twenty years before from the local convict prison. At the front door he was met, in response to repeated knocking, by Martha, with the astonishing information that Auntie was dying. Weeping, the old woman retired towards her kitchen, from which presently came the sound of running taps, the secondary sound of sizzling as water slopped over from a basin to the stove.

These sounds were, in the circumstances, most sinister, for Martha, upon her own admission, had washed many dead.

Half expecting to find a family conclave in session presided over by a brace of doctors with clanging stethoscopes, and black attaché bags, Rumbold entered the sitting-room, where Fiona sat alone, playing patience, a glass of whisky by her side.

"I hear your aunt is in a bad way," he began.

"Yes," replied Fiona. She laid down the fatal nine of spades beside its Queen. "Yes. I'm told that she won't last the night."

She took a sip of whisky; then reaching for the bottle at her feet, poured more into the glass.

"And so you've been to Aberdeen," she said and giggled. "Such funny stories they used to tell about Aberdeen, but rather dated nowadays, don't you agree?" She paused, looking at him almost shyly. "I mean," she said, "that you don't have to go to Aberdeen any more to find a miser or a money-grubber."

"No," he replied. "I daresay you don't."

"Do you know," she said. "When I look at you I am reminded of the verse of Ecclesiastes which goes . . . 'If two lie together, then they have heat: but how can one be warm alone?'"

"I'm glad," he said drily, "to see that you read your Bible."

"Let it pass," she said, "though I could cite you other texts, among them one or two even nearer to the mark. Did you have a good day in Ab . . . Aberdeen?"

"Yes, thank you. Very tolerable."

"And you were successful in your *business?*" To this last word she lent strange emphasis.

"I had no business in particular," he said. "I was merely sight-seeing."

"A lot of people seem to be sightseeing just now," she said. "A little man came to the door this morning and asked for you by name. Perhaps he was sightseeing, too? Perhaps, in Aberdeen, you also saw some sightseers?"

"Yes," he replied. "As a matter of fact, I did. I was tailed for quite a time."

"Ah, your War Office *chums*, no doubt. They seem to attach great importance to your future, don't they? Have they good reason, do you think, or is it just another example of the waste of public money?"

"The gentleman in question," said Rumbold, "looked more like a common flatfoot than the exquisite pansies to whom I'm more accustomed."

"I hope this won't interfere with your plans," she said.

"What plans?"

"Oh, have a drink," she said with sudden violence, and rising, somewhat unsteadily but with fixed purpose, she made her way towards the cupboard to fetch a tumbler and the soda syphon.

"A mouth like a prune you have," she said. "Without humour, without charity."

"Thank you," he said, and bowed ironically.

"Say when," she said, and began to fill his glass, spilling a fair part of the liquor on the table. "Yes," she continued, "astonishing how much I've gone downhill since I came here, isn't it? Just tipple . . . tipple all the day. I'm sure it isn't good for me."

"No," said Rumbold, "I don't suppose it is." He took the glass which she offered him, added more soda.

"Well . . . cheers," she said, "or is it 'down the hatch' they say in your more robust *milieu*?" She stretched out her right hand, fingers splayed, examining an emerald ring which he had never yet seen on her finger. "I feel so *wise*," she went on. "Do you ever feel wise like that? I feel as if I held the whole world in my hand. Presently, I shall set about arranging it. First I shall abolish all brass bands, then the Royal Academy, then passports. . . ."

"Yes," said Rumbold. "I've often noticed that drunkards are very sententious."

There was a silence. Rumbold, somewhat ill at ease, backed towards the fire. He stood upon the hearth and warmed his buttocks.

"An old bag . . . an ageing cow," she said. "That's what I am, isn't it?"

"I wouldn't go as far as that," he said.

"No, of course you wouldn't. You're one of Nature's Gentlemen, aren't you? Excuse me . . . I'd forgotten."

And she laughed stridently; so loud that the noise filled the room and seemed to shake the velvet curtains.

"Oh, it's funny," she said. "It's so funny that I could scream at times. At other times, I just whimper. My dear little sister . . . the pride of the family, the prude, the prig, the benefactress. You think you know a lot about this house and our family, don't you, but try going up to the old nursery just about the time the sun is setting. You want to listen carefully then because you'll hear some whispers from space time . . . *Fiona, put down that doll at once. You know it is your* sister's . . . *Fiona, go and comb your hair immediately. Why can't you be tidy like any other little girl? Fiona . . . Fiona . . . FIONA.*"

As suddenly as she had begun this tirade, she stopped. Then the tears came, but in silence, and in his scaly heart the ventricle expanded, pumping all at once more blood into his pulses.

"You don't love me, do you?" she said.

"I have great affection for you."

"Yet you sleep with my sister. Do you have nice fun and games together? Oh, please don't answer. I don't wish to hear. The other day . . . love knows no locksmiths, you must understand . . . I went into the spare room where you do what you are pleased to call your drawing. The bathroom key fits perfectly. Just a tiny scrunch and the magic cave is open. I'm so sorry that you wish to kill me."

"What makes you think that I wish to kill you?" he replied, almost steadily.

"Well . . . the Will, you know. Next time, don't leave these things about . . . even in drawers which you imagine to be private."

"Yes," he said. "I admit my intention was to kill you. Over the cliff you were to go . . . just like the other. But now . . . well, now I'm not so sure."

"Because of the detectives?"

"Yes, because of the detectives."

They stared at each other. He refilled his glass, and hers. The world stood still.

"Please tell me one thing," she said. "I'm a little drunk now so you must answer slowly. You have some sense of honour, I suppose. Please answer on your honour. *Were you going to kill me, and take my money, merely to live with Peggy?*"

"No," he said. "I had a previous engagement . . . our mutual friend Aranjuez, in fact. I was to leave about the second week in March. Spanish politics are uncertain. I saw no reason to go unprovided."

"Do you really," she said, "do you really hate and despise me so much that you would be willing to kill me in order to enjoy my money, alone? Surely you must know that I would always give it to you."

"Yes," he said, "those sentiments are beautiful in a Scottish drawing-room, but on the port at Cassis, or Juan, or St. Jean-de-Luz they might change, and change abruptly. After all, you have already had one fisherman. To-morrow, you might have another."

"Do you know," she said, "I think you must be entirely blood-

less. There are some things which you quite simply don't understand."

"Oh, I don't know," he said. "The sentimental side, which you
stress so much, is not of much importance to me. I see my way.
I follow it. Such obstacles as I encounter I remove. There was an
obstacle before you not so long ago. You employed me. I removed
it."

"Yes," she said. "I had a letter from my solicitors this morning
informing me of my son's death."

"That's bad," he said.

"Why should it be bad?"

"Because you shouldn't have heard so soon. With the time taken
to notify Australia and so on, I counted up to ten weeks before
you'd hear that news. Something has gone wrong somewhere."

In the time it takes to turn a somersault, she was sober.

Sober, and pale.

"Who *are* these friends of yours who follow you about?" she
said.

"I don't know," he said. "But don't worry. *I'll find out.* I have
a friend called Cassell, as you know. Cassell interests himself a
great deal in my private business. You ought to be grateful to him
because he's quite certainly saved your life."

And he began to pace about the room now, rearranging china
ornaments, tugging at the curtains, until at last he got a deck
of cards between his fingers . . . and shuffled, shuffled. There is
nothing better for the nerves.

"Yes," he repeated, more tranquil now. He was once again,
indeed, the theatrical "heavy" who, having heard the prompter,
slips back into his demoniac role. "Yes, but for friend Cassell you
would have been cold mutton very soon, my dear. Now, on the
contrary, if you care to transfer to me two thousand pounds I
won't embarrass you any further with my presence."

The look which she now bent upon him was one of horror. He
did not perceive it. Immersed, as always, in the adjustment of his
plans, he saw nothing untoward.

"Yes . . . two thousand," he repeated. *"On n'est pas exigeant."*

"And suppose," she said, in a flat voice, as devoid of colour as it was of warmth, "and suppose that the transactions in my bank account are watched? I understand the police have powers to do these things. . . ."

"We are not now dealing with the muddled-headed copper," he replied. "We're dealing with Cassell and his fly back-room boys who've got it into their heads that I might be leaving for certain foreign parts. I shall cash your cheque in London, on the day I leave. There won't be any trouble. If you want a personal guarantee of safety you have only to write me a receipt saying that I have advanced you the money in Spain or Portugal . . . it really doesn't matter which."

"Very well," she said, still in that same flat, heartbreaking voice. "Very well. Pass me your pen," and from her bag she took her cheque-book, smoothing down the rosy-tinted pages.

He handed her his fountain pen, and something very curious happened then: the pen nib refused to write. Blot . . . Blot . . . she tore two cheques out, unachieved, and finally succeeded.

"What date do you want?" she said.

"Oh, just put March. I'll fill in the exact day later."

She handed him the cheque, her schoolgirl script still glistening upon it. He bent, and warmed the slip of paper by the fire. At once the lustre left the sprawling commas and the dash and twiggles of the sterling symbol.

"Thank you," he said, and rising—for his knees were scorched—made as if to kiss her chastely on the forehead. But this was too much for her: with a straight left, the palm open and the fingers clawing, she pushed him away.

"*Cojones,*" she said. "*Salaud* . . . swine . . . *Dégonflé.*"

He held her wrist. His boilermaker's nails now, as always, in half mourning, pressed deep into her flesh. "Be meek and mild," he said. "It suits you better. The next few days may very well be troublesome. I think we'd better go up and see auntie."

Sixteen

AUNTIE, whose Christian name, as Rumbold now learnt, had been Ellen, died three minutes after midnight.

The doctor, a young man whose massive peasant build contrasted with his strangely foppish manners, had left about an hour beforehand, after shaking his head in the regulation manner.

"Two or three hours," he said. "Till day-break at the most. Her heart won't stand the strain this time."

Reduced to non-technical terms, auntie's death was caused, like that of King John, by simple over-eating; the fatal agency being in her case not lampreys but a caterer's box of jam and treacle tarts provided secretly by Rumbold on the previous day.

Instead of consuming her tarts in several little snacks, auntie had hoarded them until, incapable of withstanding temptation any longer, she had gorged herself to the last crumb at a single sitting.

The pastry was heavy, and auntie's digestion much impaired by age. As has been stated above, auntie was subject to severe fits of syncope, these fits taking place, upon an average, twice a month. Very probably one of these fits was due at about the time the pastry was delivered. Auntie's system, overloaded, did not this time recover.

No blame could be attached to Rumbold, who, when making his gift, had warned the old lady to go slowly. Nor can it be reasonably assumed that Rumbold desired auntie's death, which could not in any case have been very long delayed. Rumbold did not profit by this death. Nevertheless, a suspicion will remain that he was not unaware of its possibility. Like the forester who plans a new plantation, he was perhaps clearing the dry brushwood from the ground.

When all was over and the room had been cleaned and swept, the empty cake-box was discovered underneath the bed. It aroused little interest, for at the same time discovery was made of seventy-four copies of *Sporting Life* and three annual editions of *Ruff's Guide to the Turf*. Auntie's will, made almost two years previously, left everything to Martha. This, also, raised little comment, for it had been generally expected. What did however shake the sisters was the size of auntie's bank balance: over four thousand pounds stood against her name in the National and Provincial. Since her income had been tiny, the only explanation could be that her betting, so long deplored and sometimes even suppressed, had been highly successful. Other documents, found among some discarded chicken bones and a volume of Mr. James Agate's reminiscences beneath the bed, suggested that auntie also played the football pools.

However, we are anticipating ... "clearing the ground" as Rumbold might have said. Some of these documents—the bank statement for example—did not come to light until the old woman had been dead for a whole day. Let us go back in time a little while, and seat ourselves, as Mrs. Gaskell would most certainly have done, beside the death-bed.

The time is a half-hour beyond eleven. Auntie has thirty minutes left on earth. Her cheeks are blue. Her toes, beneath the multifarious blankets, are curling. The doctor has come and gone. Likewise the Minister of the Church of Scotland, a thin man with a down-drawn mouth and eyes as metallic as a chalice; who, finding little else to say, had said a prayer, drunk a cup of Martha's dreadful coffee, and departed.

The dying woman had not been fully conscious for three hours. Around the bed, between the commode and dressing-table with its load of medicine bottles, the chairs are grouped: the two sisters, Rumbold, Martha sit impassive. The women watch. The man fills in a crossword puzzle.

The breathing was now so faint, the flesh—that little of it that was visible—so waxen that the end appeared to be only a matter of moments.

A quarter of an hour before it came, however, auntie roused herself. She was clearly wide awake, in full possession of her faculties. Raising herself with surprising strength into a position semi-sitting she said a single word, but this single word three times.

"Bad," she said. "Bad . . . Bad."

None of those present knew quite what she meant, nor to whom the reproof (the exclamation was undoubtedly pejorative) could have been intended.

This was auntie's last effort. Shortly afterwards she died, and when her corpse was stiff enough, Martha, who had the water ready, washed her according to polite usage.

"Why do you never go out?" said Peggy to Fiona on the morning after auntie's funeral. (Rumbold was upstairs, shaving, yet such was their state of mind that both sisters looked towards the door as if they expected to see him enter or to leap out from behind the window curtains.)

"I don't know," said Fiona, surprised both at the question and at the irritability which she detected in her sister's voice. "I don't know. I suppose it's because the Scots don't care for women in their pubs."

"Never mind. Fill your flask. Put on your coat, and let's tiptoe down the steps and start the car."

Fiona smiled. The idea pleased her. A conspiratorial and mischievous look appeared upon her face, as of a little girl about to steal the jam or to read some long forbidden book; and Peggy, she noticed, looked mischievous also.

They observed each other for an instant: then both laughed.

"Come on," said Peggy, and hand-in-hand they tiptoed out.

"You see," said Peggy, when the car had left the drive. "You see . . . it's almost spring." She swerved to avoid a flustered robin, and pointed with gloved hand to the green fields from which the last traces of snow and ice had disappeared.

"Yes," said Fiona drily, "I daresay the first crocuses will soon be sprouting. Tell me . . . do you still keep pressed flowers?"

"No more than you do bunny rabbits," replied Peggy gazing at her sister amicably. And again they laughed.

"Many things happen in spring," continued Peggy, after a short silence.

"Yes," said Fiona. "I see what you mean."

"I've been thinking," said Peggy presently, "that I still have a husband."

"But you don't love him very much, do you?" said Fiona. She did not say this ironically: the question had intrigued her for some time.

"No, not very much," said Peggy, "but, after all, he represents an element of safety, and I'm told that Cingalese women are not really very attractive. So I think I should be silly if I lost him through my own stupidity."

"You always had a good head on your shoulders, didn't you?" said Fiona admiringly.

"Have you any idea of our guest's plans?" said Peggy. "I'm afraid, with me, he's rather uncommunicative."

"He's going to Spain," Fiona said.

"Ah?"

"Yes, he's going to Spain. I've given him a cheque for . . . well, never mind, we won't go into that now. I don't want to shock you. He's going to Spain in about three weeks time. Unfortunately, some old friends of his don't care for the idea too much. In fact, it seems quite likely that they might try to stop him . . . at least, that's what I suppose."

"Yes," said Peggy. She swung outwards to pass a lorry, swung inwards again as a touring car came round the corner. Her driving had always an element of controlled recklessness about it. "Yes," she repeated, "I've noticed a somewhat odd character hanging round the house. Tell me," she continued, "doesn't that make you feel just a little unsafe yourself? I mean . . . it wouldn't do at all for the investigations to go too far, would it?"

"Oh, I think Rumbold will manage. His life has always been a little precarious, you know."

"Rumbold may manage," said Peggy with conviction, "but in the process he'll throw away some ballast. I'm afraid you'll find that with Rumbold it's Rumbold first and all the time. That's why I've been thinking that we might ante-date your stay here by a few days."

"I'm afraid that's not much good," Fiona said. "It would be quite easy to find out that I stayed with him in London."

"Did you register under your own name?"

"No, I didn't as a matter of fact."

"Well, then. . . ."

"I'm afraid that doesn't help too much either," said Fiona unhappily. "Remember . . . he still has my cheque."

"Oh, no," said Peggy. "That's where you're wrong. More lock-picking goes on inside the house than you imagine. These clever boys are always tidy. Rumbold, for example, keeps every useful paper neatly pleated in his wallet. I took your cheque out and put in a blank one of my own. I don't mind betting you he won't see the difference till he gets to London . . . *if he ever gets there.*"

"What do you mean by that?" Fiona said.

"Never mind what I mean, dear sister. The point is that you came up here four days before you actually arrived. I'll arrange the matter with Martha. Fortunately, we don't run constant house-parties, so no other evidence is needed or available."

"And the boy?" Fiona said.

"The boy is dead. You can't help it if an adventurer killed him on spec, then tried to blackmail you. One night in Madrid . . . or Barcelona if you like . . . one night you said a little too much. Rumbold took you at what he thought to be your word."

"That's all very well," said Fiona, "but I've already heard officially from the solicitors that the boy is dead. What am I supposed to do now?"

"You don't do anything. You're frightened, don't you see? The man is in the house. He is terrorising all of us. No jury would convict you . . . I don't even think you'd ever come to trial. Just leave things to Mr. Rumbold's friends. They'll fix him soon enough."

"Do you hate Rumbold as much as all that?" Fiona said slowly.

"No, I don't hate him at all, really, though I find him presumptuous . . . and he is a bit of a *parvenu*, don't you agree?"

"Yes, I suppose I do," agreed Fiona.

The car slowed down.

"Well, here we are at the grocers'. Let's buy some delicious spam," and drawing in to the kerb, Peggy halted, put on the brake, and opened the creaking door.

When their shopping bags were full, the two ladies repaired to the Kardomah, where they drank two cups of coffee each and ate several cakes.

"It's funny to be sisterly again like this," Fiona said.

"Yes, isn't it? I was just thinking so."

"It's all the more funny, you know, because we were never very close when we were kids."

"That was *her* fault," Peggy said. "Lately, it's been *his*. I always thought we might get on very well together, for my part." She paused . . . a necessary pause brought about by the munching of a cream-stuffed bun. "Tell me," she said at length. "Do you think he's any *good*?"

"Good?" echoed Fiona, who did not understand.

"Yes, good," said Peggy. "What I mean is that, having more experience than me, you're better able to make a comparison. For me . . ." she paused again. The last of her cream bun went down the hatch. "For me," she said, "he always seems to be rather like a bull charging at a five-barred gate. I have an idea that your fisherman may have been better."

"Perhaps he was," said Fiona.

But she seemed just a little bit uncomfortable, and on the way back she took two or three small nips of whisky from her flask.

When Rumbold came downstairs and found the dining-room deserted he experienced a feeling almost of relief. Upon Fiona's plate lay a piece of half-eaten buttered toast, the teeth-marks clearly visible. Rumbold ate this toast, then strode across the room towards the chafing dish, beneath which the blue flame of the spirit lamp still burnt. He lifted the lid and removed fried eggs to the number of two, a sausage, two bacon rashers and a rhomboid of kidney. From the sideboard cupboard he took a bottle of brown beer, and filled a cut-glass tankard. "Nothing like a good old English breakfast," he would sometimes say, with obvious sincerity. Indeed, a Jorrocksian opening to the day was one of the few things of which Rumbold approved in good old England. Had the era not been one of food restrictions, he would have liked to see the sideboard heavy with hams, game pie, pickled gherkins and cranberry tarts. Nevertheless, he was not a glutton, ate only a light lunch and very little dinner. His attitude was similar to that of the great Napoleon, who although he could not be said to have any particular affection for his native Corsica, yet never could resist a well-cooked Fritto Misto.

Some totems and taboos are ineradicable. They have a lush and
verdant place in the hearts of even the most convinced expatriates.

His breakfast done with, Rumbold called the household dog,
a shaggy beast of which mention has not hitherto been made
because it was seldom present, having to be hurried out of every
room in which it chose to squat by reason of the offensive smell
which emanated from it.

"What do the ladies do in Scotland?" said Rumbold to the dog.

The dog lay down upon its back, extending its legs. Rumbold
rewarded it with a piece of sausage.

Martha came in. "Ah," she said. "Late again. It's enough to drive
a body mad, you are."

"Martha," said Rumbold, "what are you going to do with all
your money?"

"What should I be doing with it? It's decency you want, man
dear, with the old lady not yet cold inside her grave."

"Why don't you go back to your little grey home in the west?"

"My place is here," said Martha, "though I'm not saying that
there won't be many a little niece and nephew writing to me by
and by."

"Not to mention Father Farrell," said Rumbold.

"Aye, and Father Farrell, too, the dear, kind fellow."

Rumbold went out into the hall. He chose a walking stick, then
entered the sitting-room, in which the curtains remained drawn
from the previous evening. By parting these curtains gently it was
possible to obtain a fair view of all but the northern approaches
to the house. Rumbold parted the curtains and peered. At first the
scene seemed peaceful enough. The grounds were deserted. From
the chimney of the gardener's cottage the smoke rose perpendic-
ularly, for the day was windless. But Rumbold's eyes were keen:
presently he saw something which made him draw back. He whistled softly. He gripped his stick with vigour.

He did not now leave by the front door as he had previously
intended, but instead went down into the kitchen and up the cellar
steps. The dog attempted to follow, but Rumbold drove the animal
back. Behind the house there lay an apple orchard, then a low wall,
then open heath land patchy with gorse. Rumbold moved nimbly.

Disinclined to dirty himself with scoutish crawling, he made a wide detour towards the north, where a valley enabled him first to cross the road in safety, then to approach the house from the opposite direction.

About three hundred yards away from the front of the house, in the direction of the sea, upon a small knoll well covered with undergrowth and a few stunted trees, a man lay, with a pair of binoculars pressed to his eyes. It had been the glint of the sun upon these binoculars which had first aroused Rumbold's attention.

He advanced cautiously. The man, intent upon his scrutiny, heard nothing. Rumbold tapped him smartly on the shoulder with his stick.

"Having a good time?" he asked pleasantly.

Considerably startled, the man turned round.

"I asked if you were having a good time," repeated Rumbold.

The man sprang up.

"Now, now," said Rumbold. "Take it easy. Tell me how you like Scotland, for example. You must find it a bit cold lying there the whole morning, don't you? And we've met before, too, haven't we? That means we should shake hands," and he held out his own with the most charming frankness imaginable.

"You're up a gum tree there, guvnor," said the man. "I never seen you before . . . straight I haven't."

"Oh, come now," said Rumbold jovially. "Surely you remember a little encounter in a telephone box. You ought to, in any case, because as far as I remember your foot was hurt, wasn't it?" and with his stick he tapped the foot in question.

The man recoiled.

"Of course I don't want to be personal," continued Rumbold, "but I must say your employers showed very little perspicacity when they sent you up here . . . your accent I mean . . . Peckham, isn't it? . . . anyway, not exactly the language of the Highlands. And then, too, the fact that we know each other already." He paused, surveying with distaste the man's crumpled townee suit, his grey buck teeth, his deplorable signet ring inset with a fake ruby. "Ah well," he continued. "I suppose we all make mistakes. . . ."

"A chap can take a holiday, can't he?" said the man. He had

replaced his binoculars in their case and now confronted his tormentor with incipient truculence.

"Certainly he can," replied Rumbold. "And, would you believe it, that's exactly what I plan for you."

He sprang forward without warning, seizing the man first by the neck, then by the left wrist which he twisted sideways and backwards while retaining his hold upon the frayed collar. The man was now powerless.

"Move," said Rumbold.

"You leave me go or it'll be the worse for you."

"I'm afraid you must let me be the judge of that," said Rumbold. "Just keep walking, there's a good fellow. You'll find it much less painful."

The road was deserted. The pair crossed it about a hundred yards below the gardener's cottage. At intervals the man attempted to break free. When this happened Rumbold reinforced his grip and was rewarded by grunts of pain.

A fence bordered the coppice here; an old fence, of which many of the palings had come loose. Rumbold pushed his victim through a gap. The summer-house was not far distant. Very soon they were inside it. From a corner, Rumbold selected rope from among the debris of an old marquee.

"Now," he said, when the man was bound in such a fashion that any attempt to free his hands increased the pressure on his jugular and feet. "Now we can have a little talk, I feel. I'm sorry I can't offer you a chair, but you'll find the floor less uncomfortable if you roll over on one side from time to time. Incidentally, you'll also be able to look at the pretty pictures, which I painted myself."

"You'll pay for this," the man said.

"Now that's a very interesting point," said Rumbold. "Have you any evidence to support it?"

"Don't worry," the man said venomously. "They'll get you. It's only a matter of a few days now."

"I notice," said Rumbold, "that despite your alarming predica-ment you show few signs of despair. Perhaps you believe that it isn't worth my while to hurt you . . . that I wouldn't dare? A lot of representatives of law and order have been under the same childish misapprehension: it seems to be peculiar to them."

"I warn you," said the man, "that if you touch me things will go very badly for you."

Rumbold did not this time reply. Inserting, with difficulty, a hand inside the other's coat, he removed his wallet. The wallet contained money, some photographs of purely private interest, and an identity card.

"Higgins," exclaimed Rumbold delightedly. "Ernest Higgins . . . I feel sure that can't be an alias. And where is Mr. Ernest Higgins staying, if you please?"

"I'm at the Bristol, in Peterhead," the man said surlily. "What's more, if you'll stop this nonsense, I could go and have my lunch."

"No lunch to-day for Ernest," replied Rumbold. He lit a cigarette. "You don't believe me? Come now, Ernest . . . give . . . co-operate. I can see by your face that you're no hero yet I shrink from unpleasantness."

"Listen, Rumbold," said the man. "You're in a tough spot. Take my tip and cut out the play-acting. It won't pay you."

"You nasty little man," said Rumbold. "Do you honestly imagine you can measure your nasty little willpower against mine?" He pulled long upon his cigarette then held it deliberately for five seconds against his victim's knuckles. The man screamed with pain.

"More?" said Rumbold. "Do you want more? I'll show you what play-acting means, you little bastard. Come on . . . give."

"Watch," said the man. "I had to watch . . . see you didn't leave here."

"And if I did?"

"Follow." If the man spoke briefly this was because he had much difficulty in the swallowing of his saliva.

"Reporting, no doubt, from time to time, to Cassell . . . how?" said Rumbold.

"By telegram."

"And has Cassell decorated me with one of his charming code names?"

"Sugar."

"Well, well," said Rumbold. "And that's all you know, I take it. Come, come . . . don't flinch. I shan't repeat the process. When

I've had my lunch I might even bring you a little ointment to put
on your honourable scar. Meanwhile, Mr. Ernest Higgins, I'm
afraid that you stay here . . . I'm even afraid that I shall be obliged
to gag you because there's a gardener within earshot."

"For Christ's sake," said the man. "What good do you think this
does you? I tell you, they've got you, Rumbold . . . you're finished."

"Oh, it gains me a precious day or so," retorted Rumbold amiably. "Of course I quite admit that from your point of view it's
rather awkward, but don't worry . . . it's cold there on the floor
but not cold enough for you to catch pneumonia. This afternoon
I'll bring you a rug . . . even perhaps a sandwich. Incidentally, I pre-
sume you're quite alone here? It would be better to tell the truth
now, because if I discover you're lying we'll have quite a session
with a cigarette."

"There's no one else," the man said.

"Splendid. I'll send a telegram to Cassell on your behalf. I'm
sure he'll be most intrigued to know that you're following me all
the way to Glasgow." And he laughed heartily.

The situation was far from brilliant, but he had still a card or
two to play.

Seventeen

WHEN, however, Rumbold, after having lunched, returned to the
summer-house at three-thirty in the afternoon, he discovered that
the man had gone.

The thongs or bonds, expertly tied, which had secured the man
had been cut loose. Some strands of severed twine, some muddy
footprints and a common kitchen knife, abandoned near the door,
bore silent testimony of outside interference.

Rumbold made his way straight towards the gardener's cottage.
He found the gardener—who was a widower, with children long
since flown to the big cities—hanging out four pairs of socks to
dry in his backyard. In a potato bed a hungry cat made clamour.

"Where is he?" said Rumbold.

"Where is who, fine gentleman?"

"I wouldn't," said Rumbold, "adopt that tone with me. *Je ne suis pas, tu sais, à un meurtre près, à present.*"

Meanwhile, he advanced, hands outstretched, his objective undoubtedly the old man's throat. The latter sprang backwards, seized a convenient spade, and held it high in menace.

"You're not with young helpless lassies now," he said. "Stand back, or by the Great Christ above I'll crown ye."

"Very well," said Rumbold equably. "I see that I must bow to force." He turned, as if to leave; perceiving which movement the gardener lowered his spade. This was an unfortunate gesture, for at that same moment Rumbold jumped, airborne in a rugby tackle. The gardener, a much more lightly built man, fell instantly. Rising, Rumbold began to kick him in the ribs.

"Obscene old man," he said. "Do you dare to watch me? I'd fix your account now if there were only time."

And he strode off towards the house, slamming the garden gate behind him.

In the sitting-room the two sisters sat, one in tweeds, one in a house-coat. A recently unloaded log sent sparks up the wide chimney.

"Ladies," said Rumbold without preliminaries. "I'm off."

From Virginia Woolf's *Orlando* Peggy raised her eyes. "So soon?" she said. "We'd have been happy to accommodate you till Easter."

Rumbold gazed at her with hatred. "*La Grande Dame Sans Merci*, and the Dick or bounder; that's the party line now, isn't it?" he said. "I've noticed for several days that you've been working on your drunken sister."

"Well," said Peggy. "Since you raise the question, you *are* a little common, aren't you?"

Advancing, Rumbold slapped her face heavily. She did not move. She did not even raise a hand.

"Yes," she said calmly. "You're very good at that of course, but you have one mortal weakness, haven't you: you can't bear to feel yourself despised. Although you're so mean, it wouldn't surprise me at all to hear that you pay rounds of drinks to total strangers . . . 'Rumbold's *such* a good fellow,' they say afterwards, don't they?"

"You little frigid bitch," said Rumbold. "I wish to God I'd never taken you. At least she . . ." here he indicated Fiona . . . "has some warmth, some signs of human feeling. You have none. I recommend that you go into the hall and remove the antlers. They'll fit your husband when he comes."

Fiona, until this moment quiescent, passive, now leant forward. "All this serves nothing," she said with heavy voice. "Come upstairs. I'll help you with your packing."

She rose, and Rumbold followed. A last glance confirmed Peggy in her place, the small blue eyes triumphant.

"Socks . . . shirts," he said, as soon as they were in their bedroom. "Well, at least it can't be said that I'm a dandy." He stuffed his three old suits into the suitcase, but she removed and straightened them; not well, but with good will.

"No," she said. "You're not a dandy."

"Nor very consistent either."

"No," she said. "Not at all consistent."

"Nor even perhaps," he said, pausing, a pair of shoes in hand, "quite such a s—t as you imagine."

"No," she said, and there were tears in her eyes . . . her so big eyes; normally so blank. "No . . . you're not at all a s—t."

"I've been thinking," he said slowly, "that since this is the end, it would be a pity to drag you down with me. I've been thinking, for example, that we might fix things very easily."

"How?" she said, the sound of this single word almost inaudible.

"Well," he said. "We've only known each other seven weeks. It would be quite easy to pretend that I did the job because of an incautious word of yours in Madrid . . . in the false hope of a reward, can't you see? Then I came up here," he smiled wryly. "And of course it was very difficult for you to get rid of me in the circumstances."

"Do you know," she said, "I thought that was what you'd say. Ever since this morning I've been certain of it. But are things really quite so bad?"

"Oh yes," he said. "It's now largely a question of whether two should hang for the price of one. Therefore . . . well, wipe that look

of abnegation off your face. . . . People don't die for Rumbold,
though Rumbold may in the last eventuality die for them."

"Can't you get away at all?" she said.

"Oh yes," he said. "I have my plans, of course. I thought I might
go down to Southampton and get on the boat for Jersey. You don't
need a passport for that trip. From Jersey I could get across to Cart-
eret or Granville. Once in France they'll never catch me. But it's
goodbye to Spain now, I'm afraid." He gazed at her quizzically.
"Spain . . . and Mañuela."

"Yes," she said slowly, without rancour. "She was what you
really wanted, wasn't she? I'm sorry that I was bitchy at the time
but it was only because I wanted you myself. I can see now that
you'd have been better off with her."

"Oh, as to that," he said. "Well . . . does one ever really know?
These unfinished episodes always have something very alluring about them when reviewed in retrospect. Besides," here he
grinned, "who can say whether it's all over yet? If the first leg of my
trip goes well I may still join her across the Pyrenees." He closed
the suitcase, locked it, looked about the room to see if there was
anything which he had forgotten. A half empty bottle of hairwash
stood upon the mantelpiece: he threw it in the fireplace.

"There!" he said. "I'd travel lighter, but a change of clothes is
useful when there's a description of you circulating. Incidentally,
if they make enquiries you might tell them I was wearing a blue
pin-stripe when you last saw me. Every little helps to confuse the
issue."

"And now?" she said.

"Now I'm going to bump that bag across the hills and catch a
bus. Don't worry. I'll be in Edinburgh to-morrow morning."

"I could drive you," she suggested.

"And get caught by some yokel with a helmet in a road block?
No, thank you. The little man I kept in durance vile is probably
telephoning even now for reinforcements. I've got a start on him,
but if I don't use it cleverly I'm done for. . . ."

He paused. Fiona had slumped across the bed. She lay with
her face pressed hard against the pillow. Her shoulders heaved.
"Don't take on so," he said gently. "Look . . . I'll give you back

206 JOHN LODWICK

your cheque. Yes, I insist. Besides, I'm not being really chivalrous, because I daren't cash it now."

She turned her head. One red-rimmed eye appeared above the crumpled eiderdown. "Peggy's already taken it," she said. "The one inside your wallet is a blank."

"Ah," he said, and laughed. "Clever, *clever* little Peggy. You ought to watch your step with her, my dear. These sneak killers seldom stop at one success."

She sat up. The rapid evolution of this crisis, the muddled state of her poor mind, heavy as it was with the fumes of lunch and whisky, Rumbold's evident assurance and the zest with which he faced the situation . . . all these factors had combined until now to keep her passive, resigned to what appeared to be the ineluctable consequences of their association and joint action.

But now a new thought came to her. She sat up, with hands pleading, and spoke with her voice not much above a whisper. "Please tell me the truth," she said. "Please . . . *please*. Are things really so bad? Maybe they just want to prevent you going to Spain. There's nothing very terrible in that. You could stay here till they forget about you."

"No," he said. "They must have followed me to Devonshire . . . Oh, not the ordinary police, of course, but the other comrades. I was stupid not to reckon with it at the time . . . very stupid. Don't imagine that they give a damn about the boy. The odd murder's all in the day's work to Mr. Cassell. What he wants is something concrete to arrest me for when he's finished tapping all my telephone calls and correspondence. I'm afraid I underestimated Mr. Cassell."

She gazed at him piteously. "You're not lying, are you?" she said. "It isn't just that you want to get away from me, is it? Don't lie . . . I couldn't bear it."

"No," he said solemnly. "This time it's the truth: I wish to God it wasn't."

She stood up. She thrust her body close against him. Her arms met in the hollows of his shoulder blades. "Take me with you," she said. "Please take me too . . . I'll do anything you want. I won't be any trouble."

"Listen," he said. "Do you realise that if things had turned out just a little differently I might have killed you?"

"Kill me, then," she said: then, since he made no reply, "Oh, I don't care . . . I don't care at all. Do you think this is a life for me? If you don't get away I'd rather die."

"Don't be foolish," he said. "Life without any money would be hell for you, and I've only a few hundreds left. Your job is to stay here quietly. In a month's time I'll be just a dim and rather nasty memory. Then you can go to Monte for the season."

"But I love you," she said, and in her desperation she shook him, hammered with her fist upon his chest. "I love you . . . I love you . . . will nothing make you understand that?"

"It's too late now," he said gravely, and he kissed her, held her tight, swung her in his arms so that they faced the looking-glass together.

"Come," he said. "Let's have a stiff one for the road," and setting her down, he took from the cupboard a bottle, and from the wash-stand two dirty tooth-mugs.

After Rumbold had been walking for about an hour over rough and undulating heathland, he struck a modest country road, leading westwards. But he had not gone very far down this road . . . perhaps three hundred yards . . . before he heard the sound of a car behind him. It would have been perfectly possible for Rumbold to dart into the shelter of a near-by quarry, but he restrained himself, not wishing to appear more conspicuous than he was already: mud-stained and carrying a heavy suitcase in this wilderness.

This restraint on Rumbold's part was unfortunate. The car, a large coupé, stopped beside him, and Cassell leant out.

"Hullo, Rumbold," he said.

Rumbold laid down his bag. "Good staff work," he said.

"Yes," said Cassell, "but very boring. We've been going up and down among these cow-pats for an hour now."

"You've got here very quickly," said Rumbold. "I feel flattered. It isn't often you make the arrest in person, is it?"

"Oh, I wasn't far away," said Cassell. "Only in Dundee. A depressing town, don't you agree?"

"Very depressing."

"By the way," said Cassell. "The gentleman on my right, behind me, has a firearm."

"So I perceive," said Rumbold. The Colt was, in fact, levelled at his chest. "And what has the other gentleman got . . . a pair of handcuffs?"

"No," said Cassell. "The other gentleman has a warrant for your arrest."

"Oh," said Rumbold. "And what is the charge, please?"

"I'm afraid that it's one of murder," said Cassell deprecatingly.

"Ah?" said Rumbold. "Well, in that case, perhaps I'd better join you," and, picking up his bag, he moved as if to do so.

"No, no," said Cassell, and opening the car door he disembarked, followed closely by the gunman. "No, no. Put down your bag. You won't need it. Let us have a little walk and talk together," and taking Rumbold by the arm he led him towards the entrance to the quarry.

And still the gunman followed.

"It was fortunate that we should meet just here," said Cassell.

"Why so?" said Rumbold.

With a delicate gesture Cassell indicated the high walls of the quarry; the eighty feet of Grampian granite, with boulders at the bottom.

"If we had met elsewhere," he said, "I should only have had to bring you here. There just isn't any other isolated place which suits your purpose."

"I see," said Rumbold. "So this is the Tarpeian cliff, is it?"

He had grown pale, but not really very noticeably so.

"I could lend you a pistol, of course," said Cassell. "But quite frankly it would be a little awkward afterwards. People make such stupid enquiries . . . Where did he get it? . . . why didn't you stop him? I'm sure you take my meaning."

"Oh, yes," said Rumbold. "In any case, I don't like guns. Poetic justice is much better."

Beneath the bracken at the quarry's base, a single blue crocus sprouted. Cassell plucked it, sniffed it, extended it to Rumbold.

"Of course," said Cassell. "I don't want to hurry you. The decision to be made is serious. You could always choose a trial amid the pageantry of British justice. I am told that there might also be a certain amount of publicity. That, too, might please you, though I believe they cut out the relevant columns before the prisoner receives his daily paper."

"No," said Rumbold. "I think that your solution is the best."

"I'm very glad to hear it," said Cassell. "Shall we shake hands now? This gentleman," he pointed to the gunman, "will follow you to the top."

"Must he?" said Rumbold. "I don't intend to run, I promise you."

Cassell shrugged, twisted his crocus, picked another: this time a yellow one. "I'm doing my best to make the occasion as informal as possible," he said. "Unfortunately, even in my job, there's some damn fool just above you. I'm afraid it's necessary, Rumbold."

"Very well," said Rumbold. "I won't insist." He extended his hand. "Goodbye, Cassell," he said. "I always hated you, but there was some love in it as well."

"Goodbye, Rumbold," said Cassell.

They shook hands. Rumbold began to mount the slope. A few yards up, he paused.

"Aranjuez would laugh," he said.

"Yes, wouldn't he?" said Cassell.

"It's funny," said Rumbold. "There was a girl out there I was really keen on. It might have led to something. Who can tell?"

"I wouldn't worry about the one we have here," said Cassell. "There'll be no prosecution."

"I'm glad of that," said Rumbold.

He began to mount again, mounted perhaps thirty feet, then turned once more.

"Are you going to stay and watch?" he said.

"Oh yes," said Cassell. "I was looking up your dossier file the other day. It said that when you were at Ringway, on your parachute course, you made the best exits from a plane that they had ever seen."

Rumbold laughed. The earth crumbled beneath his shoes. The gunman, a much older man, followed painfully.

"You seem very out of training," said Rumbold when they reached the top.

The gunman said nothing.

"I wish you'd stand a little further back," said Rumbold. "After all, this is my affair, not yours."

The gunman retired slightly.

Rumbold looked down. Cassell and the car seemed very tiny, the road a dirty ribbon.

"I hope that everybody will observe," said Rumbold, "that the artist operates without a safety net."

And then he jumped.

The blood flowing from the broken body would have spoilt the car's upholstery. Therefore they sent an ambulance to fetch it from the town.

THE END

Saint Ydeuc, France.
February, 1947.

ALSO AVAILABLE FROM VALANCOURT BOOKS

MICHAEL ARLEN	Hell! said the Duchess
R. C. ASHBY (RUBY FERGUSON)	He Arrived at Dusk
FRANK BAKER	The Birds
CHARLES BEAUMONT	The Hunger and Other Stories
DAVID BENEDICTUS	The Fourth of June
CHARLES BIRKIN	The Smell of Evil
JOHN BLACKBURN	A Scent of New-Mown Hay
	Broken Boy
	Blue Octavo
	Nothing but the Night
	Bury Him Darkly
THOMAS BLACKBURN	The Feast of the Wolf
JOHN BRAINE	Room at the Top
	The Vodi
MICHAEL CAMPBELL	Lord Dismiss Us
R. CHETWYND-HAYES	The Monster Club
BASIL COPPER	The Great White Space
	Necropolis
HUNTER DAVIES	Body Charge
JENNIFER DAWSON	The Ha-Ha
BARRY ENGLAND	Figures in a Landscape
RONALD FRASER	Flower Phantoms
GILLIAN FREEMAN	The Liberty Man
	The Leather Boys
	The Leader
STEPHEN GILBERT	The Landslide
	The Burnaby Experiments
	Ratman's Notebooks
MARTYN GOFF	The Youngest Director
STEPHEN GREGORY	The Cormorant
THOMAS HINDE	Mr. Nicholas
	The Day the Call Came
CLAUDE HOUGHTON	I Am Jonathan Scrivener
	This Was Ivor Trent
CYRIL KERSH	The Aggravations of Minnie Ashe
GERALD KERSH	Fowlers End
	Nightshade and Damnations
FRANCIS KING	Never Again
	An Air That Kills
	The Dividing Stream
	The Dark Glasses

Lightning Source UK Ltd.
Milton Keynes UK
UKOW01f1542270218
318576UK00001B/92/P